RaeAnne Thayne

SUGAR PINE TRAIL

HQN™

W9-BUB-526

If you purchased this book without a cover you should be aware
that this book is stolen property. It was reported as "unsold and
destroyed" to the publisher, and neither the author nor the
publisher has received any payment for this "stripped book."

HQN™

ISBN-13: 978-0-373-80368-2

Sugar Pine Trail

Recycling programs
for this product may
not exist in your area.

Copyright © 2017 by RaeAnne Thayne

All rights reserved. Except for use in any review, the reproduction or
utilization of this work in whole or in part in any form by any electronic,
mechanical or other means, now known or hereinafter invented, including
xerography, photocopying and recording, or in any information storage
or retrieval system, is forbidden without the written permission of the
publisher, HQN Books, 225 Duncan Mill Road, Don Mills, Ontario
M3B 3K9, Canada.

This is a work of fiction. Names, characters, places and incidents are
either the product of the author's imagination or are used fictitiously,
and any resemblance to actual persons, living or dead, business
establishments, events or locales is entirely coincidental.

This edition published by arrangement with Harlequin Books S.A.

For questions and comments about the quality of this book,
please contact us at CustomerService@Harlequin.com.

® and TM are trademarks of Harlequin Enterprises Limited or its
corporate affiliates. Trademarks indicated with ® are registered in the
United States Patent and Trademark Office, the Canadian Intellectual
Property Office and in other countries.

www.HQNBooks.com

Printed in U.S.A.

Sma

Praise for *New York Times* bestselling author RaeAnne Thayne

"Romance, vivid characters and a wonderful story; really, who could ask for more?"
—Debbie Macomber, #1 *New York Times* bestselling author, on *Blackberry Summer*

"Entertaining, heart-wrenching, and totally involving, this multithreaded story overflows with characters readers will adore."
—*Library Journal* on *Evergreen Springs* (starred review)

"This holiday-steeped romance overflows with family and wintry small-town appeal."
—*Library Journal* on *Snowfall on Haven Point*

"A sometimes heartbreaking tale of love and relationships in a small Colorado town.... Poignant and sweet."
—*Publishers Weekly* on *Christmas in Snowflake Canyon*

"This quirky, funny, warmhearted romance will draw readers in and keep them enthralled to the last romantic page."
—*Library Journal* on *Christmas in Snowflake Canyon*

"RaeAnne Thayne is quickly becoming one of my favorite authors... Once you start reading, you aren't going to be able to stop."
—*Fresh Fiction*

"RaeAnne has a knack for capturing those emotions that come from the heart."
—*RT Book Reviews*

"Her engaging storytelling...will draw readers in from the very first page."
—*RT Book Reviews* on *Riverbend Road*

For all the wonderful readers who have been asking me for years to write Jamie Caine's book!

As always, I have legions of people to thank for helping to bring this story to life. I am deeply indebted to my editor, the wonderful Gail Chasan (and her assistant Megan Broderick); to my agent, the indomitable Karen Solem; to Sarah Burningham and her hardworking team at Little Bird Publicity, for tirelessly helping spread the word about my books; and to everyone at Harlequin—from the art department for their stunning covers to the marketing team to everyone in editorial and sales (and anyone else I have neglected to mention!).

I must also thank my hero of a husband and our three children, who have somehow managed to put up with my deadline brain more than fifty times now. I love you dearly.

Finally, this particular book would not have been possible without two amazing, brilliant friends, Susan Mallery and Jill Shalvis. I adore you both and can't thank you enough for all your help!

CHAPTER ONE

THIS WAS GOING to be a disaster.

Julia Winston stood in her front room looking out the lace curtains framing her bay window at the gleaming black SUV parked in her driveway like a sleek, predatory beast.

Her stomach jumped with nerves, and she rubbed suddenly clammy hands down her skirt. Under what crazy moon had she ever thought this might be a good idea? She must have been temporarily out of her head.

Those nerves jumped into overtime when a man stepped out of the vehicle and stood for a moment, looking up at her house.

Jamie Caine.

Tall, lean, hungry.

Gorgeous.

Now the nerves felt more like nausea. What had she done? The moment Eliza Caine called and asked her if her brother-in-law could rent the upstairs apartment of Winston House, she should have told her friend in no uncertain terms that the idea was preposterous. Utterly impossible.

As usual, Julia had been weak and indecisive, and when Eliza told her it was only for six weeks—until January, when the condominium Jamie Caine was buying in a new development along the lake would be finished—she had wavered.

He needed a place to live, and she *did* need the money. Anyway, it was only for six weeks. Surely she could tolerate having the man living upstairs in her apartment for six weeks—especially since he would be out of town for much of those six weeks, as part of his duties as lead pilot for the Caine Tech company jet fleet.

The reality of it all was just beginning to sink in, though. Jamie Caine, upstairs from her, in all his sexy, masculine glory.

She fanned herself with her hand, wondering if she was having a premature-onset hot flash or if her new furnace could be on the fritz. The temperature in here seemed suddenly off the charts.

How would she tolerate having him here, spending her evenings knowing he was only a few steps away and that she would have to do her best to hide the absolutely ridiculous, truly humiliating crush she had on the man?

This was such a mistake.

Heart pounding, she watched through the frothy curtains as he pulled a long black duffel bag from the back of his SUV and slung it over his shoulder, lifted a laptop case over the other shoulder, then closed the cargo door and headed for the front steps.

A moment later, her old-fashioned musical doorbell echoed through the house. If she hadn't been so nervous, she might have laughed at the instant reaction of the three cats, previously lounging in various states of boredom around the room. The moment the doorbell rang, Empress and Tabitha both jumped off the sofa as if an electric current had just zipped through it while Audrey Hepburn arched her back and bushed out her tail.

"That's right, girls. We've got company. It's a man, believe it or not, and he's moving in upstairs. Get ready."

The cats sniffed at her with their usual disdainful look. Empress ran in front of her, almost tripping her on the way to answer the door—on purpose, she was quite sure.

With her mother's cats darting out ahead of her, Julia walked out into what used to be the foyer of the house before she had created the upstairs apartment and now served as an entryway to both residences. She opened the front door, doing her best to ignore the rapid tripping of her heartbeat.

"Hi. You're Julia, right?"

As his sister-in-law was one of her dearest friends, she and Jamie had met numerous times at various events at Snow Angel Cove and elsewhere, but she didn't bother reminding him of that. Julia knew she was eminently forgettable. Most of the time, that was just the way she liked it.

"Yes. Hello, Mr. Caine."

He aimed his high-wattage killer smile at her. "Please. Jamie. Nobody calls me Mr. Caine."

Julia was grimly aware of her pulse pounding in her ears and a strange hitch in her lungs. Up close, Jamie Caine was, in a word, breathtaking. He was Mr. Darcy, Atticus Finch, Rhett Butler and Tom Cruise in *Top Gun*, all rolled into one glorious package.

Dark hair, blue eyes, and that utterly charming Caine smile he shared with Aidan, Eliza's husband, and the other Caine brothers she had met at various events.

"You were expecting me, right?" he said, after an awkward pause. She jolted, suddenly aware she was staring and had left him standing entirely too long on her front step. She was an idiot. "Yes. Of course. Come in. I'm sorry."

Pull yourself together. He's just a guy who happens to be gorgeous.

So far she was seriously failing at Landlady 101. She sucked in a breath and summoned her most brisk keep-your-voice-down-please librarian persona.

"As you can see, we will share the entry. Because the home is on the registry of historical buildings, I couldn't put in an outside entrance to your apartment, as I might have preferred. The house was built in 1880, one of the earliest brick homes on Lake Haven. It was constructed by an ancestor of mine, Sir Robert Winston, who came from a wealthy British family and made his own fortune supplying timber to the railroads. He also invested in one of the first hot springs resorts in the area. The home is Victorian, specifically in the spindled Queen Anne style. It consists of seven bedrooms and four bathrooms. When those bathrooms were added in the 1920s, they provided some of the first indoor plumbing in the region."

"Interesting," he said, though his expression indicated he found it anything but.

She was rambling, she realized, as she tended to do when she was nervous.

She cleared her throat and pointed to the doorway where the three cats were lined up like sentinels, watching him with unblinking stares. "Anyway, through those doors is my apartment and yours is upstairs. I have keys to both doors for you along with a packet of information here."

She glanced toward the ornate marble-top table in the entryway—that her mother claimed once graced the mansion of Leland Stanford on Nob Hill in San Francisco—where she thought she had left the information. Unfortunately, it was bare. "Oh. Where did I put that? I must have left it inside, in my living room. Just a moment."

The cats weren't inclined to get out of her way, so she stepped over them, wondering if she came across as eccentric to him as she felt, a spinster librarian living with cats in a crumbling house crammed with antiques, a space much too big for one person.

After a mad scan of the room, she finally found the two keys along with the carefully prepared file folder of instructions atop the mantel, nestled amid her collection of porcelain angels. She had no recollection of moving it there, probably due to her own nervousness at having Jamie Caine moving upstairs.

She swooped it up and hurried back to the entry, where she found two of the cats curled around his leg while Audrey was in his arms, currently being petted by his long, square-tipped fingers.

She stared. The cats had no time or interest in her. She only kept them around because her mother had adored them, and Julia couldn't bring herself to give away Mariah's adored pets. Apparently no female— human or feline—was immune to Jamie Caine. She should have expected it.

"Nice cats."

Julia frowned. "Not usually. They're standoffish and bad-tempered to most people."

"I guess I must have the magic touch."

So the Haven Point rumor mill said about him, anyway. "I guess you do," she said. "I found your keys and information about the apartment. If you would like, I can show you around upstairs."

"Lead on."

He offered a friendly smile, and she told herself that shiver rippling down her spine was only because the entryway was cooler than her rooms.

"This is a lovely house," he said as he followed her up the staircase. "Have you lived here long?"

"Thirty-two years in February. All my life, in other words."

Except the first few days, anyway, when she had still been in the Oregon hospital where her parents adopted her, and the three years she had spent at Boise State.

"It's always been in my family," she continued. "My father was born here and his father before him."

She was a Winston only by adoption but claimed her parents' family trees as her own and respected and admired their ancestors and the elegant home they had built here.

At the second floor landing, she unlocked the apartment that had been hers until she moved down to take care of her mother after Mariah's first stroke, two years ago. A few years after taking the job at the Haven Point library, she had redecorated the upstairs floor of the house. It had been her way of carving out her own space.

Yes, she was an adult living with her parents. Even as she might have longed for some degree of independence, she couldn't justify moving out when her mother so desperately needed her help with Julia's ailing father.

Anyway, she had always figured it wasn't the same as most young adults who lived in their parents' apartments. She had an entire self-contained floor to herself. If she wished, she could shop on her own, cook on her own, entertain her friends, all without bothering her parents.

Really, it had been the best of all situations—close enough to help, yet removed enough to live her own life. Then her father died and her mother became frail herself, and Julia had felt obligated to move downstairs to be closer, in case her mother needed her.

Now, as she looked at her once-cherished apartment, she tried to imagine how Jamie Caine would see these rooms, with the graceful reproduction furniture and the pastel wall colors and the soft carpet and curtains.

Oddly, the feminine decorations only served to emphasize how very *male* Jamie Caine was, in contrast.

She did her best to ignore that unwanted observation.

"This is basically the same floor plan as my rooms below, with three bedrooms, as well as the living room and kitchen," she explained. "You've got an en suite bathroom off the largest bedroom and another one for the other two bedrooms."

"Wow. That's a lot of room for one guy."

"It's a big house," she said with a shrug. She had even more room downstairs, factoring in the extra bedroom in one addition and the large south-facing sunroom.

Winston House was entirely too rambling for one single woman and three bad-tempered cats. It had been too big for an older couple and their adopted daughter. It had been too large when it was just her and her mother, after her father died.

The place had basically echoed with emptiness for the better part of a year after her mother's deteriorating condition had necessitated her move to the nursing home in Shelter Springs. Her mother had hoped to return to the house she had loved, but that never happened, and Mariah Winston died four months ago.

Julia missed her every single day.

"Do you think it will work for you?" she asked.

"It's more than I need, but should be fine. Eliza told you this is only temporary, right?"

Julia nodded. She was counting on it. Then she could find a nice, quiet, older lady to rent who wouldn't leave her so nervous.

"She said your apartment lease ran out before your new condo was finished."

"Yes. The development was supposed to be done two months ago, but the builder has suffered delay after delay. I've already extended my lease twice. I didn't want to push my luck with my previous landlady by asking for a third extension."

All Jamie had to do was smile at the woman and she likely would have extended his lease again without quibbling. And probably would have given him anything else he wanted, too.

Julia didn't ask why he chose not to move in to Snow Angel Cove with his brother Aidan and Aidan's wife, Eliza, and their children. It was none of her business, anyway. The only thing she cared about was the healthy amount he was paying her in rent, which would just about cover the new furnace she had installed a month earlier.

"It was a lucky break for me when Eliza told me you were considering taking on a renter for your upstairs space."

He aimed that killer smile at her again, and her core muscles trembled from more than just her workout that morning.

If she wasn't very, very careful, she would end up making a fool of herself over the man.

It took effort, but she fought the urge to return his smile. This was business, she told herself. That's all. She had something he needed, a place to stay, and he was willing to pay for it. She, in turn, needed funds if she wanted to maintain this house that had been in her family for generations.

"It works out for both of us. You've already signed the rental agreement outlining the terms of your tenancy and the rules."

She held out the information packet. "Here you'll find all the information you might need, information like internet access, how to work the electronics and the satellite television channels, garbage pickup day and mail delivery. Do you have any other questions?"

Business, she reminded herself, making her voice as no-nonsense and brisk as possible.

"I can't think of any now, but I'm sure something will come up."

He smiled again, but she thought perhaps this time his expression was a little more reserved. Maybe he could sense she was uncharmable.

Or so she wanted to tell herself, anyway.

"I would ask that you please wipe your feet when you carry your things in and out, given the snow out there. The stairs are original wood, more than a hundred years old."

Cripes. She sounded like a prissy spinster librarian.

"I will do that, but I don't have much to carry in. Since El told me the place is furnished, I put almost everything in storage." He gestured to the duffel and laptop bag, which he had set inside the doorway. "Besides this, I've only got a few more boxes in the car."

"In that case, here are your keys. The large one goes to the outside door. The smaller one is for your apartment. I keep the outside door locked at all times. You can't be too careful."

"True enough."

She glanced at her watch. "I'm afraid I've already gone twenty minutes past my lunch hour and must return to the library. My cell number is written on the front of the packet, in case of emergency."

"Looks like you've covered everything."

"I think so." Yes, she was a bit obsessively organized, and she didn't like surprises. Was anything wrong with that?

"I hope you will be comfortable here," she said, then tried to soften her stiff tone with a smile that felt every bit as awkward. "Good afternoon."

"Uh, same to you."

Her heart was still pounding as she nodded to him and hurried for the stairs, desperate for escape from all that…masculinity.

She rushed back downstairs and into her apartment for her purse, wishing she had time to splash cold water on her face.

However would she get through the next six weeks with him in her house?

HE WAS *NOT* looking forward to the next six weeks.

Jamie stood in the corner of the main living space to the apartment he had agreed to rent, sight unseen.

Big mistake.

It was roomy and filled with light, that much was

true. But the decor was too…fussy…for a man like him, all carved wood and tufted upholstery and pastel wall colorings.

It wasn't exactly his scene, more like the kind of place a repressed, uppity librarian might live.

As soon as he thought the words, Jamie frowned at himself. That wasn't fair. She might not have been over-flowing with warmth and welcome, but Julia Winston had been very polite to him—especially since he knew she hadn't necessarily wanted to rent to him.

This was what happened when he gave his sister-in-law free rein to find him an apartment in the tight local rental market. She had been helping him out since he had been crazy busy the last few weeks flying Caine Tech execs from coast to coast—and all places in between—as they worked on a couple of big mergers.

Eliza had wanted him to stay at her and Aidan's ram-bling house by the lake. The place was huge, and they had plenty of room, but while he loved his older brother Aidan and his wife and kids, Jamie preferred his own space. He didn't much care what that space looked like, especially when it was temporary.

With time running out on his lease extension, he had been relieved when Eliza called him via Skype the week before to tell him she had found him something more than suitable, for a decent rent.

"You'll love it!" Eliza had beamed. "It's the entire second floor of a gorgeous old Victorian in that great neighborhood on Snow Blossom Lane, with a simply stunning view of the lake."

"Sounds good," he had answered.

"You'll be upstairs from my friend Julia Winston, and, believe me, you couldn't ask for a better landlady. She's sweet and kind and perfectly wonderful. You know Julia, right?"

When he had looked blankly at her and didn't immediately respond, his niece Maddie had popped her face on to the screen from where she had been apparently listening in off-camera. "You know! She's the library lady. She tells all the stories!"

"Ah. *That* Julia," he said, not bothering to mention to his seven-year-old niece that in more than a year of living in town, he had somehow missed out on story time at the Haven Point library.

He also didn't mention to Maddie's mother that he only vaguely remembered Julia Winston. Now that he had seen her again, he understood why. She was the kind of woman who tended to slip into the background—and he had the odd impression that wasn't accidental.

She wore her brown hair past her shoulders, without much curl or style to it and held back with a simple black band, and she appeared to use little makeup to play up her rather average features.

She did have lovely eyes, he had to admit. Extraordinary, even. They were a stunning blue, almost violet, fringed by naturally long eyelashes.

Her looks didn't matter, nor did the decor of her house. He would only be here a few weeks, then he would be moving in to his new condo.

She clearly didn't like him. He frowned, wondering how he might have offended Julia Winston. He barely remembered even meeting the woman, but he must have done something for her to be so cool to him.

A few times during that odd interaction, she had alternated between seeming nervous to be in the same room with him to looking at him with her mouth pursed tightly, as if she had just caught him spreading peanut butter across the pages of *War and Peace*.

She was entitled to her opinion. Contrary to popular belief, he didn't need everyone to like him.

His brothers would probably say it was good for him to live upstairs from a woman so clearly immune to his charm.

One thing was clear: he now had one more reason to be eager for his condo to be finished.

CHAPTER TWO

"SERIOUSLY? WE HAVE Book Club in less than four hours, and you're only now checking out the book we're supposed to be discussing?"

Samantha Fremont shrugged and swiped at a lock of auburn hair that always seemed to be falling into her eyes.

"I'm sorry, but I was in the middle of a Coco Chanel biography and I couldn't put it down. Fascinating stuff, that. Anyway, I just need a copy to skim through on my lunch hour. You can tell me what happens, can't you?"

Julia sighed and handed over a copy of *Filling Your Well*, the feel-good self-help memoir that had been chosen by this week's discussion leader, Roxy Nash.

"It's all about designing your life the way you want it, about taking chances and pursuing your goals," she said,

"Oh. One of *those* books." Sam made a face. "I should have known. Maybe I'll stay home and watch reruns of *Project Runway*."

"You have to come. We had a last-minute venue change, and it's at my house."

"Ooh. In that case, I'll definitely be there. I understand Jamie Caine is living upstairs from you in all his glorious gorgeousness. How is it? Tell me everything!"

Julia rolled her eyes. "He's lived upstairs from me for

all of three hours now, and I've been working that entire time. It's a little premature for me to offer an opinion."

Samantha was a flirt of the highest order. In that, at least, she and Jamie were perfect for each other, though he was about a decade older.

"If Jamie lived under the same roof with me, I would never want to leave my house."

Funny. Julia had the opposite reaction. She was wondering if she could bring a few blankets and pillows and camp out on the sofa in her office.

"I mean, think about it," Sam went on. "He's going to be showering up there. And sleeping, too, all warm and tousled and cuddly. I wonder if he wears pajamas."

Julia's imagination began to drift into dangerous waters, until she yanked it back safely to the shores of reality.

She cleared her throat. "Do you want to check out any other books to go with this one?" she asked, holding out *Filling Your Well*.

Sam gave a dreamy sigh. "No. This will do. Unless you know any hot romance novels featuring tall, gorgeous pilots."

Julia could name several off the top of her head, but she had a feeling Samantha was only joking.

"I'll make you a list and give it to you tonight. Maybe you can pick one for the next time you lead the book group," she said, knowing perfectly well Sam's tastes usually ran to celebrity memoirs and the occasional meaty historical drama.

"Perfect. So you said Jamie's been there three hours. Has he brought any women home yet? Are they gorgeous?"

Oh, cripes. She hadn't even thought about that.

"Again. I've been working here the entire time. I don't expect I'll have much reason to talk to the man at all."

Sam looked disappointed that she didn't have more dirt to dish up about her new tenant. "I might have to find some kind of excuse tonight to borrow a cup of sugar from your upstairs neighbor."

"You would probably be disappointed. I'm not sure how many groceries he'll have on hand. He seemed to be traveling light, just a duffel and a couple of boxes. One of them might have sugar, but I have a feeling baking cookies isn't his primary goal in life."

Sam snickered. "From what I hear, that's an understatement."

Why, oh why, had she ever said yes to Eliza?

Julia sighed and finished checking out the book for Sam. "Here you go," she said.

"Thanks, sweetie."

"Bundle up. It looks nasty out there," she said, as her friend slipped the book club selection into her slouchy hand-sewn purse.

Sam tightened her scarf and pulled on matching mittens. "The perfect weather for an afternoon of cuddling by the fire with hot cocoa and a certain someone. I don't have a fireplace or a certain someone right now, so I might have to settle for hot cocoa and the latest episode in the series I'm glomming right now."

That actually sounded like a lovely afternoon to Julia, if she didn't have to work.

"Here's an idea," she suggested. "You could always actually *read* the book you just checked out. We don't meet until eight tonight."

She would have preferred earlier, but the late meeting was a concession for those who had small children and liked to get bedtime out of the way first.

"Maybe. I'll have to see. Catch you later tonight. Give Jamie a kiss for me."

She rolled her eyes as Sam gave a cheery wave and headed out the door.

Sam always made Julia feel ancient. She wasn't sure why. Yes, she was a few years older than Sam's twenty-six, but thirty-two didn't exactly make her a tottering old crone, did it?

Give Jamie a kiss for me. Why did Sam have to put that particular image in her head? The very thought of it left her feeling slightly breathless.

What was she going to do about this ridiculous crush she had on the man?

For the rest of the afternoon, she tried to put thoughts of Jamie out of her mind. It helped that the library was far busier than she expected for the Monday before Thanksgiving. She would have thought everyone in town would be too busy grocery shopping or cleaning their houses for upcoming family parties. Instead, a regular stream of patrons came through, renting videos, seeking reference information, or trying to go online. And plenty of her patrons still checked out books, much to her continual delight.

"Here you go," she said as she scanned in Muriel Randall's regular weekly allotment of cozy mysteries. "That should hold you for a few days."

"I figured I had better stock up. We've got snow coming tomorrow, plus you're closed on Thursday and Friday. I would hate to run out."

Julia smiled at the neatly dressed older woman whose late husband had once run the butcher shop in town.

"What are you doing for Thanksgiving dinner?" she asked.

Muriel slipped the books into her library bag with a smile that looked more than a little forced. "I was supposed to go to my son's house in Boise, but his wife decided they should go to her family's again this year. I'll probably cook a turkey tenderloin and cuddle in with a good book."

Julia's throat tightened, both at the lonely image Muriel painted and because it felt entirely too familiar, given her own circumstances. "I'm helping to serve at the nursing home in Shelter Springs this year," she said. "We can always use another set of hands. Why don't you join me?"

"What could I do?" Muriel held up her shaky, wrinkled hands. "I'm not much good in the kitchen these days. I'm afraid I would cut myself."

"There's plenty to do. You can help set the table or set out water glasses or be the official greeter. I would love to have the company, and I would be happy to give you a ride."

Muriel looked touched. "Thank you for the invitation. That's very nice of you. It might be better than sitting home by myself."

"Is that a yes?"

"It's a maybe. I'll think about it," she said.

She smiled. "Perfect. Unless I hear otherwise, I'll plan on picking you up about 10:00 a.m. on Thursday."

"I said I'll think about it," Muriel said in an exasperated tone. "Give me five minutes to do that, would you?"

"You can have from now until 10:00 a.m. on Thursday," Julia said.

The older woman snorted as she picked up her book bag and headed for the door.

After she left, Julia glanced at the clock. The library closed early on Monday nights and only a few patrons remained.

She walked through, reminding those stragglers that the library would be closing in ten minutes. To her surprise, in one of the alcoves in the children's section, she found two young boys she had seen come in hours earlier after school.

They must be dedicated readers, since she had seen them here Friday and most of the day Saturday, too.

As a librarian, she certainly couldn't find fault with that, though she did think it a little odd, especially since she hadn't seen them here very often, prior to the previous weekend.

They looked up when she approached them. "The library is going to be closing in a few moments," she said, glancing out the window where the gray light of early evening was punctuated by a few stray snow flurries. "Do you have someone coming to pick you up?"

The younger boy opened his mouth to answer, then closed it again with a quick, somewhat nervous look at the older boy. Up close, it was obvious the boys were related. Both had wavy hair the color of rawhide, a scattering of freckles across their respective noses and eyes the same shade of green.

The older boy, who looked to be about eight or nine, placed a hand on his brother's arm—whether in reassurance or warning, she couldn't quite tell. "Yes," he said. "We can get a ride."

"Good. It's dark out there and can be dangerous for

pedestrians, especially this time of year when the roads are icy."

"We'll be fine. Come on, Davy. Let's put these books away and get our coats on."

His brother didn't look thrilled at the order, but he obediently scooped up the large stack of picture books beside him.

"You know you can just put them in the return cart, right?" Julia said. "That way we can make sure they're reshelved in the right place."

The younger boy nodded. "If they get all mixed up, people won't know where to look if they want to read them. That's what Clinton told me."

"Clinton is exactly right," she said. She always admired when children could be respectful of others. "Thank you so much for your help with keeping the library organized."

She had other duties that occupied her attention for the next few moments, while she prepared to close down the library. Still, she kept an eye out for the boys as they returned books and loaded their belongings into two ragged-looking backpacks.

Who were these boys? She couldn't remember them ever coming in with a parent or guardian. Come to think of it, she didn't know if they had ever used a library card that might have an identifying name on it. They never checked out books, only seemed interested in reading storybooks in the library.

There was a time when she knew just about everyone in Haven Point. The town was growing so much these days, with the development of the new Caine Tech facility a few years earlier. New people were moving in all the time, and she found it hard to keep up with them all.

After she checked the library one more time, then turned off the lights and locked the door, Julia hurried outside. Her new matador-red Lexus SUV was the only vehicle in the parking lot, and when she unlocked the door, the intoxicating smell of glossy leather seats greeted her.

The engine purred to life, and she sighed with guilty pleasure. She loved this vehicle, even if it was a big reason her cash flow had slowed enough that she had to rent out the top floor of her house.

As she carefully pulled out of the parking lot, she noticed the two boys passing under a streetlight about a block down the road.

She frowned, troubled for reasons she couldn't quite identify. They had lied when they said someone was picking them up. Though in retrospect, they hadn't actually said that. *We can call someone to pick us up.* That's what the older boy said, not *we* will *call someone.*

She hoped they didn't have far to walk. Those stray snowflakes on the November wind could bite into bare skin like tiny, vicious arrows.

Where did they live? If the boys came in the next night and again stayed until closing, she would investigate further.

For now, she had to worry about the book club showing up at her house in twenty minutes.

And, of course, the man who suddenly lived upstairs.

ROXY NASH STOOD in front of the book club and gave a sharp smile that filled Julia with apprehension.

"Tonight I thought it would be fun to try something different," she said.

"You mean like actually read the book?" Samantha

asked in an undertone that made everyone sitting close enough to hear laugh.

"Since the theme of *Filling Your Well* is wringing every drop of joy out of life while you can, I thought it would be *so fun* for us to write down some of the things on our own bucket lists. We're about to head into a new year. What better time for a little self-reflection?"

Beside her, Megan Hamilton groaned. "I already don't like this," she muttered.

Julia completely agreed.

"At least the booze is good," Sam said, taking another sip of the autumn sangria Roxy had so thoughtfully provided for the book club.

Julia had to agree with that sentiment, as well.

"Ask yourself, what am I not happy about?" Roxy said to the room of twenty or so women gathered in Julia's large living room. "What would I like to change about myself? Remember, this is not about resolutions. This isn't about saying you want to lose ten pounds, though that might be a worthy goal. I want you to think a little deeper."

"Fifteen pounds?" Julia murmured, which made Megan laugh.

Roxy didn't seem to find their side comments amusing. She gave their corner of the room a stern look before she pulled out a stack of papers from a pink file folder.

"To help you out a little, I've printed out a form for each of us. At the top, it says, *This year I want to...* For this exercise, I'd like you to put at least five things on the list, things that have been hovering on the edge of your mind, things you might not even have admitted to yourself you want."

"I want more sangria. Does that count?" Megan asked, making both Julia and Sam laugh and earning another glare from Roxy, which made Julia wince.

Considering she was the hostess for the gathering, maybe she should be setting a little better example. She dutifully got up to help Roxy pass around the papers, along with pencils from a tin she kept in her kitchen.

When everyone had a paper and a writing instrument, Julia returned to her seat and gazed down at the paper, not sure what to write.

For so long, her goals in life had involved taking care of others. Her parents, her library patrons.

Maksym.

She wasn't very good at projects like this. Whenever she was forced to take a good, hard look at her life, she rarely liked what she saw.

"Can I put something involving Jamie Caine and his pecs?" Sam asked, tilting her head to look at the ceiling as if he might somehow appear there and wink down at them—and perhaps flex said pectorals.

Julia took another sip of her sangria. The man wasn't even home, though she didn't bother telling Sam that. She hadn't seen his vehicle earlier. When he did get home, he wouldn't be able to pull into the driveway, as it was filled with the vehicles of her book group friends.

"Really?" Roxy said. "Is that the first thing that comes to mind when you look at what would bring you joy next year?"

"Yes," Sam said emphatically.

Megan laughed, though Sam's mother rolled her eyes from across the room.

"What's wrong with that?" Samantha said. "You specifically wanted us to think about something missing from our lives. I would have to say that is definitely missing from my life."

"Thanks," Wynona Emmett said with an eye roll of her own. "Now we're all thinking about Jamie's pecs."

Megan snorted. "Why would you care about that when you have a hot man in uniform waiting for you at home?"

"Yes. Yes, I do." Wyn said with the sort of self-satisfied smile that made Julia ache with envy.

Once, she thought her life would turn out like Wyn's, married to a man she loved, with children and a home too small to hold in all her happiness.

Things hadn't quite turned out that way.

She gazed down at her paper as all the wasted years seemed to march across the empty whiteness.

"You can put whatever you want on your list," Roxy said. "There's no right or wrong here. It's your list. Your dreams. But be honest with yourself. Like we learned in the book, you are the chief architect of your life. No one else. I'll give you ten minutes to finish this."

To set the scene, Roxy turned on the music she had brought along, tuned to some kind of new age harp music playing Christmas songs. Julia didn't find it necessarily very helpful. Between the music and the sangria, now she just wanted to take a nap.

She stared at her paper for a long moment while a hundred thoughts chased themselves around in her brain. The sad truth was, she didn't have a problem coming up with things missing in her life. The problem was narrowing the list down so she wasn't writing a novel about it.

She took another sip of her drink and finally wrote the first thing that came to mind.

Drive my new car on the Interstate.

She had owned the Lexus for a month and so far had avoided any highways or freeways that might require her to put the pedal to the metal. That was fine when she was running around town, but it was becoming apparent to her that she was starting to go out of her way to avoid having to travel too fast. What was the point in owning such a fine vehicle, if she was afraid to drive it?

And while she was thinking about speed, another lifelong dream popped into her head, and she wrote it down before she had time to think.

Learn to ski.

She lived in the mountains, for heaven's sake, where they could have snow upwards of seven months out of the year. How could she have lived to be thirty-two and not ever have tried the area's most popular winter sport?

"Learn to ski. That's a good one!" Megan said. "Can I use that one, too?"

Julia fought the urge to cover her paper. "Um, sure. If that's your dream."

"One of many, hon. One of many."

"No peeking at each other's papers," Roxy said sternly. "You can share later if you choose, but for now I want you to do this on your own."

Megan sat back in her chair. "Wow, harsh. Roxy is as bad as Miss Chestnut. Remember her?"

"Oh, yes," Julia said. Agatha Chestnut had been the librarian in Haven Point for years. She had a dour, pinched face, a beehive hairdo and cat glasses that magnified her eyes about a hundred times. All the children had been terrified of her.

"Okay, you should have written down at least half of your list," Roxy said.

Julia had exactly two items. She looked down at her list and quickly wrote the next thing that came into her mind.

Fly in an airplane.

How humiliating that she even had to write that one down. She had more than three decades on the planet, for heaven's sake, and a long list of places she wanted to go.

Her family had taken vacations when she was young, but her father never had much time away from his business, so they usually only traveled places they could drive to in a day.

She had always dreamed of seeing India, China, Paris.

The Ukraine.

She should have gone home with Maksym.

Old, long-familiar regrets haunted her. How different her life might have been if she had followed the instincts of her twenty-one-year-old heart and chosen love over obligation.

If only she had taken a chance, once in her life.

"Okay," Roxy said. "Only five more minutes. You need to be wrapping things up now."

Julia gazed down at her mostly blank paper. She wasn't writing a stupid novel here. No one else needed to see it. She only needed to write down a few of the many things she longed to do. How hard was that?

She took a long, fortifying drink of sangria and wrote quickly, forcing herself not to self-edit.

Try escargot.

Kiss someone special under the mistletoe.

Get a puppy.

That one made her stop. Why *didn't* she get a puppy?

Her parents had never wanted one when they were alive, but they were gone now. There was nothing really stopping her, was there?

"Okay, one more minute. You've got time to add one, maybe two more things to your list."

All the possibilities crowded through her mind, and she quickly wrote one that seemed bigger than the rest.

Make a difference in someone's life.

"I know I said we were done, but now I want you to add one more."

Everyone groaned, but Roxy just gave an evil grin.

"I want you to write the very next thing that comes into your mind. Don't edit it or run it through any internal filters. Just write it."

Julia stared at the page, her mind a jumbled mix of the book they had read—of the author's heated relationship with a hot-blooded Spaniard she met on her journey of self-discovery—all tangled up with memories of Maksym and her own brief time with him, when she had been too young and naive to know herself and what she needed.

She swallowed the last of her sangria and wrote quickly, before she could change her mind.

Have an orgasm, with someone else.

The moment she wrote the words, she wanted to cross them out, but it was too late. Besides, they were written in purple Sharpie. She folded her paper, hoping like hell nobody else saw it.

"Now, wasn't that fun?" Roxy beamed at them all.

"Sure," Megan muttered. "Next time, let's all go get colonoscopies together."

"Anybody want to share something off her list? Remember, this is a no-judgment zone."

Barbara Serrano was the first to break the silence. "I want to stay home this Christmas Eve and not have to cook a single thing for anyone."

"Hear, hear," Charlene Bailey said enthusiastically. "And I'd like to go on another cruise, one to Alaska this time."

Everyone seemed inclined to share something on her list. Julia was going to remain quiet and let them have all the fun, but on impulse, when the conversation began to wane, she blurted out the least embarrassing thing on her list.

"I'd like to get a puppy. I've always loved dogs, but my parents never wanted one. My mom always had cats and my dad thought dogs were too big of a mess and bother."

"Oh, you should!" Andie Bailey exclaimed. "We adore our dog."

"What's stopping you?" Katrina asked.

Julia shrugged and poured another drink. She wasn't driving home, so why not?

"I live alone and I work long hours. I don't have time to give a puppy the attention it deserves—to train it and walk it and play with it. It wouldn't be fair."

"Get two puppies," Eppie Brewer suggested. "That way they can entertain each other."

And chew up every antique in the house, too.

"I think I'll stick with one of the other items on my list."

She would stick to driving her car on the freeway or trying escargot.

Right now, anything more seemed wholly out of reach.

THE REST OF the book club meeting was much more enjoyable. Roxy—clever girl—brought out more sangria to go with the potluck meal. By the time everyone decided to pick up their lists and go home, Julia realized that for the first time since McKenzie Kilpatrick's bachelorette party a few years before, she was more than a little tipsy.

The best kind of guests always cleaned up after themselves. And her friends were the absolute best. Julia looked around her gleaming kitchen, touched that she didn't have hours of dishes ahead of her. The only thing left was to take out the last bag of trash.

She opened the door to her guest bedrooms, where she had contained the cats for the evening so they didn't bother her company, then picked up the garbage bag and headed out, propping her door behind her.

Outside, a cold November wind blew through her sweater, making her shiver. They were supposed to have a few inches of snow that night, and the air had that funny, expectant, heavy feeling to it.

A black SUV was in her driveway, and she gazed at it for about five seconds, wondering if one of the book club guests might be in the bathroom, before she remembered it belonged to Jamie Caine.

Her tenant was home. Somehow in all the commotion of the party, she had missed his return.

Not that she had been watching for him or anything.

She shivered again, more from the lie she was telling herself this time than from the cold. Of course she had been watching for him. She had a man living in her house, and this was the first night he had spent under the same roof.

How would she possibly make it through the next six weeks?

CHAPTER THREE

HE HAD A VISITOR.

At the third plaintive yowl in as many minutes from the landing outside his new apartment, Jamie set down his book and headed to the door. When he opened it, he found one of Julia Winston's cats, the same lithe black beauty he had held earlier. She bounded inside to rub against his leg and instantly began to purr.

He chuckled and picked her up, holding her out so he could gaze into her green eyes.

"Hi there. I don't think you're supposed to be up here, but maybe you didn't get the memo."

She meowed in answer, giving him an unblinking stare.

"Are you looking for something? Did you leave your favorite toy up here?" he asked, stroking her silky fur.

She purred and rubbed her head against his hand, making him smile.

It had been a long time since he'd had much to do with cats. His mother had always loved them, but the succession of big, boisterous dogs he and his brothers and Charlotte were constantly taking home to Winterberry Lane in Hope's Crossing didn't always make for the most comfortable environment for its feline occupants.

His poor mother had put up with so much from her

brood. As always, he felt a pang when he remembered Margaret Caine, gone too young from cancer.

He petted the cat a few more moments, finding an odd sort of peace in it. He would like to have taken her in, charmed more than he might have expected by the idea of sitting by the gas fireplace in his apartment on a cold night, with a good book and a cat on his lap. He couldn't just commandeer a cat. His landlady would probably be looking for her.

"You'd better go home," he said, trying to set the cat down. She yowled in protest and wriggled to stay in his arms.

"Fine. I'll take you down myself," he said.

Jamie didn't bother with shoes as he headed down the steps to the entryway. He was about five or six steps from the bottom when the doorknob to the outside door turned and a moment later, Julia walked inside.

Her hair looked a bit messy, as if tangled by a stiff wind, and she wobbled a little as she pushed the door open. She was humming a song, and it took him a few bars before he recognized the tune. "Blue Christmas."

She didn't appear to notice him as she came inside, still humming and looking a little unsteady.

Jamie decided he had to announce himself, since she still didn't appear to notice him even when he walked the rest of the way down the steps.

"I think I have something of yours."

She shrieked and jumped a foot into the air, then whirled around with her hands in front of her in a classic martial arts defensive pose.

Whoa. Ninja librarian.

He knew the instant she recognized him. Color soaked her cheeks, and she dropped her hands.

"Oh! You scared the daylights out of me!"

"Sorry about that. I should have announced myself somehow."

"It's not your fault. I... I guess I must have been... thinking about something else."

The words *something else* came out slightly slurred and as he approached her, he noticed her cheeks seemed a little bit more flushed than he could attribute to a normal blush and her violet eyes looked a little dazed.

Unless he was very much mistaken, his prim, uptight landlady was slightly tipsy, maybe from the gathering that had just broken up down here within the last half hour or so.

He had to admit, he found this soft, flustered version of Julia Winston rather appealing.

"I had a visitor upstairs, and I thought you might be looking for her."

He held out the cat, who still seemed reluctant to leave his arms.

"Oh. Audrey Hepburn. You rascal."

He couldn't hold back his smile. "Your cat's name is Audrey Hepburn?"

"Not my cat," she corrected. "My mother's cat. They're all my mother's cats. Yes, her name is Audrey Hepburn. My mother was a big fan of *Roman Holiday*."

"*Charade* is my favorite of her work."

"Same here!" Her eyes were wide with disbelief, as if she couldn't fathom the idea that they might share a favorite movie.

It surprised him a little, too. He might have figured her for someone who preferred dry literary movies or the kind of foreign films he couldn't understand without subtitles. Then again, she was tipsy in her hallway after a wild gathering with friends on a weeknight. Maybe he wasn't as good a judge of character as he thought.

"Sounds like you were having quite a party earlier."

"Oh. I'm sorry I didn't warn you about my book club. I hope we didn't bother you."

"It sounded a little raucous for a book club." He didn't mention the fact that she seemed a little buzzed.

"We're not usually this crazy," she confided. "Roxy Nash brought this really great autumn sangria. It had apples and cinnamon and pears and was *so* good. We all got a little carried away. I think we might have underestimated slightly the alcohol content. I promise. I don't have wild book club parties very often."

"Too bad. Make sure you invite me to the next one. I'd love to see Hazel and Eppie get smashed."

Much to his shock, her gaze seemed fixed on his smile.

Or his mouth, anyway.

Now what would a prim and proper woman like Julia Winston find so fascinating about his mouth? Did he have something stuck in his teeth?

He gave her a closer look and his interest sharpened. Her lips parted and then she swallowed hard. If he didn't know better, he would swear that was a little hint of attraction he saw in her eyes.

Who would have guessed?

"You know Hazel and Eppie?" she asked after a long moment.

"Oh, yes. They're two of my favorite people in Haven Point."

"Mine, too," she said, in that same surprised tone. He had the feeling she wasn't all that thrilled at finding more points of commonality between them.

He decided to quit while he was ahead.

"Anyway, here's your cat."

He tried to hand the little beast to Julia, but once more she clung to him and yowled her protest. "Sorry. Apparently she likes me."

"Of course she does," Julia muttered darkly. "She likes you and she hates me. They all hate me."

He heard a little thread of despondency in her voice that troubled him.

"Who all hates you?" He had to ask.

"The cats. My mother's cats. Audrey hates me the least, I guess. Empress and Tabitha despise me."

"I'm sure that's not true," he answered, with no other idea of what to say in this circumstance.

"It is true. All they do is turn up their noses like they're too good to even notice me. It's not fair. I feed them, I house them, I clean up their... Well, you know. You would think they might show a little gratitude."

"Cats aren't exactly known to be overflowing in appreciation for others."

"I know, right? They act like I should be the grateful one that they're letting me clean up after them. Seriously. It's so unfair."

She glared at him, as if the temperament of the entire feline species was his fault. "Look at her. I should have known Audrey would love *you*. Everything female does."

What was he supposed to make of *that* particular statement? Was he supposed to apologize? He also wasn't quite sure what he should do about his tipsy landlady. He didn't feel right about leaving her alone in this condition.

On the other hand, he barely knew the woman. For

all he knew, maybe she went on a bender *every* Monday night.

He didn't think so, though. Julia Winston struck him as someone who rarely let herself unwind.

While he was trying to figure out his best response, she apparently decided she was done talking with him.

"Come on, Audrey. Let's go."

She stepped closer, and he caught the scent of apples and pears and cinnamon, with a heady undertone of white wine. As she reached out again to take the cat from him, her hands brushed his chest. Was it his imagination or did they linger there a little longer than strictly necessary as she tried to scoop up the reluctant animal?

That tentative touch combined with the awareness he had seen in her gaze earlier sent heat curling through him.

Seriously? He was starting to be turned on by his half-drunk, stuffy librarian?

Only because it had been way too long since he'd had a woman's soft, warm hands anywhere on his body, he told himself.

She didn't look much like a stuffy librarian now, with that soft hair slipping free and her cheeks pink and her little tongue darting out to lick her bottom lip.

Somehow seeing this unexpectedly unbuttoned side of her was more sensual than if she'd shown up at his door wearing sexy lingerie.

The cat still didn't seem inclined to leave his arms, but between his efforts and Julia's, they managed to extricate her. Julia set the cat down, and after a moment, the animal sauntered inside, probably to share her evening adventure with the other two cats.

Julia frowned after her.

"Sorry if she bothered you."

"She didn't. I like cats."

"Of course you do," she said, that grumpy tone in her voice again. She gave a heavy sigh. "Why do you have to be so gorgeous? It's not fair."

The inappropriate attraction he heroically had been trying to suppress slithered back as if someone had set a match to a detonating wire.

"It's not?" he said stupidly.

She shook her head so vigorously that more hair came loose from her messy bun. "No. Can't you do something about that? I mean, I wouldn't want you to have a disfiguring accident or something. That would be horrible. A scar, maybe. Something that would make you not quite so...perfect."

He wasn't perfect. Far from it.

"Maybe I could develop adult-onset acne," he suggested.

The scowl disappeared as her eyes widened with approval. "Yes! That would be great."

He laughed. "I'll see what I can do."

"See? You're so nice. That's why all the girls like you so much. The girl people *and* the girl cats."

He laughed again, more intrigued than he had been by a woman in a long, long time. Maybe living upstairs from the town librarian wouldn't be such a hardship, after all.

"Thanks for that. Are you going to be okay? I'm not sure I feel right about leaving you alone in your... condition."

"What's my condition?" She narrowed her gaze at him like a confused baby owl.

"Sleepy. The best thing for you right now, trust me, is to get some rest."

As if his words had planted the seed, she yawned suddenly. "I am tired. I guess you're right."

"Good night, Ms. Winston."

"You can call me Julia. If you want to."

As she stood with her hand on the door and her hair falling loose, she looked vulnerable and alone and a little lost.

He had the odd thought that the two of them just might be kindred spirits.

The moment the idea entered his brain he pushed it violently away. Kindred spirits? He and an uptight, prickly librarian?

How stupid was that?

"You got it, Julia. And I'm Jamie."

"I know," she whispered.

He had to get out of here before he did something stupid.

"Good night."

He started to close the door behind her, but she stuck her foot it in and stood with her face wedged between the door and the frame. "Wait. If we were on a date, you would kiss me."

Her lips suddenly seemed eminently kissable, plump and pink and delicious looking. What would she do if he pulled the rest of her wayward hair down, buried his hands in it and pressed her back against that door?

She was impaired, he reminded himself.

"Maybe. If you wanted me to."

"I would," she whispered.

She was impaired, plus she was a stodgy librarian

and totally not his type, he reminded himself. Still, he couldn't help wondering what it would be like to taste her.

Because she looked so lonely and because he tried to be that nice guy to girl people and girl cats alike, he leaned in and kissed her forehead.

"Good night, Julia. Sleep well."

She gave a wistful-sounding sigh and closed the door.

Heart pounding far more than it should be, Jamie headed for the stairs.

Julia Winston was trouble.

Who would have guessed? His tight-laced, no-nonsense landlady had a core of passion and heat inside of her. The man who could unleash that would be very lucky, indeed.

He wasn't that man. He could never be—no matter how hard he might wish otherwise.

CHAPTER FOUR

"How are you holding up, my dear?"

Julia managed a half smile for Barbara Serrano as she scanned her pile of library books into the system.

"I'm here and I'm breathing. That's something, right?"

Barbara laughed. "That sangria was lethal. Trust Roxy to get us all hammered, right before Thanksgiving. I haven't had a hangover since my sorority days."

The very dignified restaurant owner still didn't appear to have a hair out of place. Lucky.

"I'm doing okay so far. Over the last few hours, my headache has slipped down to *this sucks* level, which is a big improvement from this morning's, when I thought I was going to have to borrow a power drill to relieve the pressure in my skull."

Barbara chuckled. "It was a fun night, though, wasn't it? I hope we weren't too loud for your new neighbor."

At the reminder of Jamie, the vague, unsettling feeling that had been haunting her all day returned with a vengeance.

She couldn't seem to shake the feeling that something...*untoward* had happened with him the night before.

She had these odd snippets of memory, and she wasn't sure if they were real or some fantasy-fueled dream. She could picture him, clear as day, standing on her stairs in his bare feet, holding a cat.

Would she have conjured that up out of her imagination? Possibly. But what about the masculine scent of him, bergamot and cedar with a little hint of cloves? Why did that seem so clear in her memory bank?

Worse than that, somehow the words *Jamie* and *kiss* had become intertwined in her mind. That was ridiculous, of course. Wasn't it?

She hadn't seen the man the night before. She was almost positive of it. But then, she only had loose recollections of the evening from about her fourth sangria on.

She hoped with all her heart that she was imagining those little flickers of memory. It would have been beyond humiliating if Jamie had seen her in that condition.

"How are your tatted snowflakes coming for the booth at the Lights on the Lake festival?" Barbara asked.

"Fine," she lied.

The truth was, while she had loved the craft she learned from Mariah—the delicate knots and rings with thread to make lace—lately she had struggled to summon any enthusiasm. Sitting in her huge Victorian with her cats and her tatting made her feel so old and spinsterish.

"Can you believe it's Thanksgiving in two days and then all the holiday craziness is upon us?" Barbara's eyes gleamed with an anticipation that made Julia tired.

"Where did the year go?" she asked rhetorically. She knew too well. It went to working, dealing with the house, fixing the furnace, visiting her mother, then arranging her mother's estate after her death.

"Are you sure you won't come over for dinner?" Barbara asked when Julia finished checking out her books. "We'll have a full house and would love one more."

"Thank you again for the kind offer but I'll be fine. I'm already signed up to help out at the nursing home. I'm taking Muriel Randall."

"Oh, that will be good for her."

The place in Shelter Springs where her mother had spent her last few months had several patrons without families. Julia didn't love it there but also couldn't bear the thought that anyone might feel alone.

"Well, I'd better run," Barbara said after they chatted a bit more. "I would love to finish a few chapters of that new Nora Roberts book before some of our houseguests show up in the morning."

"Enjoy," she said.

Julia was busy most of the afternoon with patron questions and checkouts. She answered three phone calls to the reference desk, asking how to thaw a turkey. There would be more the next day, she suspected.

By early evening, her headache had abated, leaving just an echo of throbbing.

She made the rounds to the few groups of teenagers at the study tables to make sure they knew the library would be closing soon. When she rounded a corner of the stacks, she found Davy and Clinton, the boys from the day before, quietly playing a card game at a table.

She hadn't seen them come in. Perhaps they had entered the library when she had been taking a break.

Both boys looked up with wary expressions when she headed in their direction.

"Hi, Davy. Hi, Clinton. How are you boys this evening?"

Davy gave a dramatic sigh. "I'm hungry, but Clint

says he'll make me another peanut butter sandwich when we have to go home."

That particular statement disturbed her on several levels. Julia tried to conceal her reaction. Where were their parents? From what she had seen firsthand and from what she had inferred from Davy's comments, it seemed Clint was doing more parenting than an eight-year-old boy should.

Something was going on here, but she had no idea how to figure out what or how to fix it. She did know Davy was hungry, and she had the means to remedy that.

"You know," she said casually, "I happen to have a sandwich in the back. It's turkey instead of peanut butter, but I think you'll find it quite tasty."

"Really?" The little boy's eyes lit up. "I thought we weren't s'posed to eat in the library."

"Food isn't allowed out here in the book stacks, but you're fine to eat in the back. I do it all the time. Do you know, if we cut the sandwich in half, I think it would be more than enough for two boys."

She'd had such good intentions that morning when she packed her lunch, but her hangover had been too wicked earlier in the day to tolerate anything solid. She had ended up heating a cup of soup in the microwave.

"Did you hear that, Clint? Miss Winston has a sandwich she said we could eat!"

While the younger boy looked thrilled, his brother's reluctance showed through. He shook his head with a stubborn look. "No. We'd better not. Thanks anyway, Miss Winston."

"Nonsense," she said in a brisk tone. "You're hungry, and I have an extra sandwich that will only go to waste if you don't help me out by eating it. Think of it this way—you would be doing me a favor."

Davy looked at his brother. "Mom said we're supposed to help other people out when we can, especially this time of year. Remember? Miss Winston needs someone to help her eat her sandwich."

Clinton didn't look particularly convinced by that argument, but after a moment he shrugged. "I guess it would be okay. As long as we're helping you."

She smiled, touched beyond words that these two boys in their threadbare coats were concerned about helping others—but she was also undeniably troubled. She admired their mother's sentiment about helping people out, but where was the woman? And why was she allowing her young boys to go hungry?

"Why don't you both come to the back with me, and I'll find the sandwich for you? There might be a cookie or two in my desk, as well."

They stuffed their belongings back into their backpacks and followed her through the door that read Library Staff Only, to the inner workings of the library. Three doors down, she led them to the small room her staff used for breaks.

"Sit down and I'll find the sandwich for you."

From the refrigerator she pulled out her favorite reusable lunch bag with the pink and purple flowers and pulled out the sandwich. It was an easy matter to cut it in two and set it on paper plates for the boys.

"Look at this. There are chips and carrots here, as well as a brownie."

She had been looking forward to that brownie, a leftover from last night's book club, but she would willingly sacrifice to these two little boys, who inhaled the sandwich as if it were the best thing they had ever eaten.

Once she set the bounty in front of them, Julia took a chair at the table and sipped at the water bottle that hadn't left her side all day. Hydration was one of the best cures for a hangover, she had read online that morning through the blur of her headache. It hadn't worked yet, but she could still hope.

"I bet your mom fixes you nice lunches for school, doesn't she?"

Davy looked at his brother, then quickly back down at his plate. Neither boy answered her. They simply shrugged. Obviously this was a sore spot.

"What about your dad?"

"Our dad died," Clint said, his voice flat. "He was in the army, and he got shot three years ago."

Emotions clogged her throat at the no-nonsense tone. "Oh, no. I'm so sorry."

"I was only three," Davy informed her. "I don't even remember him much. Clint was five, though."

They couldn't have been from Hope's Crossing or even Shelter Springs. She would have heard about a soldier from the area being killed in the line of duty. And why were the sons of a dead soldier wearing such ragged coats and eating peanut butter and jelly sandwiches?

"That must have been very hard for you and for your mother."

"It was," Clinton said. "Our mom was in the army too, but she came home right away. She cried a lot. We were living with our Aunt Suzi then."

"Are you going to your Aunt Suzi's house for Thanksgiving?" she asked, trying to probe for answers as subtly as possible without it sounding like a blatant interrogation.

Clinton gave her an exasperated look. "That's all the way by Disneyland! That's too far. And she's not there anyway."

"That's in California," Davy informed her. "It's warm there all the time—not like here, where our house is cold all the time."

Clinton poked his brother, giving him a shushing sort of look that Julia pretended not to see.

"California does have beautiful weather. That's true. Why did you move away?"

"Our mom got a new job here, but then she got sick and had to quit," Davy said.

It was obvious Clinton thought his brother had said too much. He set down his napkin and slid away from the table. "We should probably go now. Our mom will be wondering where we are."

"Really?" Davy said.

"Yes," Clint said with a meaningful look. "Thank you for the sandwich, Miss Winston. It was very good."

"You're welcome."

Julia was at a loss as to what to do next. Did she tell the boys she suspected something wasn't quite right with them? That she wanted to have a talk with their mother to find out a little more about their situation, but she had no idea where they even lived?

The boys hadn't left a scrap, Julia realized. They had all but licked the plates clean, poor things.

She was suddenly ashamed of herself. She had so very much—good friends, a job she loved, a beautiful home that kept her warm in the winter.

At this time of Thanksgiving, she realized again

how very blessed she was. In the four months since her mother died, how much time had she wasted feeling sorry for herself?

What about the years and years before that?

The three of them walked out of the library offices together and out into the stacks. Very few patrons remained.

"I guess I'll see you later, then."

"We'll probably be here tomorrow since we don't have school," Davy said.

Why? She loved libraries as much as the next person. More, probably. Still, what kid with free time would choose to spend every moment of it in one?

"You know the library closes early tomorrow, right?"

Clint and Davy looked shocked and rather glum to learn this.

"What time does it open?" Clinton asked, brow furrowed.

"We'll be open from ten to three."

"That's not too bad, I guess. Come on, Davy. Let's go."

Before they walked outside, Clint stopped to zip up his younger brother's coat and tug down his beanie. It was those small, loving gestures that compelled her to action.

The wind was howling fiercely, and snowflakes swirled around the pair. She couldn't possibly let them walk home in those conditions.

She hurried over to the clerk behind the circulation desk. "Mack, do you think you can close up by yourself? I need to run a little errand."

"Sure thing." Mack Porter gave her a wide smile. "It's only twenty minutes, and I don't think too many more people will be showing up tonight. It's getting ugly out there. Be safe."

All the more reason she wanted to follow those boys. "Thanks. Have a great night."

"Same to you, my dear."

It took her three minutes to grab her coat and purse from her office, shut down her computer, lock her office door and hurry to her Lexus. Had she missed them? She scanned the direction she had seen them take the night before, fretting until she found them about a block away, walking along the lakefront road.

A cold wind blew off the water, harsh and mean, biting through her clothing with merciless teeth and hurling tiny ice pellets into her skin. She started up her SUV, spent another minute or two brushing off the new snow, then drove out of the parking lot and along the mostly empty road toward them.

She passed them and pulled off to the side of the road just ahead of them. After opening her door, she turned to face them. She had to raise her voice several decibels to be heard over the howling wind. "Let me give you a ride."

"We can walk," Clint said, that steely stubbornness she had noticed before coming through loud and clear.

"Y-y-y-es. We're f-f-fine," Davy said. His thin coat wasn't nearly enough protection to fight off that wind.

"Please. Let me give you a ride. Where do you live?"

They had reached her vehicle now, trudging through ankle-deep snow. "Can we, Clint?" Davy asked. "My feet are *freezing*, and we hardly made it a block."

The older boy looked undecided, glancing first at her vehicle, then at her, then at the road ahead of them. His mouth pursed as he tried to figure out what to do.

She gave him another push in the direction she hoped he would take.

"Come on. Get in."

"We're not supposed to take rides from strangers," he finally said, though she could hear the clear reluctance in his voice. "Come on, Davy. The faster we go, the faster we'll be home."

They took a few more steps past her vehicle. Davy looked miserable, his nose red and his chin tucked into his chest as he fought to make his way through the cold.

"I'm not a stranger. I'm the librarian. You see me every day when you come to my library," she pointed out.

"She's right," Davy said.

"It's not safe for you boys to be out here. The roads are icy, and drivers can't see you very well through the blowing snow, especially now that it's dark. Please get in."

He still looked reluctant, so she tried one more card, playing a hunch. "Would you feel better if I call my friend, Chief Emmett, to give you a ride home in his police car?"

In the glow from her open door, she saw a flash of fear in his eyes. Julia felt bad for putting it there, but not if it meant the older boy would let her give them a ride home.

"We can take a ride, I guess," he finally said.

She made sure they were buckled safely in the backseat of her vehicle before she pulled slowly onto the road.

"Where am I going?"

"Five-fifty Sulfur Hollow Road," Davy said promptly. Traffic was basically nonexistent as she drove with care to their house. The roads were slick enough that she couldn't go fast. Her hands were tight and clammy on the steering wheel by the time they made it to the address they provided.

The sight of the small, thin-walled house was not reassuring.

"Here we are. The lights are off. Where did you say your mom was?"

"She's home, I bet," Clint said. "She's probably sleeping. She works at night sometimes."

"Oh? I thought you said she lost her job. Did she get another one? Where does she work? And who stays with the two of you when she's working?"

He mumbled something she couldn't hear, unhooked his own seat belt, then his brother's and then practically jumped out of the vehicle, tugging Davy out after him.

"Thanks for the ride. We have to go. Bye, Miss Winston."

"Bye," Davy said. He beamed at her. "Thanks for the sandwich and the brownie. You're a good cook."

"Um. Thanks."

The boys hurried up the walk. Clint pulled a key out of his coat pocket, and before she knew it, they had yanked open the door and rushed inside.

Julia stood for a moment, watching a pale light go on inside.

Dropping them off at home had done nothing to ease her concerns. If anything, seeing the small, dingy house gave her fresh reason for concern.

She was trying to manufacture some plausible reason to go to the door when she suddenly spied something red on the backseat that hadn't been there before the boys climbed inside.

One of Davy's ragged mittens.

Had he left it there on purpose? She couldn't be sure, but returning it to its rightful owner seemed exactly the excuse she needed.

Apprehension settled in her stomach as she made her way through unshoveled snow to the sidewalk. She had no idea what she would encounter on the other side. Was their mother a gorgon? Maybe she was ill, and the boys were staying at the library until all hours to give her some peace and quiet.

She had to know.

She knocked, clutching the collar of her coat closed to keep out the vicious wind.

A moment later, Clint opened the door, his expression pinched and wary. He hadn't yet taken off his coat, she noticed—probably because the air inside the small house felt every bit as cold as the outside air here on the porch.

"Davy left one of his mittens in my car." She held it out.

"Oh. Thanks. Bye." He grabbed it from her and started to shove the door closed, but she pulled the old trick of shoving her boot in it before he could, and pushed her way inside.

The house was lit by only a bare bulb here in the hallway. It was clean, but there was a palpable air of neglect.

She saw a space heater in one corner and a couple of sleeping bags neatly rolled up nearby. Were the boys sleeping in here with the space heater?

She could hear no sign of their mother, or, indeed, any adult.

"Clint. I need to talk to your mom. Is she here?"

He opened his mouth, then closed it again. "No. She must be working."

"Where does she work? Can you give me her work phone number?"

He said nothing and she tried again.

"Does she have a cell phone number I could call?" she asked.

"You could try, but she's not answering."

His voice broke on the last word, but he clamped his mouth together tightly, as if afraid that once he started talking, he wouldn't be able to stop.

Something terrible was going on here. She still didn't know what, but she suddenly knew she couldn't stop until she found out.

She uttered a fervent prayer that she could figure out the best way to reach him. Somehow she sensed he would respond better if she were on his level, so she knelt down and took one of his cold hands in hers.

"Clinton," she said softly. "How long since you've seen your mother?"

He hitched in a ragged breath, eyes wide. She could see he didn't want to answer her, but his fingers curled in hers, and she saw all his bravado begin to crumble. Tears welled up in his eyes, and one trickled down the side of his nose.

"Friday. She had a doctor's appointment at the army hospital place in Boise, and she…she didn't come back. And the furnace is out, and I don't know how to make it work, and I tried to start a fire, but I couldn't do that either. It's cold everywhere except in here with the space heater."

"You said she's not answering her phone?"

He shook his head. "I tried and tried and tried to

call her, but she didn't answer. I didn't know what to do so I just took care of Davy the best I could, and we spent the days at school and the library, where it was warm and safe."

"Oh, honey."

Four days they had been on their own. She couldn't imagine what he had been going through. He was only eight years old, far too young for that kind of responsibility.

He sniffled again, and it was too much. Heart breaking, she held out her arms. "Come here. Come here."

He sagged against her, as if sharing the burden he had been carrying had left him boneless and exhausted.

"Please, don't call the cops. If you do, we'll go to foster care, and they'll split us up."

"I have to call someone, honey. Children aren't supposed to be left alone for days at a time."

"Please, don't. Just go." He slid away from her and stood looking fearful and impossibly young.

"I can't do that," she said softly. "You know I can't. You need help, and I have a good friend whose job is to help children in just this kind of situation. I'm going to call her, and she'll fix things."

He didn't look convinced as she hit her speed dial for Wynona Emmett, who used to be a police officer but was now a social worker with the state child welfare agency.

As she waited for Wyn to answer, Julia had the uncomfortable realization that an hour ago, her biggest problem was a lingering hangover and the stupid crush she had on the neighbor upstairs.

CHAPTER FIVE

"WHAT'S GOING TO happen to them?" Through the kitchen doorway, Julia eyed the two little boys sitting side by side on the tattered, raggedy sofa.

Since the moment Wynona Emmett showed up, Clinton had been visibly—and audibly—upset, full of accusations and pleas for them to go away. Davy mostly seemed confused, though he took his cues from his brother and sniffed every once in a while.

Julia felt horrible about the whole situation. Maybe she shouldn't have gotten involved, should have simply looked the other way.

How could she have, though? Any person with an ounce of compassion would have done the same thing she had, called in the state's department of child welfare. If ever two children's welfare needed looking after, it was Clint's and Davy's.

The boys couldn't stay here in this cold, cheerless house. Their mother was nowhere in evidence, and it looked as if they hadn't had a decent meal in days.

"I don't know what will happen to them," Wynona admitted. Her eyes were soft with compassion as she looked through the doorway at the boys. "They'll go into foster care, definitely, probably a short-term facility in Boise for now, until we can find a longer-term placement."

"So they'll have to leave their friends and their teachers? While we were waiting for you, Clinton was so pleased to tell me about how well he's doing in school."

"I wish I could find something closer to Haven Point. Believe me, there's nothing I would love more. It would be better, all the way around. But local foster families are in short supply, especially this time of year when the need outpaces the available resources. There is a chance I could place one of them in the area, but not both."

Out in the living room, Clint put an arm around his brother, who had started to sob—whether from fear or exhaustion, she didn't know.

"You'll have to split them up?"

"Most likely," Wyn admitted. Julia could tell she wasn't any happier about that idea than Julia. Wyn's expression plainly conveyed her frustration with the situation.

"Any idea where the mother might be?"

"We've put out a BOLO on her. Be on the lookout. Sorry. I forget not everybody knows cop-speak."

"I watch TV occasionally," Julia said. "I know what a BOLO means."

"She never showed up for her appointment at the VA. We've been able to figure that much out."

Wyn gave a careful look toward the boys, then turned her body away and spoke in a low voice. "I really hope we can locate her. Her counselor at the VA couldn't tell us much because of privacy laws. Reading between the lines, though, it sounds like Mikaela Slater has been struggling the last few weeks."

"Oh, I hope she's okay. They've already lost their father. I hate thinking they might lose their mother, too. What about extended family? Clint told me the boys lived with an aunt and uncle while their parents were both deployed."

"It might take us some time to track them down. Clinton says they're working in a country that starts with an A or an I. He couldn't remember which one. That doesn't narrow it down much."

In the other room, Davy sobbed, and Clint patted his back and said something to him.

Julia's distress must have shown on her features. Wyn reached out and squeezed her arm. "You did the right thing, honey. You know you had no choice. I'll see the boys find a good placement."

"You'll let me know what happens?"

"Absolutely. I won't know anything definite until tomorrow anyway. Tonight they'll go to the temporary facility in Shelter Springs, where they'll be well taken care of, I promise."

"Thank you."

Wyn squeezed her arm again, and Julia recognized the gesture as one of both comfort and dismissal. Wyn had more important things to do than allay her concerns.

Feeling helpless and superfluous, Julia walked out into the living room to say goodbye to the boys.

Before she could open her mouth, Clinton threw her a look of deep mistrust.

"This is your fault," he said, voice vibrating with anger and his eyes dark with betrayal. "We should never have let you give us a ride. No, we shouldn't have gone to the library in the first place."

"Oh, honey. I'm sorry."

"We were doing just fine. I heard what the lady said. Now they're probably going to split us up."

"I'm sorry," she said again. The words seemed wholly inadequate.

"We thought you were our friend, but you're not. You're just a big...poopie," Davy cried. That was probably the worst word he could come up with. Right now, it felt pretty accurate.

"Just go," Clint said.

Julia wanted to gather both boys close to offer what little comfort she could, but she knew they wouldn't welcome the gesture right now.

Oh, she hoped Wyn was able to find their mother—and soon. She couldn't bear considering the alternative.

Her heart felt as cold and heavy as the wind blowing through Sulfur Hollow as she walked out to her car.

ALL HE WANTED was a lousy shower. Was that too much to ask?

Jamie knocked hard again on his landlady's door, willing her to answer, even though all the evidence indicated the woman wasn't home.

He had made two trips to California that day, transporting Caine Tech employees who had family there home for Thanksgiving. The last one had been through a vicious storm.

Okay, he wanted a shower and a beer, maybe, and his nice, warm bed.

He knocked one more time, though he already knew it was futile. Inside, he could hear a couple of cats meowing at him, but no approaching footsteps.

She wasn't home, which meant he wouldn't have hot water.

Okay. No hot shower. He could either suck it up and

have a cold one or heat up some water in the microwave so he could at least wash up.

He had been deployed to the Middle East twice. He had survived much worse conditions.

He turned away from the door and was about to head up the stairs to his apartment when he noticed headlights pulling into the driveway and into the detached garage on the property.

A moment later, the front door opened, and Julia Winston walked in, moving slowly, as if her bones weighed more than she could support. Something was wrong. He wasn't sure how he could be so confident when he barely knew the woman, but he knew it at a glance.

Surprise flickered in those hauntingly lovely eyes when she spotted him. He saw a quick flash of something that looked suspiciously like dismay.

Was she thinking about the night before, about those heated few moments?

You're so nice. That's why all the girls like you so much.

He had been thinking about her all day. He had done his best to push those thoughts away, but it hadn't worked very well.

At random moments, he would remember those beautiful eyes of hers and the tousled bedroom hair and the way her tongue had darted out to lick at her plump bottom lip.

Now those same lips tightened. "Oh. Hello. I'm sorry. You're looking for me. Have you been waiting long?"

"A few minutes."

He immediately wanted to demand she tell him what had upset her but that would probably sound ridiculous.

"I was…held up after work. Did you need something?"

Yes. For you to tell me what's wrong. He couldn't say that, of course.

His real reason for knocking on her door seemed silly, and suddenly he didn't want to burden her with one more thing. It was obvious she had greater worries than his hot water—or, more specifically, the lack thereof.

Without telling her the truth, though, he couldn't think of a good excuse for standing outside her door.

He sighed. "It's not a big deal, and I hate to bother you with it. I don't have any hot water. I was heading into the shower and ran it for about ten minutes, and the temperature seemed to only get colder."

"Oh." She looked totally defeated, as if all color and light had leached away from her world.

"I'm sure it's something simple. Do you mind if I take a look at your water heater? I might be able to figure it out."

"I…no. Of course not."

"Is it inside your apartment or…" He let his voice trail off.

"Oh. Yes. You want to go inside." She unlocked the door and pushed it open. "I'm sorry. It's been a…long day."

She unlocked the door and pushed it open. Immediately, a trio of cats rushed past her to greet Jamie.

She didn't blink at that, as if their defection was all she deserved.

Inside her house, he had the same impression as the other night, one of fussy tidiness. Some instinct told him the decor on this floor of the house wasn't the real her, that she was only maintaining the antiques and collectibles out of obligation. She would fit much better among the delicate, feminine furnishings upstairs.

Saying nothing, she led him through the living area to her kitchen, where she opened a door and flipped on a light. Stone steps led the way down to a large stone basement that had likely once been the root cellar of the house. Now, as Julia led the way down the stairs, he discovered a furnace and water heater that both looked new.

He looked around the space. "This is quite a cellar."

"I know. I hated coming down here when I was a girl. I'm still not that crazy about it, if you want the truth. I avoid it as much as possible."

As soon as she spoke the words, she looked as if she wanted to take them back, as if she hated revealing a weakness about herself.

He wanted to tell her he found it charming. It also made him wonder what she had been like as a little girl, all gorgeous, serious eyes and long, dark braids. He didn't know how he knew she had braids, but he could picture them, clear as day.

"The water heater shouldn't be having trouble. It's brand-new and still under warranty," she said. "I had it installed when the furnace went out this fall."

"Let me just take a look."

He didn't know much about water heaters, but he figured if he could fix some of the tricky mechanical problems of his airplanes, he should be able to figure this out.

He tinkered for a moment and quickly realized the pilot light had gone out on the water heater.

After trying the regulator on the pilot a few times with no success, he sought an alternative.

"Got a match?" he asked.

"Not on me," she answered with a rueful look. "But my father always kept some down here to light the pilot on our old furnace."

She went to a shelf along the wall that still held dusty preserves. After rooting around a moment, she pulled out a box of long matches. "I can't guarantee they'll still light," she said. "My dad's been gone three years now."

"I'm sorry," he said. His pop was still going strong. Jamie hated thinking of a world that didn't have Dermot Caine in it.

"Thank you. He was a good man, even toward the end. Some people with Alzheimer's get mean, but my father was always the sweetest, most gentle man."

Alzheimer's. That was tough. He knew how heartbreaking that damn disease could be.

Her mother had recently died, he remembered. Eliza had mentioned her mother had spent her last few months in a nursing home after a series of strokes, which meant she had been through more than her share. Eliza had also told him Julia was an only child. That must have been a heavy load to carry alone.

He couldn't fix that for her, but at least could get the hot water going again. Turning his attention to the task at hand, Jamie adjusted the gas to the pilot light and quickly lit a match to it. The light ignited with a whoosh that made her gasp a little and step back.

When it appeared the water heater was working correctly, Jamie stood up. "That should do it. My shower should be hot in no time."

"If you have more trouble, let me know, and I'll call the company in Shelter Springs that installed it."

"You got it."

"Thank you for fixing it. I wouldn't have known the first thing to do."

"I didn't do anything except check the pilot light," he said.

"My mother always called a neighbor every time something went wrong. I'm trying to be a little more… independent. Obviously I have a long way to go."

She mustered a smile, but her eyes still looked haunted. Something was wrong, he thought again. He had a feeling it had nothing to do with her parents.

"There's nothing to lighting a pilot light. See that regulator valve? Just turn that to pilot and hold it down for about a minute. If it doesn't light, you can use a long-handled lighter or match. Just keep your eyebrows out of the way. If you're fond of them and want to keep them, anyway."

That teased a little smile out of her, but it slid away quickly.

"After it's lit, you have to hold down the valve to heat the thermocouple for about a minute, then release it and you should be good to go."

"I'll probably just end up calling the neighbor, but thanks for the explanation. I guess that's it, then. Enjoy your shower."

The big tank wouldn't have enough hot water for a shower for hours yet, but he didn't tell her that. "Thanks."

He replaced the door on the control panel, then the two of them headed back up the stairs.

When they were once more in her kitchen, he couldn't ignore the bleak sadness in her eyes any longer. "Is something wrong? Besides the hot water heater, I mean?"

Her eyes widened with surprise. "I don't…why would you ask that?"

"You seem troubled."

He wanted to tell her she appeared very different from the soft, appealing, tipsy woman she had been the night before. That hardly seemed appropriate, though, so he held his tongue.

"I'm fine, Mr. Caine. It's been a very long and difficult day, and the only things on my mind are my comfy pajamas, a cup of tea and a good book."

He had no right whatsoever to push her to tell him what was wrong, as much as he might want to.

"I understand," he finally said. The truth was, if he switched the pajamas for sweats and the tea for a beer, his evening would be just about the same.

"Good night, Mr. Caine," she said woodenly.

What happened to *Jamie*? he wondered, as he let himself out and headed back up the stairs. Did she remember that she had asked him to call her Julia?

He had to admit, he liked the sweetly soused woman he had met in the entryway the night before much better than this forlorn version. He would even prefer the stiff, prickly librarian she had been when she showed him around the apartment.

CHAPTER SIX

SHOULD SHE OR shouldn't she?

Julia gazed at her cell phone as she gnawed her lip in indecision. She had already called Wyn four times that day and ended up with her friend's voice mail each time. Phoning her yet again might be verging on harassment.

She had to know, though. What was going on with Davy and Clinton? Had Wyn found a foster care placement for them? Where? Would they have to spend Thanksgiving in a cheerless facility somewhere?

These questions had haunted her all night long. As exhausted as she'd been the night before, she expected that once she slipped into those comfy pajamas she had mentioned to Jamie Caine and finished her chamomile tea, she would be out like a light. Instead, she had paced and worried and paced some more, under the watchful eyes of three sulky cats.

It hadn't helped when she finally heard the shower upstairs start up. Her stupid imagination wandered in dangerous waters, and she couldn't seem to stop thinking about him up there, all wet skin and hard muscles...

She owed the man an apology.

Jamie had offered her only kindness, fixing the water heater and showing concern and asking if something was wrong. In return, she had been stiff and cold, as dismissive as her cats to his efforts at kindness.

What was it about the man that left her feeling so completely flustered? She could carry on casual conversations with her library patrons all day. Strangers, friends, children, senior citizens. But around Jamie, she couldn't seem to string two coherent sentences together. She was awkward and tongue-tied.

His easygoing manner should have helped her feel more comfortable around him. Instead, it seemed to have the opposite effect, heightening her awareness of him and her own ridiculous crush on the man, until she couldn't seem to think about anything else.

She wasn't sure why she found it so surprising that he could be full of charm. Every woman in Haven Point was enamored with Jamie. To draw that sort of adoration, he had to possess more than simply good looks.

She found him entirely too appealing—but right now her crush on her upstairs tenant was the least of her worries.

Julia pulled out her phone again, staring at Wynona's contact info. She would call one more time, she decided, then stop hounding her friend.

This time, the phone rang only twice before the call was answered.

"Julia!" Wyn sounded breathless and harried. "I'm so sorry I haven't returned your calls. I've been in meetings all morning long."

Julia could feel her cheeks turn pink, and she shifted in her chair. She should have waited for Wynona to call her back instead of hounding her. "I'm sorry to be a pain. I've been so worried about the boys. How is everything going? Did you locate their mother? Have you found a good placement for them?"

A long pause met her question, and she knew the answer even before Wynona replied.

"That's one of the reasons I haven't had time to return your call. I've been in contact with different agencies all across the southern half of the state. So far we've had no luck locating the mother. Everyone is out there looking. Meanwhile, I'm doing all I can to find an in-home placement for the boys, at least for Thanksgiving. Even the various group facilities are packed. I've found two available foster homes, one in Pocatello and one in Burley. Unfortunately, they can each only take one boy."

"You have to separate them."

Wynona's sigh clearly conveyed her frustration. "I know it's not ideal. It's not my preference either, but I don't have other options right now. I'm sorry. This is the best I can do."

"You can't split them up," Julia declared. "They need to be together. They're so close. The bond between them is remarkable. You've seen them together. Clinton is so worried about his little brother, and Davy tries his best to watch out for his brother in return."

"You're right. They're sweet together. It's impressive, especially given the chaos they've been through the last few years. Their father's death, their mother's PTSD, moving here away from family. I think all that hardship has only made them closer."

"Then why would you even consider splitting them up and potentially risk compromising that bond?"

Wyn sighed again. "It's not up to me, honey. Nobody's made me queen of the world yet, darn it. I'm doing the best I can. I don't want to split them up either, but separate home placements are really more beneficial than a temporary, overcrowded facility in every way.

Trust me on that. Those facilities are usually packed with children who are hard to place for a reason. Usually they're much older and more world-wise. Under those circumstances, separate home placements would be better in the long run for two young boys."

Her heart hurt when she tried to picture the two boys being driven away in separate directions. Those poor kids had been through so much already. This seemed more than they should be asked to endure.

"Isn't there anything we can do?"

"I wish I had a better answer for you," Wyn said softly. "I've been racking my brain all morning."

The completely preposterous idea that had come to her in the night—the real reason she hadn't been able to sleep—suddenly didn't seem as impossible as it had at 3:00 a.m.

"What if I took them?"

The words slipped out before she could think better of saying them, and she instantly wanted to snatch them back. She couldn't take two little boys. The idea was mad.

Wyn must have agreed. For a long, painful moment, her friend said nothing. The silence dragged on so long, Julia wondered for a moment if the connection had been lost.

The social worker probably had been so shocked, she dropped her phone in her coffee.

"You?" Wyn finally said.

"I know it's not practical. I'm not a certified foster parent or anything. But these are unique circumstances. These boys lost their father, who gave his life serving our country. We have an obligation to take care of them, don't we? Surely this case merits an exception to the rules."

She gripped the phone tighter. She was out of her mind. She had to be. This made no sense, yet here she was arguing her cause like a seasoned attorney. "I have a huge house with plenty of room. I can provide a safe, warm, comfortable place for them to stay for a few weeks, where they can continue on with their friends and school, until you can find something more permanent."

"It definitely is an intriguing idea, one I hadn't even considered. Are you sure about this, Julia?"

Far from it. She hadn't been *less* sure about anything in a long time. But she couldn't shake the sense of obligation she felt for those two lost little boys. She wasn't responsible for their predicament; she was only the one who had discovered and reported it. She understood that intellectually, but she couldn't shake the image of Clint the night before.

This is your fault, he had snarled, accusation in his eyes and his fists balled.

It wasn't. She knew that. Like it or not, though, she had a connection to them now. Besides, they were alone in the world right now, something she understood too well.

"I wouldn't have suggested it if I didn't mean it," she said briskly. "I have the room and I want to help. I'm involved in this and have been since they started using my library as their safe haven. I don't feel right about standing by and doing nothing while they are split up, especially if I have the ability to help. No matter how good the separate placements might be, I feel strongly that these boys *need* each other."

"These are two young boys who have already had a rough time. It's not like taking on a couple of stray puppies."

"I understand."

"I hope you do. I can't even guarantee how long it might take until we can find the mother or the uncle and aunt they've talked about—or until we can locate a different foster placement. It could be weeks."

"That's fine," she said. "Do you think it's even possible, considering I'm not a relative or a certified foster parent?"

"It's possible. It's definitely possible." From her initial shock, Wyn's tone began to take on a growing enthusiasm. "I would have to pull some strings. It won't be easy, but maybe, just maybe, we can swing it—at least on a temporary basis through the holidays. Because you work with children at the library, you already would have gone through the necessary background checks, security clearances, fingerprints, etc. Isn't that right?"

"Yes. My background check was just renewed a few months ago."

"Perfect. That definitely will stand in our favor. Give me an hour or so to talk to the powers that be and see what we can work out."

"Okay."

Now that the option was out there on the table, her hands were shaking, she realized, and her stomach jumped with nerves. Even so, she was also aware of a bubbling sense of anticipation that had been missing from her world for a long time.

"I can't believe you're willing to do this, but I have to tell you, I like this idea so much better than the alternative," Wyn said. Julia could hear audible relief in her friend's voice. "I always knew you were an angel. This just proves it."

Julia wasn't so sure of that. After she and Wynona severed the connection, with Wyn's promise to call her as soon as she knew anything, Julia gazed off into space, unable to find comfort from the stacks of books that surrounded her.

Now that the adrenaline rush of taking such a huge chance had begun to fade, all her doubts rushed back.

What did she know about making a home for two little boys? And right before Thanksgiving, too!

She had to be crazy. This was the stupidest thing she had ever done, and was destined to end in disaster. The boys would hate her. She was sure to screw up, would probably scar them for life…

She caught herself before the wheel of negative self-talk could totally carry her away. She couldn't lose sight of two boys who needed help, who needed a home. She had the ability to make a real difference in their lives. This wasn't some token effort. Serving at the nursing home or making crafts with the Helping Hands was all for the good. This was something real—opening her home, her *life*, to two boys who needed her.

As long as she kept that in mind, she could handle anything.

THIS WAS GOING to be an utter nightmare.

Davy and Clinton were staring at her as if she were a Dementor, a Heffalump and an orc rolled into one.

"No!" Clinton exclaimed. "You didn't tell us we were coming to *her* house. We don't want to stay with her! You can't make us."

He turned back to the door, but Wynona placed a

hand on his shoulder. "Why would you say that? This is a beautiful house, and Julia is one of the nicest people I know. And look! She has cats!"

That might not have been the most effective argument, since all three cats were perched on the back of the sofa, watching the proceedings with various expressions of disinterest.

"I like cats," Davy said. He looked at his brother uncertainly. Julia hadn't missed the smile that lit up the younger boy's expression when he walked into her house and spotted her, but that smile had quickly dripped away in the face of his brother's objections.

"So what if she has cats? She tricked us, Davy! If she hadn't stuck her sneaky nose in our business, we would still be at home. She made us think she was nice, but then she called child welfare and now they're trying to split us up."

"Not unless we have to," Wyn said. "That's the whole reason you're here. Miss Winston has agreed to take you in temporarily so you can stay together. We don't have a lot of other options here, kiddo."

"I didn't want you to have to move away from Haven Point either," Julia said. "You told me how well you are doing in school, and I hated the idea that you would have to start over with new teachers and classrooms."

Davy gave her a half smile, then quickly hid it when Clinton glared. "You should have minded your business. We were doing fine. I was taking care of Davy. He wasn't going hungry, was he?"

"You're a wonderful brother, Clint," she said softly. "Nobody is saying otherwise. I can't believe how well you watched out for Davy, all on your own."

Though she might not ever have proof, Julia sensed

that while their mother had been missing for less than a week, the older boy had been watching out for his brother far longer than that.

"Here's the thing," she went on. "You're only eight years old. It shouldn't be your job to make sandwiches and tuck him in and help him get ready for school. Right now your job is to go to school and play with your friends and have fun being eight years old."

He opened his mouth to answer but apparently couldn't think of anything to say, because he clamped his jaws closed again and looked down at the ground.

"If you and Davy want to stick together, you need to give Julia a chance," Wynona said.

"I want to go home," Clint muttered.

"That's not an option right now," Wyn said gently. "You understand that, don't you?"

Clinton crossed his arms across his chest and stuck out his chin, plainly not happy with that answer.

Wyn's phone rang, and she glanced down at the caller ID with a harried expression. "This day just won't stop. I have to take this. I'm sorry."

"No problem," Julia said. "You can go in the kitchen if you need quiet."

When Wyn hurried away, she turned to the boys with a bright smile. "Do you want to see the room where you'll be staying?"

Davy nodded, but Clint just looked stone-faced. She decided to ignore him for now and led the way to the biggest bedroom, the one her parents had used.

It had been empty since her mother had went into the nursing home. In the few hours since she spoke with Wyn, Julia had scrambled to figure out bedding for them. She had put out a call to the Haven Point Helping Hands, and Megan Hamilton had offered a bunk bed she had bought for one of the rooms at the Haven Point Inn but ended up not using. Her maintenance guy had dropped it off but had been on his way to visit family out of state and hadn't had time to set it up for her.

"Tonight, you guys might be sleeping on mattresses on the floor, until we can put together the beds for you."

"Like camping!" Davy said.

"Exactly," she said with a smile. "But warm and without the bugs, I promise. You can leave your things in here. There are two dressers. You can decide which one each of you would like. I have two guest rooms down here, but I thought you would like to be together. If you'd each rather have your own room, we can do that, too. Whatever you'd like."

"We'd *like* to go home," Clint said. "We want our own beds and our own dressers and stuff."

"For the next few weeks, I hope you can consider this your home."

"We won't," Clinton snapped.

"Nope," Davy echoed.

She decided to ignore their objections for now. "I'm afraid I don't have any boy comforters since no boys have lived here in many years, since my father was little, but I tried to find a few quilts that might work for now. Maybe this weekend we can have the time to go to the store and pick up something you both like."

"We won't like anything you pick," Clint said, stubbornly determined to oppose anything she said.

"Nope," Davy said, crossing his arms just like his brother.

She sighed. It was going to be a long few weeks if she couldn't break through this antagonism.

"We'll all have to make the best of the situation," she said calmly, leading the way back to the living room as Wyn wrapped up her phone call and joined them, expression grave.

"I don't want to just drop them off and run, but I have to, uh, drop them off and run," Wynona said. "I've got another emergency. It's that time of year."

"Don't worry. We'll be fine."

If she said that enough times, Julia just might begin to believe it.

"I'll call you later to see if you need anything," Wyn said.

"Thanks."

"Thank *you*. It's a good thing you're doing here, Jules."

She had to hope she wasn't making a terrible mistake.

"Davy, Clinton, it's been a pleasure getting to know you the last few days," Wyn said. "I'm so happy you will have the chance to stay together, as you wanted. Julia's one of my favorite people, and I'm sure the three of you will get along just great."

Neither of the boys said anything, just continued scowling.

Wyn didn't appear to let it bother her. She simply smiled at them both and headed for the door. "I'll definitely call you Friday, but don't hesitate to contact me before that if you need anything. Happy Thanksgiving!"

Thanksgiving. Oh, fiddle. Julia closed her eyes. That had totally slipped her mind in the last few hours. She hadn't planned on cooking a Thanksgiving dinner. And she had promised Muriel Randall she would pick her up to go together and help out at the nursing home in

Shelter Springs. She would just have to figure something out.

Something told her she would be saying that a great deal while the boys were here.

"Happy Thanksgiving," she said, giving Wyn a hug. "Call me if you run into any problems."

As Wyn walked out into the lightly falling snow, Julia couldn't shake the feeling it wasn't so much a matter of "if" they would run into problems but "how many."

CHAPTER SEVEN

WHAT THE HELL was going on downstairs?

Jamie looked down at the floorboards as another round of wails worked its way up.

Someone down there was *not* happy—which was a bit of an understatement. The wailing had been nonstop for the half hour he had been home, echoing through the house as if two or three of Julia Winston's cats were in labor.

Whatever was happening on the floor below, he couldn't hear any words, only the occasional high-pitched shouting, slamming doors and those piercing cries, with the occasional cat yowl thrown in for fun.

So much for renting a quiet apartment with a reserved, well-behaved librarian for a landlady.

Should he go down and see if she needed help with something?

The night before, she hadn't seemed all that grateful for his help with the water heater. Julia Winston struck him as someone used to solving her own problems, mechanical problems notwithstanding.

He supposed he could put on some noise-canceling headphones. A little head-banging rock would probably drown out the commotion. On the other hand, he couldn't shake the suspicion that something might be seriously wrong, that Julia Winston possibly could need his help.

It was none of his business, Jamie tried to remind himself. She could carry on with all kinds of caterwauling creatures if that was her thing. It was her house, after all.

What if she was hurt?

If Pop could see him up here minding his own business, he would definitely have a thing or twenty to say about it. Dermot Caine had taught all his sons not to stand by when a woman might be in distress.

"Nooo," he heard a high-pitched voice cry out. That decided him. She might not welcome his help, but a real man offered it anyway.

The commotion grew louder as he headed down the stairs. In the vestibule outside her door, he could pick out three distinct voices, though he still couldn't hear the words they were saying.

He raised his hand to knock, but before he could, the door jerked open. A young boy of about seven or eight stood there. His cheeks were red and tear-stained, and his eyes glittered with temper.

He didn't appear to notice Jamie standing there.

"We can just walk to our house," he said defiantly. "I know the way and you can't stop us."

From inside, Jamie heard his landlady. "Clinton Slater. For the last time, you can't go anywhere. I know you don't want to be here, but right now, none of us has a choice."

"Do so," the young boy retorted. "Come on, Davy."

Before Jamie could move, the kid rushed through—right into Jamie—followed by another one who looked like a carbon copy but a few years younger.

"Clint, Davy. Get back in here," Julia snapped as the older boy looked up at Jamie, those intense blue eyes wide with shock.

"There's a guy out here," Davy called. "Is he your boyfriend?"

An instant later, Julia's surprised face popped around the door. Her color was high, too, and her hair was again falling out of the little updo thingy she wore. When she spotted him, he thought that color rose another inch or two.

"Oh. This is Mr. Caine. He's lives upstairs. He probably came down because you both were making so much noise, with your tantrums."

"It's true," Jamie said helpfully. "I thought the cats were fighting down here. Or maybe having kittens. What's going on?"

"We don't want to stay here, but she won't let us leave," the older of the two boys said, crossing his arms across his narrow chest.

Jamie raised an eyebrow. "Kidnapping, Ms. Winston?" he teased. "That's a felony."

"Yeah," the younger boy said, crossing his arms just like his brother. "A fella-me."

"You're not helping," she snapped, her chest rising sharply.

"Why don't we all go back inside?" he suggested. "We can all sit down, and you can tell me what's going on."

The boys eyed the doorway, but must have sensed they couldn't juke past him. He hadn't been a linebacker on the Hope's Crossing High School championship football team for nothing.

They reluctantly turned around and went into her living room.

"I'm Jamie."

"My name is Clinton Scott Slater, and this is my brother David Joshua Slater."

"Clint and Davy are going to be living with me for a while," Julia said.

"Only until we run away and go home and find our mom," Clinton responded.

"You know your mother is not at home," Julia said through her teeth. Something told him they had covered this ground a few times already that evening. "You can't go back to an empty house."

"Why should we believe you? We thought you were our friend, but you were just spying so you could call the welfare people on us."

"I'm hungry," the younger boy whined.

Julia sighed and ruffled his hair. Despite his alleged unhappiness, Davy leaned into her hand a little.

"I know you are, buddy. I'm working on dinner. I'll remind you both that I would have been done twenty minutes ago, if I didn't have to keep coming out to make sure you weren't trying to sneak out the door when my back was turned."

She tried to tighten her mouth into a stern expression, but something about the quiver in her lower lip stirred all the chivalrous instincts ingrained in him since birth. She appeared very much like a woman completely out of her comfort zone.

"Tell you what," Jamie said, "we can help you finish that delicious-smelling dinner. With all of us working together, the work will go faster—then you can invite me over to eat with you, since I'm starving, too. See, it's a win all the way around."

He winked at the boys, earning a giggle from the younger one. While the older boy didn't look as convinced, he appeared a little less belligerent.

"We can't ruin your whole evening," Julia protested.

"What are we cooking?" he asked, ignoring her to lead the way into the kitchen. "Smells like spaghetti."

Julia and the boys both followed him. It was obvious she didn't want to accept his help—just as it was obvious to both of them that she needed it.

"Lasagna, actually. It should be done in about fifteen minutes."

"What can we do in the meantime? Besides wash our hands, of course."

"I only need to make a salad and set the table."

"You sit down. You've done all the hard work on the lasagna. Clint, Davy and I can handle the salad."

"Can you?"

He had plenty of nieces and nephews and was quite an accomplished child-wrangler, if he did say so himself, but he decided to let his skills do the talking.

"No problem," he said. "Just watch us."

"I'll set the table," she said, looking disarmed and more than a little overwhelmed.

"Excellent division of labor."

He steered the boys over to the sink, where he supervised while they washed their hands, then washed his own.

"All right, guys. What do we need for salad?"

"Lettuce," Davy said promptly.

"And tomatoes. Except Davy doesn't like tomatoes."

"We'll put those on the side, then."

All the necessary ingredients for a good tossed salad were in a colander draining in the other sink from the one where they had washed their hands. Jamie put the boys to work ripping up the lettuce into bite-sized pieces while he found a knife and started cutting up the tomatoes, green onions and celery for the salad.

After a few minutes, Julia wandered over to see how they were faring.

"You can handle a kitchen knife," she said with surprise as she watched him.

He smiled, cutting the avocado in half and slicing it into strips inside the skin with an expert flourish. "My family has a café back home in Colorado. My Pop is more than seventy but still works there every single day. My parents made sure all of us knew our way around a kitchen, so I spent most of my school breaks working there—busing tables, washing dishes, prepping food, working the grill. There's not much I can't do."

What he hadn't learned at the Center of Hope Cafe kitchen, he taught himself after he first went to school, then military training. A guy could only eat at the mess hall so often—and he quickly got tired of frozen pizzas.

"I can cook," Clint boasted, bony chin up in the air.

"He makes super good toast and mac and cheese and microwave popcorn," Davy attested.

"That's an excellent start. Now you know how to make a basic green salad, too," Jamie said.

Who were these boys and what were they doing in Julia's kitchen?

A hundred questions chased around his brain. When she introduced them to him, she said they were staying with her for a while. There was obviously a story here.

You know your mother is not at home. You can't go

home to an empty house, Julia had said to them. Where was home? And where was their mother?

The timer went off before he could figure out a subtle way to probe for some of those answers.

"That's the lasagna," she said unnecessarily. She slid on oven mitts then opened the oven, releasing a delicious meaty tomato smell that made his stomach rumble in a rather embarrassing way.

She pulled out a pan full of a gooey, wonderful-looking lasagna, set it on a waiting rack on the stovetop, then slid in another foil-wrapped bundle.

"Boys, I put the plates out, but we need silverware now. Forks and knives. Four of each."

"I was only joking about you inviting me for dinner," Jamie said, a little embarrassed about his forwardness.

"You saved the day. Feeding you is small repayment," she said. "There's plenty of lasagna, as you can see. We'll have enough leftovers for a week."

"It does look delicious," he said.

"Please stay. It's the least we can do after we made such a ruckus earlier." She glanced at the boys, and pitched her voice low. "Anyway, your presence appears to be distracting them from how angry they are with me. Maybe they can forget long enough to actually eat something."

"Why are they so angry?" he asked. He had a dozen other questions. Who were they? Why had she taken them in? Where were their parents? He would start with the one he had asked.

"It's a long story," she said. With her cheeks rosy from the heat of the oven and her eyes that vivid violet color under the kitchen lights, she looked completely delectable. The prim librarian was nowhere in evidence tonight. "They blame me for calling in the child welfare department, taking them out of their home."

"Why would they blame you?"

"Because that's exactly what I did," she answered.

He wanted to press her, but the boys came over before he could.

"Can we eat now?" Davy asked plaintively.

"The garlic bread will be done in a moment and the lasagna needs to sit a bit, but we can start with the salad. Why don't you pour everyone a glass of water?"

The younger boy hurried to comply, even as Jamie had a feeling what Julia Winston needed more than anything was a stiff glass of something bracing and alcoholic.

JULIA SUSPECTED THE other members of the Haven Point Helping Hands would never believe how brilliant Jamie Caine was with children. Within five minutes of sitting down to dinner, he had the boys laughing uproariously at a story he told about a disastrous meal he and his brothers fixed their parents when they were kids.

She was beginning to see there was much more to the man than a charming smile and sexy eyes.

By the time they finished eating, Clint and Davy were acting as if he was their new best friend. She tried to ignore the little pinch of envy at how easy he was with them. Better to be grateful. As she had hoped, Jamie's presence at dinner seemed to have distracted the boys from the trauma of moving in with her.

"That was a delicious meal," he announced, setting down his napkin beside his plate. "Thank you for inviting me. Guys, what do you say to Julia for fixing us such fantastic lasagna?"

That seemed to remind Clint, at least, that he was still angry with her. He sent her a cold look, then looked down at his plate.

She thought he might snap at her, but instead, he apparently didn't want to upset his new friend.

"Thank you," he mumbled.

"Yeah. Thanks," Davy said, one side of his face smeared with red sauce. "That was the best 'sagna I've ever had."

"You're very welcome," she said, dabbing at his cheek with her napkin. "And your salad was perfect. Good job ripping that lettuce."

"When I was growing up, my mom and dad had a rule," Jamie said. "Whoever didn't cook the meal has to clean it up. Since Julia did most of the work, that means us. Why don't you guys give me a hand clearing these dishes away?"

"I can do it," she protested.

"So can we. Go put your feet up. Read a book. Throw a ball of string for your cats. Whatever relaxes you."

She would love to play with the cats, if they weren't snotty brats.

She cleared her own plate and silverware, then grabbed some of the foster parent documentation Wyn had left and sat at the kitchen table to go through it, where she could watch him interact with the boys—and maybe learn a thing or two in the process.

He really was brilliant with them. To her relief, he didn't seem in a hurry to say good-night. He turned cleaning the kitchen into a game and had them laughing through the whole thing. When Davy mentioned they would be sleeping on mattresses on the floor until their bunk bed could be set up, Jamie immediately went to their room to check out the situation.

"Oh, we can put this together in a minute," he said after examining the wood and hardware that had confounded Julia. "Nothing to it. I've got just the tools we'll need."

"This wasn't the way you planned to spend your evening," she protested.

"I didn't have any plans at all," he assured her. "I'll try to get the boys good and tired, so you don't have to stress about them sneaking out to wander home in the night."

"I hadn't been worried about that until you said it. Thank you. I needed one more thing to stress about," she said tartly, which earned her a grin that made her toes tingle.

He was right about one thing, anyway. The bunk bed didn't take long to throw together, and she was impressed at the way he let the boys help him figure out what went where.

Jamie was actually perfect with them. Why didn't he have children of his own? she wondered. Or maybe he did somewhere. What did she know about the man, anyway?

After the drama of the day, the boys both seemed worn out by the time they finished the project. Julia ushered them through showers and into their pajamas and had them brush their teeth. She didn't want to admit it, but she was quite relieved that Jamie stayed through the whole bedtime routine, providing moral support to her on this first night until they were tucked into their new beds.

Both were asleep almost immediately, leaving Julia utterly drained by the time she closed the door.

"Why do I feel like I've somehow survived a hurricane?" she asked as she collapsed onto the sofa.

"My parents always said they never loved us as much as they did when we were asleep and couldn't get into trouble."

She smiled, trying to picture him as a boy Clint's or Davy's age. It was tough, especially when he was so very masculine. "You were wonderful with them."

He made a face. "I don't know about that."

"I do. You were brilliant. Before you showed up, I was nearly in tears, completely at my wit's end. We survived the first evening, which gives me hope that maybe we can make it a few weeks."

"You will," he said.

She was a little more confident about that than she might have been a few hours earlier, when Clint had been in tantrum mode and Davy had followed his lead.

"I do have one question," she said.

"Oh?"

"How are you so good with them? Tell me your secret."

"No secret. Just practice. You know I come from a big family. Seven kids."

"Seven! I can't even imagine it!"

One evening with two boys had left her completely exhausted. She shuddered to think of a houseful.

"It was noisy and chaotic and pretty wonderful. As a result of all those siblings, I have been blessed over the years with multiple nieces and nephews, and I guess I've picked up a thing or two about dealing with rug rats over the years."

Her own childhood couldn't have been more different. When they adopted her, Julia's mother had been in her midforties, her father ten years older. She had adored them both, but now, through the filter she had gained as an adult, she saw that they had always treated her as a miniature adult. Their home life had been quiet and orderly, without anything resembling chaos.

Sometimes she wondered about all she might have missed.

"Now that the boys are in bed, can you tell me what's going on? Who are Clinton and Davy, and why are they suddenly living in your house?"

After everything he had done that evening to help them all survive this first night together, he deserved a few answers.

"It's a very long story. It all started when two little boys walked into my library."

By the time she finished telling him everything that had transpired over the last few days, he was shaking his head in disgust. "So the mother just took off, leaving two little kids for days, in a freezing-cold house with no food?"

"In her defense, I don't believe the furnace was out when she left."

"That's not really a defense."

"I know." Julia frowned. Oh, she hoped their mother was found quickly. Bad enough they lost their father. She hated thinking of them without a mother, too.

"I have to think something drastic must have prevented her from keeping that appointment at the veteran's hospital, but I don't like thinking about the possibilities. Police have tried all the hospitals and treatment centers in the region. They haven't found her vehicle yet."

"What about the airport or the bus station?"

"Both have been checked. They have an aunt and uncle out there somewhere, the same ones they lived with when both parents were deployed, but the phone number Clint had has been disconnected. All we know is the aunt's name is Suzi, and they're living out of the country right now."

"Those poor kids. They've been through hell. You did the right thing, calling in child protective services. Don't doubt it. You couldn't leave them there."

Hearing that validation from him brought the sting of tears to her eyes. "Thank you for saying that," she said softly. "At least I've done one thing right in this whole thing."

"You did plenty right," he answered. "You opened your home to them, so you could keep them together. When they get past the initial trauma, they'll understand that."

"I hope so. As you clearly saw tonight, I have no idea what I'm doing when it comes to children. Unlike you, I don't have much experience with children. I was an only child of two only children—our family reunions were basically the three of us having a picnic."

He chuckled at that, the sound low and rich and delicious.

She tried not to notice, focusing instead on the little tendrils of panic curling through her as the reality of what she had done began to soak through once more.

"I'm in so far over my head, I can't see sunshine. What do I know about kids? I should never have opened my mouth. This house isn't set up for children. *I'm* not set up for children. I don't have clothes for them or shoes or so much as a game of Chutes and Ladders to entertain them."

"Kids don't need much."

She appreciated his efforts to calm her, but the reality of everything two young boys might require, even for a few weeks, was suddenly daunting. "And tomorrow is Thanksgiving! Cripes. I don't have a single thing prepared."

He raised an eyebrow. "Weren't you already planning to celebrate Thanksgiving before you knew the boys were coming to stay with you?"

"I had volunteered to help serve Thanksgiving dinner at the nursing home in Shelter Springs, where my father was for a time and where my mother spent the last few months of her life. They serve a big meal for their residents and families and any senior citizens who don't have anywhere else to go."

She didn't add that *she* didn't have anywhere else to go. That was the reason she had agreed when the director asked if she might be available. She had plenty of friends who had invited her to their houses, but this first year without either of her parents seemed like a good chance to help someone else.

"They're counting on me. I can't back out at this late date."

"No. That wouldn't be right."

"Maybe I can see if Clint and Davy can go hang out at one of my friends' houses. Maybe Devin's or Andie's. If not, I can put them to work helping me in the kitchen, and then we can come back here and cobble something together for ourselves."

"I have an alternative idea."

She barely registered his words, her mind racing with all she had to do. "How late is the grocery store open, do you know? Is there any chance you could stay here in case the boys wake up while I run over to see if I can scrounge up a fresh turkey for us? I've got potatoes I can mash, so that won't be a problem. I'll have to buy yeast to make rolls and maybe some cranberry sauce as I can't stand the stuff. Okay. I can do this."

She jumped up, ready to throw on her shoes and coat and rush out the door, but Jamie laid a restraining hand on her arm.

"I have an alternative," he said again, more firmly this time.

"I'm sorry. I cut you off," she realized.

"Aidan and I are making a quick run to Hope's Crossing in the morning to pick up some of our family members, then we're bringing them back to Snow Angel Cove for Thanksgiving. Aidan is planning to take Maddie with us on the plane, to keep her out of Sue's and Eliza's way."

She wanted to shake her head at the casual way he talked about making what would be a nine-hour trip by car. She couldn't imagine being able to hop in a private jet to pick up family for Thanksgiving—but then, Aidan Caine was the founder and CEO of Caine Tech and one of the wealthiest men in the world.

More than likely, Jamie was probably also ridiculously wealthy, since she knew he ran the air fleet for Caine Tech.

"We could easily take Clinton and Davy along with us," he went on. "There's plenty of room. My brother Brendan is coming back with us, and he has kids around their age. I'm sure they would get along great. Clint and

Davy can come with us to Hope's Crossing in the morning while you do your thing at the nursing home, then you all can join us at Snow Angel Cove for Thanksgiving dinner tomorrow afternoon."

She stared at him, astonished at the offer. "Why would you... You don't even know the boys. That's an extraordinarily generous offer."

"You don't know the boys either," he pointed out. "Not really. Yet you've opened your entire home to them. The least I can do is entertain them on my plane for a few hours."

Could he surprise her any more that evening? Apparently there was much more to Jamie Caine than just a handsome face. The more time she spent with him, the more she found appealing.

For that very reason, a wise woman would probably refuse such a generous offer. She could always go buy three turkey TV dinners for her and the boys. But how could she turn down an adventure that Clint and Davy would probably love?

He wanted to do something nice for two boys who had been through a tough time. She didn't see how she could be anything but gracious about it.

JAMIE WAITED FOR her answer with an anxiousness that he didn't quite understand.

The idea had been one of those spur-of-the-moment things, but it suddenly seemed vitally important that she say yes.

"What do you say?" he pressed, when her silence dragged on. "Think the boys might enjoy an airplane ride? Aidan and I can keep a close eye on the three kids on the flight there. On the way back, there will be a dozen more Caines to watch them on the plane."

"I'm not concerned about that."

"Then what? Do you worry about my flying skills? I'm a good pilot, Julia."

"I'm sure you are," she answered. "It's just…it seems such an imposition."

"Not at all. I offered, which I wouldn't have done if I didn't sincerely want to take them with us."

"All right," she said after a moment. "I'm sure they'll be thrilled at the adventure. Who knows? It might even help them forget they're so angry with me."

"Terrific! I'll just take them with me to the airstrip in the morning. I'm probably leaving early, around eight."

"That should be fine." She paused. "As for the rest of it, while it's kind of you to invite us to Snow Angel Cove, I'm not completely comfortable intruding on your family's Thanksgiving."

"Don't worry about that for a minute. You know Eliza. She opens the house to everyone. She would be on the phone in a heartbeat inviting you herself, if she had any clue what was going on."

"She already did invite me, weeks ago. Before I had the boys here."

"There. You see. It won't be a problem, I promise, but I can have Eliza call you and issue a formal invitation, if that would make you feel better. When we get back to Lake Haven, Aidan and I can take the boys to his place along with everyone else, and you can meet us there when you're done with your thing in Shelter Springs."

"You've thought of everything."

He shrugged. "When you're a pilot, you have to think

three or four steps ahead. I just want the boys to have a good holiday."

"They will. It sounds great. I'm envious, if you want the truth."

"Envious?"

Her cheeks turned that soft pink he was beginning to find completely adorable. "I've never been on an airplane. It's on my bucket list."

For a moment, he thought he must have misheard her. How was that even *possible*?

"Never?"

"My parents were homebodies and didn't like to leave Lake Haven. When I was young, we went on a few vacations—one to Yellowstone and another to Seattle—but they preferred sticking close to home."

"What about later, when you became an adult? You didn't ever want to jaunt off to Paris for a week?"

"Not Paris. The Ukraine, maybe," she said, then her blush heightened, and she looked down at her hands.

That was an odd choice for a vacation. Apparently Julia Winston had a few secrets. "What was in the Ukraine?" Or, more likely, *who*?

"Nothing," she said quickly. "It was impossible, anyway. My parents both had health issues toward the end of their lives. With my dad's Alzheimer's, it was tough for him to travel, and I didn't like to leave my mom alone to care for him as she wasn't very strong herself."

Jamie had a fierce urge to bundle her up along with the two little boys and fly her somewhere exciting. Tahiti would be lovely this time of year.

He wouldn't believe her parents allowed her to sacrifice so many years of her life for them.

"You could always bow out of the nursing home thing and come with us."

Her eyes widened. "I don't… I can't. I gave my word. They're expecting me."

Did she always do what was expected of her? He had a purely naughty urge to entice this quiet, reserved librarian into doing all manner of wild and dangerous things.

He did his best to rein in the impulse. Julia Winston appeared to be a nice woman—caring, compassionate, willing to offer a home for two boys going through a rough time, simply because she saw a need.

She seemed sweet, vulnerable, maybe a little needy herself—exactly the kind of woman he tried his best to avoid. He didn't quite understand why he was having such a hard time resisting this particular temptation.

"Next time, then. Meanwhile, I'll take the boys with me and get them out of your hair, then you can come join us for turkey. It's the perfect solution."

"Are you always so sure of yourself?" Though there was a hint of tartness to her voice, like taking a bite out of a pie cherry when you were expecting a Bing, he also sensed it was sincere.

He shrugged. "Sometimes the best course of action is to come up with a plan, then try your damnedest to make it work. It's a military thing."

"Full throttle ahead?"

He smiled at her aviation reference. "Exactly. I'd like to be wheels-up by eight tomorrow morning. Do you think Clint and Davy could be ready by seven thirty?"

"I'll make sure they are."

"There's always room for one more," he cajoled.

"Don't plan on it," she said.

"Fine." He rose to leave, surprised at his reluctance to go back upstairs. Julia was turning out to be far more intriguing than he ever would have guessed when he moved in—which was probably the very reason he should leave, before he made a mistake he couldn't take back.

"Thank you again for dinner," he said.

She rose, as well. "We both know I'm the one in your debt. You calmed the waters, *and* you helped put their bunk bed together. I know dealing with two rambunctious little boys wasn't on your agenda for the evening, but I truly would have been sunk without you."

"My pleasure. Really." He was quite looking forward to seeing the boys with his family. Pop would take one look at the two cute, needy little boys and want to tuck them under his considerable wing.

"I'll see you in the morning when I pick up the boys and then later at Snow Angel Cove as soon as you're done volunteering at the care center."

"How many of you did you say would be there?"

He laughed. "There's only one of me, darlin'. But I think Eliza's planning for upwards of twenty."

"Good gracious," she exclaimed. He didn't think he ever heard a woman of his generation say that particular phrase before. He found it rather adorable.

"Every time my family gets together, I think the exact same thing," he lied. In truth, his imprecations were usually a little stronger than *good gracious*. "We always have a good time, and the food is invariably delicious. And then when you leave, you can have one more thing to be thankful for tomorrow—that you're not stuck with us."

Her mouth lifted into a soft smile, and Jamie had a

sudden wild urge to press his lips to that lush bottom lip, to see if it tasted as delicious in reality as it did in his imagination.

What was *wrong* with him?

"Good night," he said quickly. "I'll see you in the morning."

He hurried away before he could do something both of them would regret.

CHAPTER EIGHT

WHEN THE DOORBELL rang the next morning, Julia felt as if a hundred butterflies were dive-bombing in her stomach.

"He's here! He's here!" Davy raced for the front door, while Clint followed a little more cautiously.

"We're really going on an airplane?" the older boy asked, for probably the fiftieth time that morning. He couldn't quite seem to accept the idea, which she didn't find all that unusual, considering it had all happened on the spur of the moment.

"That's the plan," she answered, giving him a reassuring pat on the shoulder. "Isn't it nice of Mr. Caine to take you on a quick ride?"

"I suppose," he said, though he didn't sound at all convinced of it.

"Airplane. Airplane. Airplane," his brother exclaimed with glee, as he yanked open the door.

"Hi, Mr. Caine. Hi. I'm all ready to go on your airplane. See? I even have an airplane on my shirt."

"I see it. That's a great-looking shirt."

He smiled down at the boy, and Julia tried not to notice how completely gorgeous Jamie looked that morning. His hair was damp from the shower she had heard running earlier, and he was freshly shaved, with none of that irresistible stubble he'd had the night before.

She didn't know which version she found more appealing: fresh-out-of-the-shower Jamie or sexy pirate Jamie.

Neither, she told herself sternly. She had no business finding either of them appealing.

He looked up from Davy and spotted her and Clinton. "Good morning," he said brightly. Before she realized what he was about, he stepped forward and kissed her cheek.

He smelled delicious, that irresistible combination of cedar and bergamot and pine from his soap.

"Morning," she murmured, blushing when she heard the breathy sound of her own voice. She was an idiot. So the man had kissed her cheek. Big deal. That was the sort of meaningless gesture guys like him did all the time.

"Happy Thanksgiving. Are you two ready to go?"

"I am!" Davy declared. He pulled out the paper airplane he had folded over breakfast out of a piece of scratch paper and zoomed it around in circles.

Clint, Julia noticed, said nothing and appeared more subdued than she had seen him.

Was he nervous? Or upset about something else?

"Are you sure about this?" she asked Jamie. "Last chance to bow out."

"Absolutely sure. I talked to Aidan about it last night, and he's thrilled to have a few other children aboard to keep Maddie company. When she doesn't have someone her own age to entertain, she tends to talk both our ears off."

He seemed to have a particular skill of twisting a situation where he was doing something nice for someone else to make it seem like the recipient of the gesture was actually doing *him* a favor.

Both of them knew it was the other way around.

"Let's go!" Davy said, tugging Jamie toward the door.

He laughed. "We will. Hold your horses. The plane can't go anywhere without me."

As she had predicted, the boys had been vibrating with excitement after she told them Jamie's plan for the day. They seemed to have forgotten their anger with her, and Julia had to work hard to get them to eat.

As they'd finished breakfast, though, Clint grew quiet, his responses increasingly monosyllabic. She'd tried without success to get him to tell her what was bothering him.

"Grab your coats," she said now. "It's as cold in Colorado as it is here."

Davy immediately complied, but Clint seemed to be dragging his feet. As she found his parka and helped him into it, she decided to try one more time.

"Did you change your mind about going?" she asked quietly. "I thought you'd be excited about having a fun adventure."

"Why aren't you going?"

"I told you. I have a commitment already. I'm helping serve Thanksgiving dinner to some older citizens of Lake Haven."

He drew in a ragged-sounding breath. "Are you sending us away because we were bad last night?" he asked, his voice miserable. "Tell me the truth."

Her heart twisted. Poor thing! She should have realized the anxiety behind his sudden distance.

"Oh, honey. Of course not!" She knelt down in front

of him. "Jamie thought you might enjoy a ride in his airplane. That's all it is. He'll bring you back, I promise. This afternoon we're having Thanksgiving dinner with his family, and I'll see you there."

"You swear?" His eyes were fierce and protective. "I only ask because Davy likes the bed and said how nice it was not to be cold when he woke up."

Her heart twisted in her chest. These poor children had little reason to trust the adults in their lives.

"I swear on every bookshelf in my house. And I'm a librarian. You know how much I love books."

At her words, the tight set of his features started to relax. "Good. My mom needs to be able to find us when she comes back. If we go to some other town, she won't know where to look for us."

Where was their mother? Julia sent up another wordless prayer that Mikaela Slater could be found safe so these children didn't have to endure another heartbreak. "You'll be here in Haven Point. Right here. I made a promise to take care of you when I asked Mrs. Emmett if you and Davy could stay with me, and I intend to keep it."

It seemed important to remind him that she had volunteered to take the boys in. Maybe if he understood that, he might come to accept the situation.

"We're really going on an airplane?"

Some of her tension trickled away at his wondering tone. "Yes. And I want you to remember every moment of it so you can tell me about it later, okay?"

He nodded, and she took a chance and gave him a hug. He didn't return it, but he didn't try to wriggle away either.

"Everything okay?" Jamie asked, while the boys were grabbing their mittens.

"Crisis averted for now. He's afraid you won't bring them back here. And if they're not in Haven Point, he worries his mom won't know where to find them when she comes back."

His handsome features softened with sympathy. "Poor kids. They've had a rough break. I'll take good care of them, I promise. I wasn't being cocky when I told you I'm an excellent pilot."

She didn't doubt it for a moment. Something told her Jamie Caine would be excellent at everything. And she meant *everything*.

Her cheeks suddenly felt hot, and she had to look away. This was what happened when she read too many steamy romance novels. Her dratted imagination took her brain in wild directions.

To her relief, Clint and Davy rushed out of their room before she could say something stupid.

"There are the boys' booster seats," she said, pointing beside the door where she'd pulled them from her vehicle. "They can be tricky. Do you need me to help you hook them into your SUV?"

"I have hundreds of nieces and nephews, remember? I can figure it out."

"I'll see you this afternoon, then."

"Thanks. Have fun at the nursing home. It's still not too late for you to come with us," he said.

She shook her head in answer, and he grinned and ushered the boys outside.

The house seemed eerily quiet after they all left. How was that possible when Clint and Davy had only been there since the previous afternoon?

She fed the cats, straightened up a bit, threw in a load of laundry. She had never minded her alone time before but suddenly felt at loose ends until it was time to pick up Muriel to drive to the care center at Shelter Springs.

"WELL, THAT'S OVER for another year." Lani Tucker collapsed into a chair in the kitchen. "Good job, us. Everybody seemed to have a great time."

Julia smiled at the other woman, who was a nurse at the regional hospital positioned halfway between Haven Point and Shelter Springs.

"Yes," Julia agreed. "We didn't have any fistfights this time, and Eugene Peterson only tried to goose me three times."

Lani laughed. "That's because you spent most of the time in the kitchen. I was out here on the front line. I'm going to have bruises from that old lech."

Julia grimaced in sympathy. "On the plus side, your mom seemed happy today," she commented.

The other woman sighed. "She had a good day—so far, anyway. Who knows? In five minutes, everything could change. Alzheimer's sucks."

"This I know too well," Julia said. "I'm so sorry."

"It is what it is. I just wish you could have known my mom before this cursed disease took her. She was the most amazing woman."

"She must have been, to raise such a loving daughter," Julia said with a smile as she wiped down the countertops in the kitchen. "You take such good care of her."

"It's not easy. But I don't have to tell you that."

The two of them had met when Julia's mother had been here the last year before her death. Julia had been impressed that Lani visited twice a week and played an active role in her mother's care. She was the youngest of four children and the only one in the area, so the bulk of the care fell on her, which couldn't be easy.

"Can I ask you something?" Lani asked.

"Sure."

"Why are you doing this?"

Julia held up the dishcloth. "I felt something sticky. Guess I didn't wipe them well enough earlier."

"Not that. I mean, why are you here? Now that your mom is gone, you have no reason to keep coming to the care center and helping out. It's nice of you and all, but I can think of much more enjoyable ways to spend Thanksgiving than in this depressing place."

"I helped out last year, and when the volunteer director asked if I could help out, I didn't have any reason to say no."

This had been her first holiday without family. While Eliza and others in the Helping Hands had invited her to join them, she hadn't felt right about inserting herself into someone else's family dinner, but why hadn't she thought about hosting her own celebration for others who might not have anywhere else to go? She had at least a half-dozen friends she could think of who might have enjoyed having somewhere to go.

It made her feel small and selfish that the idea had never even occurred to her.

Next year, she told herself. She would start keeping a list of potential guests now—and Lani would be close to the top of her list.

"Thanksgiving is for counting your blessings, right? My mother spent the last months of her life here, surrounded by people who took good care of her. That's a huge blessing for me. I'm glad I had the chance to give back a little."

"That's sweet of you." Lani smiled. "Look, a couple of my friends are getting together later this evening to play games and watch a chick flick. Why don't you join us?"

They had both been so busy with dinner, Julia hadn't had a chance to tell Lani about the radical life change she'd undertaken the day before.

"I can't. I'm so sorry. It sounds like fun. A few days ago, I would have jumped at the offer, seriously, but my life has become…complicated."

Lani looked intrigued. "That sounds promising. Do tell. Is there a male involved?"

"Two of them, actually." Three, counting Jamie. Not that she was really involved with him—and not that she wanted to mention anything about him to Lani.

The nurse's eyes widened. "Two? My goodness. For a shy, retiring librarian, you've got an interesting life, honey. No wonder you said things were complicated."

"Two very *young* males," she amended. "I'm temporary guardian to a couple of little boys who needed a home for a few weeks. They're eight and six and have been through a rough time."

Lani's pretty features softened with compassion. "Oh, the poor things. But where are they? You should have brought them with you today. You know how the residents dote on little lost lambs."

"A…friend offered to take them while I was busy here. I'm meeting them all to have Thanksgiving dinner with his family."

"Even more exciting. Is he cute? The friend, not either of the boys, I mean."

Cute didn't begin to cover it. "I suppose," she said. "As I said, we're just friends, though."

It was an odd thing to say about Jamie Caine, especially when he made those butterflies stampede in her stomach every time he smiled at her, but it was true. Who would have guessed she would become friends with him?

"Anyway, I wish I didn't have another commitment. You have fun with your movie night. It sounds great. Maybe another time."

She didn't have that many friends in Shelter Springs, mostly in Haven Point. It would be fun to branch out.

"You got it. We get together once a month or so. It's always a wild party."

"I'll look forward to it," she said.

After they finished cleaning up, Lani returned to her mother's room, and Julia said goodbye to the nursing home staff before heading out to the parking lot. Muriel had decided to take up a last-minute invitation to have dinner at a cousin's house in Shelter Springs and had caught a ride there after helping out with things at the care center, so Julia didn't have to take her back to Haven Point. She could go straight to Snow Angel Cove from here.

The blue skies of the morning had given way to gathering clouds while she had been inside, and she had to brush a light film of snow off her windows.

Her hands tightened on the steering wheel as she drove toward the two-lane road that circled vast Lake Haven toward Haven Point and Snow Angel Cove.

She didn't like driving in the snow, even though her vehicle had four-wheel drive. She focused on the road, trying to ignore the nerves zinging through her from both the weather and her destination.

A big SUV loaded with kids pulled in behind her, following entirely too close on the slick, winding road. Apparently the driver was in a big hurry to go over the river and through the woods this Thanksgiving afternoon.

She was going about ten miles below the speed limit, but she didn't dare speed up, not when conditions could be slick.

The driver of the SUV grew impatient after another mile. Though there was a double yellow line on the winding road, he disregarded the law and pulled over to pass her.

Julia's hands tightened on the steering wheel as he gunned it, swerving the wheel in front of her mere seconds before a sedan came around the bend in the opposite direction.

Another five seconds and the SUV would have caused a head-on collision, all because the driver was impatient that Julia wasn't driving the speed limit.

The near-miss did nothing to calm her nerves as she negotiated the final curve to Snow Angel Cove, the beautiful, sprawling glass and cedar lodge Aidan had bought when he first moved to Haven Point.

Being nervous was stupid. Eliza was a dear friend. She had visited them many times and had even met other Caine family members at various events over the years and considered a few of her sisters-in-law more than casual acquaintances, almost friends.

So why this panic?

She could answer that in one word. Jamie. The two

of them might have forged a tenuous friendship, as she had told Lani, but she was still fiercely attracted to him.

Oh, she had to stop this right now. The man had gone out of his way to do a favor for her by taking the boys with him to Hope's Crossing while she volunteered at the senior center.

She refused to repay him by acting like a brainless, quivering spinster who had never spoken with a man before. She wasn't—far from it. If fate hadn't intervened, she would be long married right now, probably with a houseful of children, as she and Maksym had often discussed.

She could think of no reason why she couldn't be casual and friendly with Jamie, treating him the same way she did Aidan, Bowie Callahan, Ben Kilpatrick. All her friends' husbands.

They didn't make her palms sweat or her thoughts scatter like withered leaves in a November wind.

Anyway, she thought as she parked in front of the house, Jamie told her there would be dozens of people here. Odds were good she wouldn't even have to talk to him.

If she could make it through this dinner without making a fool of herself, she would truly have something for which to be thankful.

JULIA WINSTON WAS LATE.

Jamie checked his watch one more time before shifting his gaze in the direction of Aidan's huge front door, as if he expected her to materialize simply because he willed it.

He didn't know the woman well, but he had a feeling tardiness was extremely out of character.

She was supposed to have been here nearly an hour ago. Road conditions were quite treacherous out there. Maybe she slid into a tree or something…

"What do you think?" Aidan asked. "Should we start without her? The natives are growing restless. You know how Carter gets if he doesn't eat on schedule. Looks like the two boys you brought along take after him."

The day had actually been a delight, the most enjoyable he had spent in a long time. The boys had adored the airplane, especially when he let them into the cockpit and explained some of the controls to them.

As he had suspected, they hit it off with Carter like gangbusters. No big surprise there. Brendan's youngest son was a funny, kind, imaginative kid. It was hard not to like him.

Just now, they were setting out place cards under the watchful eye of Sue, Eliza and Aidan's longtime housekeeper.

"She'll be here," he said now to Aidan. "She texted me forty minutes ago that she was on her way."

He wasn't sure what was taking her so long, though. The drive between Snow Angel Cove and Shelter Springs should only take twenty minutes, and that was with slow traffic.

"I still can't believe you've invited a woman for Thanksgiving dinner," his brother Dylan said. "You never bring anybody to family events. I mean *ever*."

"I believe that's on the first page of the Jamie Caine handbook," Brendan said.

He rolled his eyes, though his skin prickled with heat. How had his usually clueless brothers picked up on that?

Yeah, it had been a conscious effort. You only brought the keepers home to meet the family—and he never dated keepers.

His family was irresistible. He never wanted to run the risk that some unsuspecting woman might fall for his family, which would only complicate things when he broke up with her.

"Not only is he bringing a woman, but he spent all day babysitting a couple of boys for her. Personally, I can't wait to meet this Julia Winston," Brendan said.

"You've met her," his wife, Lucy, told him as she set a vegetable tray down in the middle of the massive table Aidan had bought specifically for these family gatherings.

"Have I?" Brendan frowned, obviously trying to figure out when.

"She was here at Liam's christening last year and the Fourth of July party we had," Eliza said as she carried in a bowl of creamy mashed potatoes that made Jamie drool.

"Is she one of your Helping Hands?" Genevieve, Dylan's wife, asked from the seat she had been firmly relegated to. Gen was hugely pregnant, a few months further along than Lucy, and gloriously beautiful—especially in contrast to Dylan, with his eye patch and scars.

Dylan used his remaining hand to refill his wife's water glass from the fruit-infused pitcher on the table. As Jamie watched his brother, long-familiar guilt pinched at him. He acknowledged it, then shoved it back to the dusty corner with all his other demons.

"She'll be here," Eliza said. "If there's anyone in this world you can trust to do what she says she's going to do, it's Julia Winston. She's the most dependable, steady person I know."

Eliza made Julia sound like a golden retriever. He frowned, but decided he probably shouldn't call his sister-in-law out about it without drawing even more attention from his annoying brothers.

The doorbell rang before he could, anyway.

"I'll get it!" His niece Maddie raced past him toward the door.

Jamie felt stuck. He didn't know how to play this. He *had* invited Julia and the boys to the Caine family dinner, but he hadn't realized how his brothers would put some kind of romantic spin on the gesture.

If he paid too much attention to her, they would tease him mercilessly—and worse, probably her, too. But ignoring her seemed unnecessarily rude.

For now, he would leave Maddie to welcome her, he decided.

The eight-year-old beamed at Julia, grabbed her hand and tugged her inside. "Hi, Miss Winston! You look so pretty today!"

"I...thank you, honey."

Julia had a dazed, what-have-I-gotten-myself-into look as the wall of sound probably crashed over her. Still, she managed a smile for Eliza's daughter as the girl took her coat with perfect manners.

"We had so much fun flying to Hope's Crossing today. I wish you could have come with us. Davy and Clint were scared at first, but I told them I've been on Jamie's plane like a billion times and never even had a crash."

"Did you?" This time her smile looked a little more

natural. She had a truly lovely smile. It lit up her features from the inside, making her glow with life.

"Uncle Jamie even let me hold the rudder. That's the thing that helps you steer the plane. I only got to do it for like three seconds because Clint wanted a turn."

"That does sound exciting. I'm sorry I missed it." She looked around the room until her gaze found his. He wanted to think the nervousness in her eyes seemed to calm a little when she spotted him, but that might have been a trick of the light.

"You're all waiting for me. I'm sorry. The snow is coming down, and the roads were turning to slush. It took me longer than I expected to make it around the lake."

"You're here now. That's the important thing."

He supposed he shouldn't have been surprised when his father hurried over to make the newcomer feel welcome. Dermot grabbed her hand and hooked it through his arm, then led her into the room, pouring on the Irish charm, as he always did in the company of a pretty woman.

Apparently Julia was no less susceptible than any other woman. Her cheeks took on that rosy glow he was coming to enjoy so much, and those glorious eyes gleamed.

Dermot might be past seventy and very happily married to the dear friend he had finally wed a decade after his first wife died, but that didn't prevent him from charming all women, young and old.

He was a little surprised when his father led Julia straight to him, as if by some mysterious master plan. He was also intrigued when her color seemed to heighten.

"Jamie. Hi. Um, how did things go today?"

"Great, at least from my perspective. Maybe you'd better ask Clint and Davy, though." He turned to the boys, who were jostling to find a space at the overflow table. "Guys, how was the airplane?"

"It was awesome," Davy exclaimed. He ran over to them, his gap-toothed grin wide. "You should have been there, Julia. We were higher than the clouds. I'm not even lying, am I, Clint?"

His brother, not far behind, shook his head. "Jamie said we were going six hundred miles an hour. Six hundred! Can you believe it?"

She looked duly impressed. "That's amazing. I want you to tell me all about it, but why don't we wait until after dinner. It looks like everyone is ready to eat. I'm sorry again to keep you waiting."

"You didn't," Eliza assured her. "We're only now setting everything out."

"Can I help with anything?"

"You can sit down and enjoy yourself. I understand you've been helping all day at the nursing home in Shelter Springs. I think you've earned a rest."

Julia looked as if she wanted to argue, but Eliza— ever the consummate hostess—urged all of them to take their seats.

"My handsome helpers have put out turkey place cards with everyone's names on them. Go ahead and find yours."

"Hurry up," Carter said. "I'm starving."

Jamie quickly realized Eliza had seated him next to Julia.

Oddly, he couldn't remember a Thanksgiving dinner he had looked forward to more.

"THAT WAS A fine meal, wouldn't you say?" Dermot said to the kitchen in general—which contained Jamie and most of his brothers, charged with cleaning up after the big meal.

As he had told the boys, cleaning up together was a Caine family tradition, one he enjoyed almost as much as the turkey—though he would never admit it, even under the threat of torture.

"Delicious, as always," Dylan said. "Thanks for hosting again, Aidan."

"You know Eliza." Aidan's smile was smitten as he put silverware back in the drawer. "She's always up for a party."

"You picked a good one there." Pop beamed.

"Don't have to tell me."

All of Jamie's brothers had married well. He adored each of his sisters-in-law.

"It was nice to have a few fresh faces, too, just to liven up the conversation," Dermot said. "Julia seems very nice. I like her."

Of course he would like her—Pop loved everyone. Anyway, he was lucky. Julia had at least *talked* to Dermot. She seemed to have made it a point through dinner to virtually ignore Jamie, unless it was to ask him to pass the potatoes.

He wasn't sulking, he told himself.

"She is very nice," he agreed, scrubbing a little harder at a small glob of potatoes on a plate. He really didn't want to talk about Julia with his brothers, but couldn't think of another topic quickly enough to shift the conversation.

"I believe this might be the first time you've dated a librarian," Brendan said.

"We're not dating," Jamie said.

"You mean you're not checking her out?" Dylan said, a pun that earned groans of disgust all around.

"Julia is great," Aidan said, an unmistakable hard note in his voice. "She's one of Eliza's dearest friends. We would hate to see her hurt."

The implication that Jamie might be the one doing the hurting rankled. Did his family really think him so heartless?

"No one is going to hurt anyone," he said stiffly. "I told you, we're not dating."

Aidan didn't seem to believe him. "I'm just saying, Julia is not your usual love-'em-and-leave-'em sort. She's had a rough time of things and seems a little more...breakable."

He fought the urge to dunk his brother's head into the dishwater. His brothers were his closest friends. Did they really think him so cavalier that he would purposely set out to make a soft, innocent woman like Julia fall for him, just so he could break her heart?

"She's my landlady. That's all. We happen to be living under the same roof for the next few weeks, until my condo is finished."

"Your landlady that you invited for Thanksgiving dinner," Dylan put in.

"I was being nice! She was stressing about the boys coming to live with her, which all happened at the last minute yesterday, so I offered to entertain them for her today by taking them with us on the plane. It only made sense for all of them to join us for Thanksgiving dinner. That's all there is to it. We are not romantically involved whatsoever. I don't know why you all think I can't be nice to a woman without having some sinister ulterior motive, but it is possible. Aidan, you can go back and report to Eliza that you heard it firsthand. I have no evil designs on Julia. I don't intend to seduce her, to debauch her or to break her heart. Okay? Are you happy? Would you all back off now?"

The kitchen fell silent for several awkward seconds before Drew cleared his throat. "Clear enough. I guess we've been told."

What the hell? Where had that come from? He had been way too emphatic, and now everyone was looking at him like he was one can shy of a six-pack.

"So. Informal count. Who's planning on coming back here for Christmas?" Aidan asked.

To his relief, the conversation shifted to the upcoming holidays and the big gala fund-raiser in a few weeks for Spence and Charlotte's charity, Warriors of Hope, that provided recreational therapy for injured veterans.

Little by little as the dishes were done and dried, the kitchen emptied of all but him and Pop. Jamie had a feeling his father had hung back on purpose.

That hunch was verified when Dermot finished drying the last dish, then gave Jamie a stern look. "I know you said Julia Winston is only your landlady, but I just wanted to say I think she's a lovely girl."

"I… She is."

"And maybe a lovely girl is exactly what you need."

"Pop," he began, but Dermot cut him off.

"You need to start thinking about your future, son. You're out of the military now, with your own successful business. Do you want to spend the rest of your life as a carefree bachelor, dating a different woman every week?"

Was that so terrible? Half the married men he knew

would trade places with him in a heartbeat. Not his brothers, of course. They were all happily married, but he considered that an anomaly.

"I appreciate your concern, but I'm doing fine. I have a pretty damn good life."

"Do you? Are you really happy? Have you looked ahead to a decade from now, two decades?"

He didn't want to talk about this, so he chose to remain mute.

"Katherine told me not to say anything, that it's not my business. I agree, but I keep thinking of your dear mother and how it would break our Margaret's heart to see you alone. You need a family of your own. Children of your own."

"Not everybody is cut out for the white picket fence."

"I agree. Some are alone by choice or by circumstance and have wonderful, meaningful, beautiful lives. If that's truly what you want, you know I will accept and support you. But I can't help thinking that you're still punishing yourself, all these years later. I worry you don't think you deserve to be happy."

He felt himself go cold as the ghosts of the past rose up once more. "Pop."

"What happened with Lisa was not your fault. I've said it to you many times and I'll say it again now. No matter what story you tell yourself, you weren't to blame."

He and his father would never agree on that. "You think I'm punishing myself because of something that happened nearly twenty years ago?"

"I think somehow you've convinced yourself you don't have the same right to the happy-ever-after that your brothers have found."

He was saved from having to answer when Eliza came in looking for something to cut the pie. Not for the first time, he would have gladly kissed his sister-in-law for her excellent timing, and he hurried back to the great room before Pop could hound him further.

CHAPTER NINE

"So you had a good Thanksgiving?" Julia asked the boys as she pulled the Lexus into the driveway of Winston House.

"Yes. It was the best one ever," Davy said, voice brimming with excitement.

"What about you, Clint?" she pressed when the older boy said nothing, keeping his eyes focused on the darkness outside the vehicle window.

"It was okay, I guess," he finally mumbled.

"Just okay?"

He shrugged as she pulled into the garage, turned off the engine and started helping the boys out of their seat belts.

"You looked as if you were having a wonderful time playing with the other children. Carter and Faith and the others were so nice, weren't they? And I can only imagine how exciting the airplane ride was."

"Riding on an airplane was fun at first, then it got kind of boring," he answered.

"You weren't bored! You loved it just as much as I did," Davy said.

Clint glowered at his brother as they went up the steps to the house. "Shut up. I did not."

"You said it was fun!"

"You don't know what you're talking about."

They were still quarreling as Julia let them all inside the kitchen and flipped on the light. She felt wholly inadequate. How did parents deal with these squabbles? She feared taking sides would only make things worse.

This parenting gig was *hard*.

"*You* shut up," Davy said. "I heard you say it was fun before, and now you're lying when you say it wasn't. Why are you being such a jerk?"

"You're a jerk."

"Boys. That's enough. You shouldn't call each other names. Also, it's rude to tell someone to shut up."

"It's rude to tell a lie, too. Clint's a big, dumb liar."

"I am not!" his brother protested. "I didn't have fun. There were too many people and food I didn't like. The mashed potatoes tasted weird, and they didn't have any blueberry pie. I wanted to have Thanksgiving like we always did. I want my mom."

His chin quivered, and in that moment, Julia wanted *her* mom, too. Mariah would know how to handle these boys. She would be her calm, loving self and get to the root of the problem.

Her mother wasn't here, and neither was the boys' mother. She was it for them right now and would have to fix this herself.

Julia sat on one of the kitchen chairs and pulled Clint toward her in what was probably the world's most awkward hug. He didn't seem to mind. After a moment, he hugged her back, and some of the tension seemed to seep out of his small frame.

"I know you miss your mom," she said softly. "That's normal."

That was the root of his rude behavior. She didn't need Mariah to help figure out that. He was worried and upset. How could she blame him? Everything in his world suddenly had changed.

"Sometimes we can't have everything we want," she said, her voice soft. "It stinks, I know. But simply because everything isn't perfect doesn't mean you should throw out the good things you *do* have. Imagine that I gave you a really delicious chocolate chip cookie, but it only has three chocolate chips, not the four you wanted. Would you throw it on the ground and stomp on it and refuse to eat it?"

"No," he scoffed. "That would be stupid."

"Right? But it's kind of the same thing here. You didn't have everything you wanted today. You miss your mother and are worried for her. I don't blame you at all for that. In fact, I completely understand. I miss my mom, too. This is my first Thanksgiving without either of my parents, just like you, and it hurts."

"I just want everything to be okay."

"I know. Remember that Thanksgiving is about being grateful—for airplane rides and nice people who invite us to dinner and leftover turkey we can have for sandwiches tomorrow. It's okay to be sad about what you don't have, but don't let your sadness ruin what you *do* have. Okay?"

"Okay." For just a moment—one small, precious slice of time—he rested his cheek against her. Julia tightened her arms, her heart swelling at the warm, sweet weight of him.

"It's been a long day, and I'm sure you're both tired. Why don't you take your baths and get in your pajamas, then we can look through the bookshelves in your room for something you'd like me to read to you before bed."

"Can you read *Green Eggs and Ham*?" he asked.

"You've got it. That is definitely a book I know we can find on the bookshelf."

"What about the *Wild Things* book?" Davy asked.

"I have that one, too. I'm going to put these leftovers Eliza gave us in the refrigerator. You two take care of your part, and we'll meet in your room when we're all done. Can everyone be nice, now?"

They nodded and went together to prepare for bed.

They were both so sleepy after their exciting day, their eyelids were drooping by the time she finished the first of the five stories they pulled out for her to read.

"Why don't we stop there?" she said softly as she closed the book.

"But what about the other books?" Davy asked, forcing one eye open.

"They will still be here in the morning. We can read them tomorrow."

They made a token protest, too sleepy to put much force into it. Clint climbed up to his top bunk.

This wasn't so bad, she thought as she tucked them in and smoothed a hand over each boy's head. She could handle story time with a half-asleep but appreciative audience.

"Good night, both of you. Sleep well."

"Can the cats stay in here?" Davy asked.

Empress and Tabitha were curled up at the foot of his bed.

"For now," she said. "I'm not sure they'll stay here all night. They sometimes like to wander, but I can leave the door open a bit so they don't wake you up when they leave."

"Okay. G'night, Miss Julia," Davy said.

"Night, Miss Julia," Clint echoed.

"You know, since you're living with me, you don't have to call me Miss Julia, right? You can simply call me Julia."

"Good night, Julia," both boys said in unison, as if they had rehearsed it.

She smiled and left the room, closing the door a crack, as she had promised.

The bathroom was a disaster of wet towels, wet floor, dirty clothes. The mess trailed out into the hall and into the living room. She picked things up, wondering how two boys possibly could generate so much clutter, especially when they had come to her without much in the way of belongings at all.

She was going to have to do something about that. They needed more clothing, books, a few toys to call their own at her house.

They might have to make do for a few days. The last thing she wanted to do was take them shopping on Black Friday.

She was hanging the last towel on the rack when she thought she heard a soft knock on her door.

Jamie.

It had to be him. Any other visitors would have rung the doorbell out front.

She tucked a wayward strand of hair behind her ear, grimly aware of the fierce punch of her heartbeat.

Stop it, she told herself as she went to the door and pulled it open to find Jamie wearing a fawn-colored leather jacket and holding a plastic container.

She had only left Snow Angel Cove an hour earlier. How was it possible that she somehow forgot how delicious he smelled?

"Hi. Did we forget something?"

He held out the cardboard. "Pop wanted to make sure you had a few extra slices of boysenberry pie to enjoy later."

"Oh, how sweet! He must have seen me inhale some earlier. It was quite possibly the best piece of pie it's ever been my pleasure to taste."

He smiled. "That is one of his specialties."

He handed over the container, and though she was more stuffed than she'd been in a long time, her mouth watered in anticipation for the future treat.

"Your father is a lovely man. I hope you know."

"He is. And I do. Mind you, I didn't always think so, especially during my rebellious teen years."

"I'm trying to imagine you as a rebellious teen, but I'm afraid I can't quite picture it."

"I have photographic proof, if you'd like to see it. Long hair, surly expression and all."

"I would. Very much."

He looked startled for just a moment before he laughed, which sent shivers down her spine and made Audrey wander in from parts unknown to see what was happening.

"Do me a favor and don't tell my sister that. She loves any excuse to whip out the photo albums."

She smiled, resolving to ignore him and do just that. Charlotte, his only sister, was a dear. The first time Julia met her, it had come as quite a shock to discover she was married to Smokin' Hot Spence Gregory, who used to pitch for the Portland Pioneers. Over the last few years, she almost had gotten over being tongue-tied around the man.

Now Jamie was the only one who left her flustered.

"All of your family is wonderful," she said softly. "You're very lucky."

"I know. And if I ever forget, they're all quick to remind me."

"Good. You should remember it always. It was a wonderful dinner. It's obvious you all love each other very much."

"Again, it hasn't always been that way," he answered. "The fighting among us boys could be epic when we were growing up. Our mom used to grab whoever was arguing and force us to sit on the sofa together until we could work things out."

"Did it work?"

He shrugged. "Aidan and I once slept there all night in a spat over ownership of a Stretch Armstrong, but then we got hungry, and Pop was making pancakes, so I gave it back to him."

She smiled a little at that, completely charmed to picture one of the world's most powerful geek gods fighting his younger brother over a toy.

He gazed down at her for a long moment with an odd expression, then cleared his throat. "Anyway, if you hold on, I have a few other things in the car."

"More leftovers? Eliza and Sue already filled a bag for us. I've got enough stuffing, mashed potatoes and turkey to last through the weekend."

"No. These are for the boys. You can blame Eliza for that. After I told her the situation, she put out the call to my family and friends letting everyone know about the boys. We thought they might need a few things while they're staying with you. Clothing, coats, toys, books. That sort of thing."

Her insides went all soft and gooey at the idea of

Jamie Caine calling in the troops to outfit a couple of schoolboys.

Resisting him was proving harder by the minute.

"Right before you showed up, I was wondering if we could get by until next week so I don't have to brave the Black Friday shoppers."

"I can't guarantee you'll have everything you need, but there are two suitcases full of clothes and a couple plastic bins of toys. That should get you started. Can I start bringing them in?"

"Of course. Let me grab some shoes, and I'll come help you."

"No, stay here, where it's warm. I can take care of it."

"I don't mind," she assured him. After she threw on her boots and shrugged into a coat, they walked into the cold night air. Across the street, the neighbors had turned on their Christmas lights, hanging from every shrub and tree branch. They glowed a lovely blue and white against the lightly falling snow.

Everyone else in her historic neighborhood went all out for Christmas, decorating their multistory Victorian houses with ribbons and lights and evergreen branches.

As in all things, her parents had been subdued in their holiday celebrations. When she was a girl, she remembered wreaths in the windows and a few lights around the porch, but since Julia's father died, her mother hadn't even wanted to bother with a tree, claiming the cats would only pull off the ornaments.

But Julia had two young boys living with her now in this sprawling museum of a house. She couldn't let the holiday pass without some outward show. They needed some Christmas spirit now more than ever, especially with their mother missing and their world filled with uncertainty.

Perhaps they could go that week and cut down a tree at the farm in Shelter Springs. She would have them help her go through boxes in the attic to find leftover decorations.

"It's a beautiful night," she said, lifting her face to the barely perceptible brush of snow on her cheeks.

Jamie, opening his cargo door, glanced around the area. "It really is. I'm looking forward to seeing Haven Point all decked out for the holidays."

He pulled a couple of suitcases from the back of his SUV and handed them to her, then reached in himself for two large black plastic totes before shoving the door closed and locking it with his key fob.

"Can I ask you a question?" she asked as they headed back to her house.

"Shoot."

"You're very close with your family. I saw that today."

"I guess so."

"Most of them live in Hope's Crossing. Why, then, would you decide to locate your charter business here, in Haven Point?"

"Aidan's here," he pointed out. "He's family."

"Only half the time. He and Eliza split their time between Haven Point and California."

He gave a short laugh. "I believe I'm aware of that, since I'm usually the one flying them back and forth between locations."

"So why settle here and not in California? You just… don't strike me as the small-town sort."

"Don't I?"

She shrugged, wishing she hadn't said anything. "I'm sure you know you have a bit of reputation."

He raised an eyebrow. "What sort of reputation?"

Cripes, she had a big mouth. "Nothing. Forget it."

"No. I'm interested. I'd like to know what the Helping Hands are saying about me."

She sighed. She would have to just brazen through. "Nothing bad. Only that you, um, date. A lot."

"A player, do you mean?" He sounded vaguely insulted.

She quickly shook her head. "No. Not at all. Just that you rarely date the same woman more than a few times."

A player was someone who manipulated women and used them for his own gratification. She'd never heard anything like that about Jamie, merely that he liked to go out with a lot of women and always seemed careful to keep things casual.

"That's probably true. I always figured the world is a garden, filled with beautiful blooms." He paused with a rueful expression. "And hearing myself say that out loud, I realize I sound like an idiot."

She had to laugh as she shrugged out of her coat inside her living room. "No. Just like the player you say you're not."

"The women I date know I'm not looking for anything serious. I'm always clear about that up front."

He spoke with an intensity she didn't quite understand.

"Why not?" she asked, then immediately regretted the question. "Sorry. None of my business. Still, if your end goal is variety, I wonder why you didn't base your flight operations in California, where the, er, flowers grow a little more abundantly than a small town in

Idaho, where your dating and business expansion opportunities are limited."

"I enjoy Haven Point. It's a charming little town in a stunning location. I love the lake and the mountains and all the recreational opportunities here, from hiking to boating to fishing to snowshoeing. I can't say I miss the traffic or the cost of living in northern California."

Something told her there was more to the story, but she also sensed he wouldn't easily reveal himself.

"What about you?" he asked. "Were you born and raised here?"

"In this house, actually. Not the born part. I was born in a hospital, of course, but the rest of it. I've lived here my whole life, except the three years I lived in Boise while I was in college."

His eyes widened in shock. "You haven't ever wanted to live anywhere else?"

Julia thought about the dreams of her youth. She had talked with friends about backpacking across Europe after graduation or even joining the Peace Corps, just to widen her horizons a little. She loved reading about adventures but had a compelling urge to live a few herself, to see something beyond this small spot on the map.

Then, the last half of her senior year, she had met Maksym in an Eastern European literature class. During their whirlwind courtship—a hazy, surreal time that now seemed as if it had happened to someone else—they had talked about moving to his country and building a future together as soon as he finished his degree and his year of mandatory military service.

Maksym had proposed a month before finals, spurred by the urgency of having to return to the Ukraine days after graduation.

Her parents had both freaked. They had been fiercely opposed to the marriage—so opposed, they even refused to meet Maksym. They weren't exactly xenophobic, but they couldn't see how a sheltered, quiet girl from a small town in Idaho could possibly be happy with someone from a completely different background and culture. She thought their objections were largely based in fear, that their only daughter would move to another continent and they would never see her again.

Julia loved him, though, as wildly and impulsively as a twenty-one-year-old could. She defied her parents, the one and only time she had.

Sadness pinched her heart for those dreams and the choices she had made, the bitter reality that had taken their place. "I never thought I would end up here, but life doesn't always work out the way we plan," she said instead.

"True enough."

Enough about the past. This was still Thanksgiving for a few more hours, a time for focusing on gratitude, not missed chances and fate's cruel twists.

She turned her attention to the bags of clothes, boots and other items, some that looked almost new.

"This is wonderful. Please, tell your family how grateful I am. I'll make sure to keep track of what we use, so I can return things after the boys are either back with their mother or end up with a more permanent placement."

"That's not necessary," he assured her. "All of these things were eventually headed to Goodwill, so it was no sacrifice, believe me. Send them on with the boys if you want or find another home for them here in Haven Point or at one of the thrift stores in Shelter Springs."

"I'll do that. Thank you."

"No problem. We had to guess on sizes, so I'm sure some of it won't fit. Just donate what you don't need or want for the boys."

"Sounds good. Please, tell everyone thank you for their generosity. And thank you very much for thinking of it in the first place—and for everything else you did today."

"It wasn't much."

"I disagree. You took what could have been a rough day for me and for the boys and turned it into something memorable."

His smile was wide and genuine. "I'm happy I could help out a little."

"More than a little," she insisted. "Once more, I'm in your debt."

"I guess I'll have to figure out a way you can repay me," he said. She was quite sure he didn't intend his voice to come out all low and seductive, but it still sent goose bumps rippling over her skin.

"Good night," she murmured. "Happy Thanksgiving."

"Same to you." He leaned in to kiss her cheek.

She had about half a second to react, while the delicious scent of him swirled around them. She had no idea why she did it, but without giving herself a chance to think about it, she turned her mouth at the last second and his mouth found hers.

In that first shocked instant, he inhaled sharply, and then he was kissing her for real. His mouth was warm and tasted of berries and vanilla ice cream, and the taste completely took her breath away.

This couldn't be happening. She couldn't really be standing in her living room kissing Jamie Caine!

And what a kiss. Her thoughts whirled like the snow-flakes falling outside, with just about as much staying power, and her heart fluttered in her chest.

It had been so very long since she had kissed a man, *really* kissed a man. What a tragedy that was. She had forgotten how utterly decadent it could be, far more lus-cious than Dermot Caine's boysenberry pie.

She had missed this surge of her heartbeat, the nerves dancing through her, the slow churn of her blood.

Jamie Caine could write books about kissing. If he did, she would be first in line at the bookstore to buy every copy. He knew just how to coax and tease and inflame her senses. A nibble here, a glide of his tongue there, all while his big, warm hands held her tightly against his muscles.

She wanted to stay here forever. She might have, if not for the sudden jagged pain in her leg that felt very much like cat claws.

It was Audrey, of course. She gave Julia a haughty stare, then rubbed against Jamie's leg and started purr-ing loudly.

Jamie's gaze met hers, and she wished with all her heart she could decipher the jumble of emotions there. She thought she saw surprise and maybe awareness, but he was a mystery beyond that.

"I wasn't expecting that," he murmured.

She stepped back, aware her hands were trembling and her face was on fire. What would he think of her? She had started that kiss, had leaned in to steal something she'd been wondering about since before he moved in.

"Audrey has always been the jealous type," she said,

deliberately misinterpreting his words. "Apparently she has claimed you for her own and wants to make that unmistakably clear."

"I guess I've been warned." He looked down at the cat for a moment, then back at her, searching her expression. "And that kiss? I wasn't expecting that either."

She would have to brazen this out. "Half the women in Haven Point are in love with you. Maybe I just wanted to see what all the fuss is about."

"You're exaggerating."

The sad thing was, she really wasn't. "Don't worry. I won't accost you again."

"You didn't accost me. You kissed me. And it was one hell of a kiss."

"Which won't happen again, I promise."

Too bad, she thought she heard him mutter, but Audrey mewled at that moment and she couldn't be sure.

"Thanks again for everything today. Good night."

Leaving him no chance to answer, she quickly shut the door to the vestibule in his face and snicked the dead bolt shut, then rushed to the sofa and sank down.

Oh. My.

She had kissed Jamie Caine. What had she been *thinking*? She gazed into space, trying to process what had just happened. She *hadn't* been thinking. That was clear enough. She had been lost in the moment—of him close to her and the intimacy of the quiet house and the feeling that had been lingering since Roxy's book club, that life was going on without her.

She had resolved to try new things and be open to exciting opportunities. Never, in her wildest dreams, had she imagined kissing a man like Jamie Caine might fall into that category.

Though her lips felt achy and swollen and the scent of him still lingered on her skin, she felt like those moments had happened to a stranger. One minute, she had been telling him good night, the next she was wrapped around him like one of her cats around the scratching post.

How would she face him ever again?

When she did, she knew she would remember the taste of him, the scent of him, the incredibly seductive sensation of being in his arms.

It was done. She couldn't jump into the way-back machine and change those few moments; she could only move forward.

And since she couldn't change it, what was the point in regretting a kiss that had been magical? She might as well savor the moment, since she would likely never have the chance for a sequel.

What was happening to her? In the last thirty-six hours, she had reached completely out of her comfort zone. First, she had taken on two foster children and now, instigating a kiss with Jamie Caine, of all people!

If she were honest with herself, she kind of liked this unusual boldness. For too long, she had been living her life according to what others, especially her parents, had expected of her.

She had loved her parents and had felt a great duty to them for adopting her, for providing her with love and kindness and possibilities. They were gone now. She missed them dearly, but maybe it was past time she tried to create her own future.

CHAPTER TEN

How HAD HE ever been foolish enough to think Julia Winston was staid and boring?

Jamie climbed the stairs to his apartment, still reeling from that shockingly hot kiss. For a quiet, reserved librarian, she kissed with a passion and intensity he had found incredibly arousing.

Why had she kissed him? He had the feeling she had been as startled by the impulsive gesture as he was—and somehow the spontancity of it made the kiss even sexier.

He couldn't seem to stop thinking about the little hitch in her breathing as he kissed her, the trembling of her hands against his chest, her soft, enthusiastic response.

And how much he wanted to kiss her again.

No. He couldn't think about it. Enticing as she might be in that mysterious, under-the-radar way, Julia Winston was *not* the kind of woman he should spend even five minutes thinking about.

She was far too breakable.

Jamie let himself into his apartment, with its soothing walls and feminine furnishings. She had created this space, and every inch of it screamed she was a romantic at heart.

He had been clear with her that he only allowed himself to become involved with women who were good with casual, easy relationships—women who understood he didn't want anything serious. It was an iron-clad rule, from the time he was nineteen. He stayed miles away from vulnerable innocents with soft eyes and fragile emotions.

He plopped onto the sofa and turned on the television, then immediately switched it off again, restless and edgy and still half-aroused from that kiss.

What was it about Julia that tugged at him so unexpectedly?

She took in those two lost boys, even as the reality of being responsible for them obviously terrified her. That told him there was far more to her than he had thought when he first moved in.

Maybe she intrigued him simply because she was so very different from the women he usually dated. She *was* quiet and reserved—maybe a little uptight. Her house was fussy and formal, her clothing bland to the point of boring.

Yet her mouth was soft and warm and delicious, and she kissed him back with an innocent passion that made him ache to explore all those hidden depths.

He wouldn't. He couldn't. The risk was far too great. He couldn't be the cause of more heartbreak, no matter what Pop had said.

So what now? He lived upstairs from the woman. He couldn't exactly avoid her. He could for a few days, though. In the morning he was taking most of his family back to Hope's Crossing, then he would be flying Ben Kilpatrick and Aidan to Asia for meetings.

He hadn't been looking forward to the overseas trip in particular, expecting it to be exhausting and demanding, with long hours in the cockpit, but now he faced it gratefully. He would be away from Haven Point for several days, which just might help cure him of this sudden fascination for the unexpected temptation that lived downstairs.

SHE WAS DYING.

Julia tried to lift her head from the sofa pillow, but her skull suddenly weighed a hundred pounds. Everything hurt, from her temples to her chest to her toes. She was by turns hot, then clammy, and her stomach ached from hurling everything up over the last twelve hours.

"I brought you a drink of water," a small voice said. She propped one eyelid open to find Davy standing in front of her, holding out a clear glass.

"Thank you," she croaked out. "But, remember, you need to stay away from me. I don't want you catching this."

"I'm being careful," he said. "And I'll go wash my hands again."

"Leave it on the table. Thank you."

Over the past twenty-four hours, she had tried to insist the boys stay on the other side of the room from her after school or play in their bedroom. Yesterday had been rough. Today was torture. All she wanted to do was curl up into a ball, pull the covers over her head and sleep for weeks.

How did other parents handle being sick, having to care for others when they wanted the whole world to leave them alone so they could feel wretched in peace?

"I'm going to make a couple of peanut butter and jelly sandwiches for us," Clint said from behind his brother. "Do you think you might want one?"

Just the thought of it made her stomach twist into

greasy knots again. Even tiny sips of water made her stomach hurt. She had never been this sick in her life. The flu had come on hard and showed no sign of leaving her in peace.

Clint's words suddenly echoed in her mind, familiar and haunting. That's exactly what he had been doing when she found him—taking care of his brother. That wasn't the way this foster care arrangement was supposed to go.

She forced herself to sit up, then had to catch her breath as the room twisted and turned like a violent, horrible roller coaster. "I can make sandwiches for you," she said.

She had signed up to take care of them. It was her responsibility. Mothers—even temporary foster mothers—couldn't take the day off, even when suffering from a bug that knocked them out.

She was all the boys had right now, and she couldn't let them down.

"Don't get up," Clint said, his voice firm. "It will just make you yack again. Stay there. I make super good PB&J sandwiches. Davy can stay in here to keep an eye on you while I do it."

His words made her eyes sting with unshed tears. He had been so sweet to her through the course of this vicious illness, bringing her an extra blanket, making sure she had warm washcloths close at hand, even taking over story time duties for his brother to give her a break.

She couldn't believe the difference a week made. Both boys were settling in to their new home, coming to terms with the situation.

"You're a good boy," she said to Clint, voice quavering. He gave a half smile, but she couldn't tell whether he looked pleased or embarrassed at her words. "Try to drink some water if you can. You'll feel better."

She knew he was right, as distasteful as she found everything right now. She sipped the straw but couldn't manage more than a swallow or two. She was gearing up for a third when she heard a sharp rap on her door.

"I'll get it," Davy called out. Before she could tell him she was in no state to receive visitors, he raced to the door and yanked it open.

Just when she thought she had hit bottom on the misery scale, she slid down another few inches. If she'd had an ounce of energy, she might have shriveled away from the humiliation. She was wearing her grungiest pair of sweats, her hair was lanky and smushed on one side, and she was fairly certain she hadn't showered that day.

Jamie Caine, on the other hand, looked as if he had casually decided to swing by after a photo shoot for a cologne advertisement.

She hadn't seen him since Thanksgiving night, since that shocker of a kiss. Over the past week, she had visualized a dozen different scenarios for what might happen when they did meet again—how casual she would act, smooth and put-together. She imagined being polite and friendly, but making it absolutely clear to him she hadn't spent an instant obsessing about those magical moments she had spent in his arms.

Never once had she envisioned this particular scenario—with her feeling like death warmed over on the sofa.

Jamie didn't appear to even notice her, too busy greeting Davy. "Hey!" His face lit up when the boy answered the door. "If it isn't one of my favorite copilots. How are you doing?"

Davy giggled. "Hi. We're good. Well, Clint and me are good. Julia thinks she's dying."

He must have spotted her then. His alarmed gaze landed on her, and she told herself it was the flu making the room spin again.

"I might have exaggerated a bit," she said. In her head, she spoke with confidence and good humor, but her ears—and most likely, his, too—heard a weak, pitiful whisper.

"What's going on?"

"She's sick," Clinton said, peeking his head in from the kitchen. "She had a fever and chills, and she's been throwing up all day. She says it's stomach flu."

If she had an ounce of strength left, she would drag herself into the fetal position, stuff her head under her pillow and pray that Jamie would leave her to her abject humiliation.

"Oh, no," he exclaimed, his expression softening with compassion. "I'm so sorry. That's the *worst*. Can I do anything for you?"

"Going away would be a good start."

He obviously didn't think she was serious. He smiled and moved closer. "I hate to state the obvious, but you should be in bed."

The idea of curling up under the covers and blocking the world out called to her with more ferocity than a free weekend and a stack of new releases by all her favorite authors. "I'm okay," she lied.

"Are you?" he challenged.

"I'm feeling better than I was earlier." That was marginally true, considering she hadn't emptied the contents of her stomach in about an hour. "I'll be fine. I'll go straight to bed when the boys do. I have to make sure they eat and do their homework."

Jamie gazed at the boys for a moment, then at her. "Why don't you let me take care of that tonight?"

Her brain felt fuzzy and exhausted. That must have been why she couldn't make sense of the offer. "You?"

"You have a better chance of regaining your strength more quickly if you rest as much as you can instead of pushing yourself to the limit."

She didn't tell him she had reached that limit about twelve hours earlier and was only hanging on by sheer willpower.

"These flu bugs can be vicious, but they're usually short-lived. By morning, I'm willing to bet you'll feel a hundred times better—but only if you give your body a chance to recover."

"You only just returned from traveling," she protested. "You've been gone for a week, and you must be jet-lagged. The last thing you likely want to do is spend the evening here."

"Are you kidding? I didn't have anything planned, only a quiet evening at home. It would be much more fun to catch up with my favorite copilots."

The boys both grinned back at him, and the sweetness of this big, macho guy being so kind to these needy boys was more than Julia could take. The tears of misery she had been holding back since Clinton and Davy came home from school began to leak out, and she couldn't seem to do anything to stop them.

"Why are you being so nice to me?" she sniffled.

He gave a short laugh. "I'm a nice guy. Besides, Pop would never forgive me if he found out I let you suffer down here on your own without lending a hand."

She did adore his father. Julia pictured the elder Mr. Caine, with his bushy eyebrows and those kindly eyes. She would hate for Jamie to get into trouble with his dad.

"Here, honey. Dry your eyes." When he handed her a tissue, she suddenly realized those tears were dripping out.

"It's going to be okay. I promise," Jamie went on. "You'll feel better once you get some rest. I'll help the boys with dinner and homework and get them settled for the night, and you focus on getting better. By morning, you'll be a new woman."

"I hate being sick."

"It's the worst," he agreed. "Let's get you to bed."

Before she quite realized what was happening, he scooped her up, blanket and all.

"I don't want to get you sick," she protested.

"I wouldn't worry about that. I've got the constitution of an ornery bull."

"You're not ornery. You're so sweet."

The room was spinning again, but she wasn't sure if the light-headedness stemmed from being in his arms again or from the medicine she had taken.

She did know she wanted to stay right here all night, with his strong arms holding her close and her own arms around his neck. That wasn't too much to ask, was it?

He apparently thought so.

"Here we go. Into your bed."

She tried not to be embarrassed again at how hideous she must look as he helped her beneath her quilt, adjusted her pillow, smoothed her hair away from her face.

Nothing in her life had ever felt as tender and sweet as that tiny moment of gentle caretaking.

She was so ridiculously crazy about him.

"I'll bring in some water for you. You rest now."

He smoothed that stubborn lock of hair away again, and she couldn't resist leaning into his hand as more tears swelled. "You're a lovely man, Jamie Caine."

He gave a sharp bark of laughter. "I do believe you're the first woman who has ever called me that."

Oh, she highly doubted that. "You are. And you're so cute, too."

She didn't realize she had said that part aloud until he gave a strangled cough. "Um. Thanks. Close your eyes and rest now. Everything will be fine with the boys, I promise."

"Thank you."

She was so very tired, and the bed felt incredible. She wanted to sleep for days.

Her last thought before she fell asleep was shock all over again. Had she really kissed Jamie Caine, that gorgeous, sweet man who treated her with such kindness it brought her to tears? Or had she dreamed that, too?

CHAPTER ELEVEN

SHE WAS ALREADY asleep by the time Jamie eased out of the room and closed the door softly behind him.

Poor thing. He hated being sick, especially when he had people counting on him. He couldn't make her feel better, but at least he could take the worry of caring for Davy and Clinton from her shoulders.

He found the boys on the floor of the living room petting two of the cats while the other cat watched them from the sofa Julia had recently vacated.

Clint and Davy both looked up, wearing matching expressions of concern. "Is Julia gonna die?" Davy asked, fear in his eyes.

These boys had too much experience with death and loss for such young ages.

"No! Of course not," he said firmly. "She has the flu. That's all. It's very contagious, though, so you two need to wash your hands a *lot*, and don't touch your nose or mouth."

"Hear that?" Clint said, eyeing his brother with a teasing look. "Don't pick your boogers and eat them anymore. Jamie said not to."

Davy thrust his jaw out. "Shut up! I never did that in my life. You're the booger head."

"Better than being a booger mouth."

They went on trading insults a few moments longer. He well remembered many similar conversations among his own brothers when they were this age—and how those conversations inevitably devolved into physical retaliations.

It was probably better to head things off before they reached that point.

"What do you guys feel like for dinner? How about pizza? I know an excellent place in town that delivers."

That plan was met with an enthusiastic response that didn't surprise him in the least. Pizza. The great peacemaker. Since his cell battery was nearly dead, he picked up Julia's landline and dialed Serrano's.

Barbara herself answered, and when he identified himself, her voice sharpened with suspicion.

"Jamie Caine. What are you doing, calling me from Julia's house?"

"Um. I live here."

"You live upstairs, yet according to my caller ID, you're calling from her phone number."

He wanted to ask what business it was of hers, but things didn't work like that in Haven Point. Right. She was good friends with Julia through the Haven Point Helping Hands. He should have remembered that. Women in this town tended to stick together.

In Haven Point, like his hometown of Hope's Crossing, people watched out for each other. That's what he was doing, Jamie reminded himself. He had absolutely no reason to feel guilty.

"Julia is feeling a little under the weather, so I offered to help out with the boys who are staying with her to give her a break."

In an instant, Barbara's suspicion shifted to concern. His head spun a little with how rapidly her tone changed. "Oh, no! Is she okay? What can I do?"

"For now, pizza for the boys should cover it. She seems to feel pretty rotten, but I'm sure with a little rest she'll be back to herself in no time."

"Oh, the poor dear. And aren't you the sweetest thing, to step up and help in her moment of need?"

"I'm not doing much. Just helping Davy and Clint with homework and feeding them. Can we get a large pepperoni?"

"You got it. And you're in luck. Today's soup of the day is chicken noodle. I'll send a big, healthy portion for Julia. You make sure she eats it, you hear me?"

"Yes, ma'am," he answered meekly. What else could he say?

"I'm serious. Homemade chicken noodle soup is documented to cut the duration of any sickness. It's better than going to a doctor."

"I've heard," Jamie said. Pop was a big cheerleader for soup in all times of crisis. Barbara reminded him a little of his father, which was more than a little frightening.

"How long on the pies? I've got a couple of starving dudes who are about to start gnawing the original woodwork here."

She laughed. "Twenty minutes. I'll put a rush on it for you."

"Thanks." He hung up and turned to the boys. "Okay, guys. What's the homework situation?"

"We don't have any," Clint said promptly.

"Are you sure?"

"Positive."

Jamie narrowed his gaze and studied them closely.

Clint looked back at him guilelessly, but Davy pressed his lips together tightly and looked down at the floor, a clear indication that some level of deception was going on here.

"Truth time. I have to be able to trust my copilots are one hundred percent honest with me. I'll ask one more time. What's the homework situation?"

They looked at him, then each other. "It's only Friday," Clint said. "We have all weekend."

"Why don't we get it out of the way, then you won't have to wait until the last minute."

Clint gave a heavy sigh. "I have to finish my math, and Davy is supposed to read aloud for twenty minutes every night."

"Perfect, since that's how long the pizza will take. I'll read with him, you work on your math and by the time we finish, dinner should be here."

"When we're done, can we go get a Christmas tree?" Clint asked. "Julia said we could cut one down last night, then she didn't feel good enough, so we had to go to bed early."

He had noticed the house seemed singularly devoid of Christmas decorations, unlike most of the others in town. "That might be something she wants to do herself," he said warily.

"Please?" Davy begged. "We really want to have a Christmas tree. We didn't have a very good one last year."

"Our mom was kind of sad last Christmas, plus we had just moved here and didn't have much money," Clint said. "We bought a little one and hung some ornaments we made, but Davy and me kind of wanted a big one this year. We thought maybe if we had a bigger tree, and we wished hard enough, Santa might bring our mom back for Christmas. That's okay, though. We don't really need one."

He spoke in such a matter-of-fact way, Jamie felt his heart squeeze. Either this kid was a master manipulator, or he really didn't realize how sad his situation was from the outside. Jamie had a feeling it was the latter.

These boys had been through so much. He wanted to give them whatever they wanted, but he knew it wasn't that simple.

"Not tonight," he said. "But tomorrow is Saturday, and I don't have to fly anywhere. If Julia's still feeling under the weather in the morning, we'll talk to her about picking one out. If she's okay with it, I'll take you then. Deal?"

The boys' faces both lit up. "Yay!" Davy exclaimed. "We're gonna have a Christmas tree tomorrow!"

"That's a maybe, remember? For now, our first order of business is homework. Let's see if we can get it done before the pizza arrives."

The boys hurried off to find their work, and Jamie collapsed into a kitchen chair, hoping he hadn't just made a huge mistake.

Two hours later, he closed the door to the boys' bedroom, headed back into the living room and eased into the big formal wing-back chair that was surprisingly comfortable.

He couldn't remember when he had been so exhausted. If one of his brothers happened to stop by right now, he could easily think Jamie had been in a brawl. His shirt had a big pizza stain courtesy of Davy, his jeans were soaked from cleaning up the bathroom after them and his hair was a mess from Davy tugging on it while Jamie gave him a horsey ride into bed.

This child-caring gig was harder than he ever imagined. He'd hung out with his nieces and nephews plenty of times, but only when their parents were around to supervise. It was an entirely different undertaking when he was the one in charge.

The boys had fun, though. That was the important thing. He smiled as he recalled the grand, elaborate paper airplanes they had folded after the homework and pizza had both been tackled, then their fierce competition to see whose could fly farthest off the landing into the foyer.

He had figured out a few things that worked with them. Both boys loved to be helpful, he discovered, so he had used that shamelessly. They had fought each other to see who could pick up more toys from the living room, who could wash more dishes, who could be the first in and out of the shower.

They were good boys. Davy had a really funny sense of humor and found humor in even the silliest things, and he found it so sweet to watch Clint watch out for his younger brother.

When he thought of what they had survived, he wanted to punch something. Where the hell was their mother? It would break their hearts to find out she was dead of an overdose somewhere—or, worse, that she had taken her own life.

When he had seen them on Thanksgiving, both boys seemed to have a few reservations about staying with Julia. After a week, they seemed to have settled into a comfortable routine, and Davy had been quick to correct anything Jamie did that might veer away from that.

They were also obviously worried about her health. Several times, he'd had to dissuade them from going in to check on her—though he had let them peek in before they went to bed, and they seemed content to find her sleeping soundly.

He had done his good deed for the day. Now he could head up to his apartment and go to sleep with a clear conscience.

One of the snooty cats—Empress, he thought, though it was tough to tell her from Tabitha—suddenly jumped on to a side table, but she must have misjudged her landing because she knocked several books on to the floor.

He glanced toward Julia's room, hoping the clatter didn't awaken her, but her door remained closed and he could hear no sign of movement behind it.

After the boys worked so hard to pick up their mess, he couldn't leave a pile of books scattered on the floor. Not to mention, it would probably severely offend Julia's librarian sensibilities.

He reached to pick them up and realized a piece of paper had fallen from one of them, a new age feel-good kind of book about filling wells—which always seemed kind of a dumb phrase to him. Wells were supposed to automatically replenish, weren't they? The whole point of having a well was the ability to take stuff out of it without having to worry about refilling it, otherwise it would be Filling the Reservoir.

He picked up the paper and recognized Julia's handwriting from a shopping list he'd seen on the refrigerator, though it looked a little less elegant here, as if she'd scrawled the words in a hurry.

He was about to put it away when the words "Have an orgasm with someone else" jumped out at him.

Why, Julia Winston. You naughty thing.

He grinned a little as he smoothed the list out. How could he resist reading further after that tantalizing snippet? Across the top he read, "This year I want to…"

Ah. It was a bucket list of sorts. What kind of things—besides orgasms—did his quiet librarian landlady dream about?

The orgasm was the last thing on the list. Personally, he would have ranked it way at the top, but that was him.

He scanned the rest of the list: Fly in an airplane. Learn to ski. Try escargot. Drive new car on the freeway. Kiss someone special under the mistletoe. Get a puppy. Make a difference in someone's life.

As far as wish lists go, hers was quite simple. In fact, with a little effort, she could accomplish all those items before the new year. Wasn't she already making a difference in someone's life, by helping Davy and Clinton?

An idea whispered into his mind, simple but compelling.

He could help her with the rest—except the orgasm part. He would be wise not to let his imagination travel too far in that particular direction.

He could certainly take her on an airplane, though—who better to do that than him? He suddenly didn't want to let any other pilot have that particular privilege.

And he couldn't think of a better place to teach her to ski than the Silver Strike ski resort, which just happened to be in his family's backyard in Colorado.

The more he thought about the idea, the more he liked it. Julia was a sweet, caring woman. She was stretching way out of her comfort zone to take in Davy and Clinton.

When had Jamie ever done the same for *anyone*?

He wanted to help her tick off her wish list, wanted it more than he might have believed possible ten minutes earlier.

What about his vow to keep his distance from a soft, sweet, *vulnerable* woman like Julia? That nagging internal voice made him pause.

A week ago, after that unexpectedly wild kiss, he had decided playing it safe and staying away from her would be his best option. Now he wasn't so certain. Those boys had just about broken his heart earlier, talking about how the year before had been such a tough Christmas.

Maybe Make a Difference in Someone's Life needed to be at the top of his own particular bucket list. He could do both things at the same time—help Julia tick items off her list while also helping her provide a memorable Christmas to two boys who didn't know what that meant.

Excitement sizzled through him. This would be perfect. He couldn't wait to see those beautiful eyes light up with exhilaration on the ski slope and with delight at butter-drenched escargot.

He couldn't let her know he'd seen the list. With the last bit of battery on his phone, he snapped a quick picture of it, then slipped the paper where he had found it, inside the book at the bottom of the stack.

He decided to check on her one more time. With slow care, he opened her door. She had rolled over onto her side, and in a pale slice of moonlight he could see her profile, the lovely high cheekbones and delicious mouth.

He felt a strange ache in his chest, a softness he didn't want to examine too closely.

She murmured something that sounded like "peppermint," but he couldn't be sure. He closed the door and returned to the living room.

He stood there for a long moment, conflicted. He didn't feel right about leaving her alone with the boys, when she felt so lousy. What if she needed help in the night, and the boys didn't hear her cry out? Or what if one of them had a bad dream and needed *her*?

Better safe than sorry. He would just stay here, he decided.

He retrieved a soft throw from one of the other chairs, rounded up a couple of pillows and adjusted them to his liking, then undid the top button on his jeans.

After he stretched out on the sofa, Audrey Hepburn jumped on top of him. He rearranged her on the back of the sofa, then settled in.

He'd slept in far worse places than Julia Winston's fancy Victorian sofa, he thought, then fell asleep while the cats snored softly and the graceful old house creaked and settled around them.

OKAY, APPARENTLY SHE hadn't died in the night.

Julia opened her bleary eyes to see dappled sunlight glinting through the lace curtains of her bedroom.

Work. She needed to call in sick to work. She felt a quick burst of panic, wondering what time it was and how she had slept through her alarm, then she remembered it was Saturday, and she wasn't scheduled to work. She had arranged her schedule around the boys' school day until after Christmas, which was one of the perks of being the head librarian.

The boys!

She finally glanced at her alarm clock, and that panic returned in full force. Oh, no. It was 10:00 a.m. on Sat-

urday morning. Surely the boys had been up for hours—
and she had left them completely unsupervised.

Give her the foster parent of the year award.

Why hadn't she set an alarm?

Come to think of it, she couldn't really remember
going to bed. The events of the day before were a bit
hazy. She had a vague recollection of Jamie being there
and a strange feeling of comfort when he insisted on
taking over, but that must have been impossible. Why
would he? Anyway, he was out of town, wasn't he? His
apartment had been empty all week.

She had to get up. She had to check on the boys.
She forced herself to sit up, pushing the covers away.
The room only spun a little, which she considered a
good sign.

Though she felt as weak and wrung out as a soggy
paper towel, she threw her robe on, shoved her feet into
slippers and moved as quickly as she dared toward the
door, expecting to find total pandemonium.

When she opened it, she had to blink several times,
disoriented as the unmistakable scent of bacon and
maple syrupy pancakes drifted to her.

What on earth? Had Clint cooked breakfast for him
and Davy? Oh, dear! Had he used the stove all by himself? That was completely against the rules.

Her head spun with images of all the disasters that
could befall two young boys alone in a kitchen. With
her heart in her throat, she ignored her wobbly knees
and made her way to the kitchen as quickly as she could
manage.

In the doorway, she stopped, arrested by the scene
in front of her.

Jamie, Clint and Davy sat at the kitchen table eating pancakes and chatting about superhero movies.

Davy was the first one to notice her. He beamed and waved.

"You're finally up!" Davy chirped. "Yay! Now we can go get a Christmas tree, right? You said we could on Saturday."

At his words, Clint and Jamie both turned around, and she wanted to disappear. If she looked half as disgusting as she felt, it was a wonder he didn't jump up and run screaming from her house.

He, on the other hand, was as gorgeous as ever. He smiled at her, and her knees threatened to give way.

"Morning. How are you feeling today?"

"Better," she croaked. It was true enough, though *better* still seemed a long way from *human*.

"You're looking a little wobbly on your pins there. Let's get you to a chair."

As he grabbed her arm and helped her to a kitchen chair, she felt ancient, as old as the residents of the Shelter Springs nursing facility, where she'd served Thanksgiving.

"What are you doing here?" she asked, aware she sounded as if she'd been chain-smoking a pack of unfiltered cigarettes. "Did I sleep through the doorbell?"

"Jamie slept on the sofa in the living room," Clint announced. "We found him this morning when we went in there to watch TV."

She stared. "What? Why?"

He shrugged, looking more than a little embarrassed. "I was worried about leaving you and the boys alone when you weren't feeling well. I was worried you might wake up in the night and need help."

A delicate, sweet warmth seeped through her. Her entire adult life, she had been the one watching over her parents. It felt inexpressibly lovely to know that he had been willing to step up to watch over her, to inconvenience himself all night long just in case she might need something.

"I… That was very kind of you. Thank you."

"How are you feeling this morning? You still look fairly pale."

"Better," she said.

"So *can* we go get a Christmas tree today?" Davy asked. "You said we could before, then we didn't because you were sick."

The logistics completely overwhelmed her. Going out in the cold, picking a tree, tying it on to her Lexus, then bringing it home and setting it up. She barely had the energy to make it from her bedroom to the kitchen. How was she going to handle setting up a tree?

"I'm afraid that might have to wait," she admitted.

"But you promised!" Davy said. His voice had a hint of a whine, and she had to remind herself that all children disliked disappointment, and he and Clint had endured more than their share.

"I know, but that was before I got sick."

She hated to see the disappointment in both boys' eyes, but she didn't know how she could give them what she had promised.

"It's okay," Clint said. "We understand. Plans change sometimes."

There was a brief pause, then Jamie spoke. "If you trust me to pick out your Christmas tree, I can take the boys. We can set it up and put the lights on for you today, then when you have a little more strength and are feeling up to it, you can decorate it with them."

It took her several seconds to process the offer, and she still couldn't quite believe he had made it. "Really? You would be willing to do that?"

"I totally understand if you want to have the fun of picking the tree out yourself. I have the day free, though, and would be happy to help out, if you want."

This man was utterly impossible to resist, on so many different levels.

"Can we, Julia? Can we?" Davy asked. "I can't *wait* to have our Christmas tree!"

Clint didn't say anything, but he looked just as eager as his younger brother to add a little festive spirit to their home.

In the face of their excitement, how could she refuse Jamie's kind offer?

"I… Yes. That would nice. As long as you're sure you don't mind."

"I wouldn't have offered if I didn't want to do it," Jamie assured her.

He turned to the boys. "Finish up your breakfast and load your plates into the dishwasher, then bundle up. This will probably be a crowded day at the Christmas tree farm, and we want to go as early as we can, while they have the best selection."

"I'm done," Davy said, jumping up to clear his plate before racing from the room.

"Me, too." Clinton followed his brother's lead, scraping his plate into the garbage, then rinsing it and loading it. Before he left the room, he turned as if on an afterthought. "Thanks for breakfast," he said to Jamie. "It was really good."

With that, he raced out, leaving the two of them alone in the kitchen. She again wanted to disappear. If she had at least showered, maybe she wouldn't be feeling at a complete disadvantage.

"You don't have to do this," she said. "The boys will survive if we don't pick up a tree until later in the week."

"I hope I'm not depriving you of some kind of Winston family tradition you were looking forward to sharing with them."

She shook her head. This time the room only jiggled a little. "My parents didn't do much to decorate for Christmas. I suppose they didn't see much reason to fuss."

They had been set in their ways by the time she came along. Julia often wondered how her life might have been different if she had entered her parents' world five or ten years earlier.

They had been wonderful parents in their quiet way, just perhaps without the same energy of younger parents in their twenties and thirties.

"I can't say they didn't have any traditions," she went on. "My mom always made me a new stocking on Christmas Eve, and filled it with little gifts. Nothing grand, just things that held special meaning."

She had, in turn, done the same thing for her parents after she reached adulthood. She would have to make stockings for the boys this year. For now, they had to start with a Christmas tree.

"This will mean a great deal to them. Thank you for being willing to take them. And thank you also for staying the night—though if I had been aware of it, I would have told you it wasn't necessary."

Actually, the very nature of that statement probably

indicated it *had* been necessary. A man had spent the night in her living room, and she'd had absolutely no idea, which probably meant she hadn't been in anything resembling a fit state to care for two little boys.

"My pleasure, on both counts. Now, I hope you don't take this wrong, but you look like you're going to fall over. While we're gone, why don't you take advantage of the quiet and go back to bed for a few hours?"

Her head had begun to pound again, just in these few moments she had been sitting here.

Before she could answer, the boys came rushing in, jostling each other through the door to be first inside.

"I'm ready!" Davy said, proudly holding up his mittens.

"So am I," his brother said.

"Give me five minutes to go up to my place for my coat," Jamie said.

"Okay, but hurry," Davy said. "I can't *wait* to get our Christmas tree."

Jamie laughed and rubbed his head. The sweetness of the gesture made her insides quiver, which she tried to chalk up to the flu.

After they left, she considered doing as he suggested and sliding back beneath her warm covers. As strongly as her bed called her, she thought perhaps taking a shower would be more prudent. That way she could at least feel somewhat normal again.

It turned out to be a good choice. The steam helped unclog her headache, the hot water worked magic on her aching joints, and by the time she dressed and combed through her wet hair, she felt stronger than she had in days.

Something warned her it was a temporary improve-

ment, but she figured as long as she was upright, she
might as well take advantage of her renewed strength by
finding the Christmas tree stand and box of lights Jamie
would need when he and the boys returned. It would be
easier to find it for them than to explain where it was.

Julia managed two trips from the garage to the living room before her small burst of energy seeped out,
and her headache returned. Her bed called to her, but
she knew if she gave in she would be there all day. Instead, she decided to curl up on the sofa with a book
and wait until she caught her second wind.

CHAPTER TWELVE

"Okay, here's how this is going down."

In the driveway of Julia's house, Jamie turned around to face his two partners in crime.

"How?" Davy asked eagerly, as if they were planning a bank heist together.

"I'm going to lift the merchandise down from the vehicle, give it two or three good shakes, then it's your job to make sure we get all the snow off—every bit of it—before we take the tree inside."

"Why?" Clinton asked, his features concerned. "What happens if it still has some snow on it?"

"The snow would melt all over the floor, which Julia probably wouldn't like very much."

"She wouldn't," Davy said. "If our boots have snow on them, she makes us leave them in a little tray in the mudroom."

"She says we have to protect the wood floors because they're antique."

"Exactly. We have to do this right. Are you ready?"

The boys both nodded solemnly, and Jamie grinned at them. "We can do this."

He climbed out of the vehicle, then opened the back door for them. A moment later, he lifted the big tree down and tapped it hard several times on the concrete of her driveway, releasing a shower of snow that made Davy laugh.

It was a lovely scotch pine, about eight feet tall, with soft needles and a perfect conical Christmas tree shape.

"What do you think? Did we pick a good one?"

"Maybe it's too big," Clinton said, brows knit with worry.

"It's not."

"Are you sure? Julia won't like it if we bring home a tree that doesn't fit in her house."

"This one will be perfect. Trust me. You'll see. Julia's house has high ceilings, so this tree will be exactly right. A smaller tree would look weird. Okay, now help me brush off the snow while we're out here. Gently, so you don't knock any more needles off than necessary."

The boys took their charge seriously, batting at any remaining clumps of snow with their mittens until the tree had been completely cleared.

"I cut a tree down with our dad once," Clinton confided. "We went to a farm and used a chain saw and everything. It was the last Christmas before he died."

"I was too little to go," Davy said. "Or at least I don't remember it."

His heart ached for both of them.

"Do you think our mom has a tree, wherever she is?" Clinton asked seriously.

How was he supposed to answer that? He had no idea where their mother was. He could only pray police found her soon and could get her the help she obviously needed.

"I hope so," he answered, his voice gruff. "Are you guys ready to take this inside?"

"I have a question," Davy said. "How does the tree stand up by itself?"

Shoot. He hadn't given that a thought and felt stupid now for not picking up a stand at the Christmas tree farm. "We'll have to see if Julia has a stand. If she doesn't, we might have to run over to the hardware store."

"You go ask her. Davy and me will watch the tree to make sure nobody steals it."

That suspicion probably stemmed from living in Sulfur Hollow, where people quite possibly *could* steal an unattended Christmas tree. This quiet neighborhood wasn't immune from crime, but he wasn't too worried about it.

"She might be asleep," he warned. "There's a good chance we'll have to wait until she wakes up."

The boys didn't seem to have a problem with that. "Go see," Clint ordered. His bossy tone made Jamie smile as he hurried to comply.

He knocked softly on the back door. When she didn't answer after a minute or two, he let himself inside and made his way through the kitchen to the living room.

It took his eyes a moment to adjust to the darker interior, but when he did, he discovered Julia stretched out on the same sofa where he had spent the night. She was fast asleep on her side, one hand tucked under her cheek like a child. The throw had slipped down, and so he carefully drew it back up to cover her shoulders.

He didn't have the heart to wake her. He would try to convince the boys they could wait a little longer to set up the tree.

When he turned to go, he discovered a couple of cardboard boxes across the room. He also spied a

Christmas tree stand, situated in a perfect spot for a tree, directly in front of the bay windows. She had even repositioned a rocking chair to make room.

He went to investigate and discovered the boxes were filled with fairly ancient lights, but since he had picked up four new strands at the store next to the tree lot, he wasn't too worried about that.

They could do this. It would be tough, but he wanted to think he and Davy and Clint were up to the challenge. The look on her face would be worth it.

He hurried back outside to where the boys were now struggling to form snowballs out of the loose, powdery snow. "Guys, good job watching the tree. Anybody try to take it?"

Davy shook his head. "The neighbor's dog wanted to come over and pee on it, I bet, but we scared him away."

"Good work. We have a little situation."

"Do we have to go buy a Christmas tree stand now?" Clint asked in a resigned tone.

"Actually, no. There's one in the living room. Julia must have found it, but then she fell asleep on the sofa. If we try to set it up, I'm afraid we'll wake her up."

"We won't!" Davy assured him. "We can be super quiet."

"We can be as quiet as ninjas," Clint added, which made Davy laugh and reminded Jamie of that night Julia had tried to take him on in the entryway of her house.

"I don't know. Setting up a tree and hanging lights might be hard to do without making a sound."

He had vivid memories of the process during his childhood, listening to Christmas music while his mother made cookies and Pop gave the occasional Gaelic curse when the light strands didn't work and his brothers and Charlotte squabbled about whose turn it was to hang the star.

"Can we try?" Davy begged. "Maybe we could put the lights on in the glass room and then carry the tree into the living room."

That would probably end up spreading needles all over the house.

"Use your quietest voice. We'll try," he said.

He had a feeling she must be out of it on flu medicine. It was the only thing that explained how she possibly could have slept through the ruckus they made. Though the boys tried to be quiet, they were boys, after all. They bickered in stage whispers about whether the tree was straight, about how even the lights were, about which of them was more hungry for lunch.

She moved positions a few times but didn't awake in the forty minutes it took them to set up the tree and string the lights. Just as they finished, big, fat snowflakes began to fall outside.

He was about to suggest they go find some lunch when one of the cats wandered in and jumped onto the sofa before he or the boys could stop her.

"Hey. Get off," Julia mumbled, batting at the cat, which made Davy giggle.

Something about that particular giggle did what all the others couldn't. She blinked a few times and opened her eyes. For a few seconds, she seemed disoriented as she looked at them standing by the glowing tree, then her eyes widened.

"What? How did you…?"

This time, both boys giggled.

"We did the whole thing, and you didn't even wake

up." Davy grinned. "Jamie said you would, but you didn't! We were so quiet."

"You must have been." She sat up and tucked a strand of hair behind her ear. Her eyes began to lose that unfocused look, and she smiled at them. "That is a beautiful tree. Good job."

"Me and Clint picked it out," Davy informed her. "It was the prettiest tree on the whole lot—and they had about a jillion of them."

"That many?"

"More like three hundred," Clint said honestly.

"I can't imagine how hard it must have been to choose. You did well. All of you."

Her smile included him, and he felt that odd tenderness again.

"We had fun, didn't we? Thanks for having the stand out. I ended up replacing your lights, since most of them wouldn't have worked unless we replaced half the bulbs."

"They're ancient. I was afraid of that. Thank you." She gazed at the tree with astonishment in her eyes. "I can't believe you did all that without making a sound."

"We made plenty of noise, trust me. You were sleeping pretty soundly. How are you feeling?"

"Better," she said after a moment. "I think I'm through the worst of it. Thank you for stepping up."

She smiled, and he couldn't seem to look away. She looked adorable, all sleepy and mussed, with her cheeks flushed and those gorgeous eyes bright.

She was lovely. Why didn't she seem to realize that?

He thought again of that list he'd seen the night before and how he wanted to put the wheels into motion to help her reach some of those goals.

Not all of them. There was one particular item he *really* had to stop thinking about.

"You're welcome. I'm glad you're through the worst of it. We left the tree for you to decorate—though if you want to point me to your ornaments, the boys and I can tackle that, too."

"You've done enough for today," she said firmly. "I'm sure you have plenty of other things planned for your day."

He really didn't, other than a quick trip to his hangar in Shelter Springs to check on the progress of some work being done to one of his planes.

"I don't mind," he said.

"I appreciate that, but the rest of the decorations don't have to go up today. I'm feeling much better, and I'm sure by tomorrow I'll be back to normal and we can finish all the festifying."

She seemed quite determined to send him on his way. Was it his help in particular she didn't want or would she react the same way if, say, somebody from the Helping Hands were to stop by and offer to decorate her tree?

The memory of that kiss the week before that he couldn't shake from his memory seemed to swirl between them. Did she remember it, too? Was that why she wanted him gone?

As he was quite sure he couldn't change her mind, he decided to gracefully exit. "Is there anything else you need before I take off?"

"I don't think so. Thank you."

"Do you have to go?" Though Davy was the one who spoke, Jamie saw a matching look of disappointment on Clint's features.

She spoke up before he could. "Guys, Jamie has been

here since last night. He's hardly had five minutes in his own apartment since he came back to town yesterday. Let's give the guy a little break."

He didn't really need a break, but he didn't want to argue with her.

"Once we finish decorating the tree, we can invite him down to take a look at it," she added.

The boys' disappointment was gratifying, he had to admit. It was nice to know at least some of the downstairs neighbors wanted him around.

"I can't wait to see it," he said truthfully. "You two be good and let Julia rest this afternoon, okay?"

The boys nodded, though they still looked dejected.

"Thanks for taking us to get the tree and helping us put on the lights and stuff," Clint said.

"Yeah, thanks," Davy said. To Jamie's surprise, the boy threw his arms around his waist.

"You're welcome." Touched to his core, he patted the boy's head a little awkwardly. He had long ago decided kids weren't for him, for many strong and compelling reasons. Once in a while that decision left him with a hollow ache in his chest.

"I'll see you guys later."

With a final wave, he let himself out and headed up the stairs, wondering why the prospect of a free afternoon suddenly held so little appeal.

BY THE MIDDLE of the following week, the bug that had knocked Julia to her knees seemed to have moved on to torment somebody else, much to her relief. She still had a tendency to tire easily but no longer felt as if she'd been run over by one of the notoriously sloppy Haven Point garbage trucks.

She felt good enough to throw together some white chicken chili before she left for the library. The Haven Point Helping Hands were set to gather for one of their lunchtime work parties at McKenzie Kilpatrick's store. Whenever they met, Julia liked to add the ingredients for soup to her slow cooker in the morning before work, then take it with her to the library. There, she could plug it in to further meld the flavors before the lunch work party.

As she was finishing up in the kitchen, she sensed movement outside the window and looked out to find Jamie with a snow shovel in his hand. He had cleared her driveway both times it had snowed in the last week, and she had also seen him help some of the neighbors with their snow removal.

She was finding it increasingly difficult to resist the man. How was she going to make it through another month of him living upstairs?

On impulse, she found a disposable container and filled it with soup from the slow cooker, snapping the lid closed just as she heard the front door open. She grabbed it and hurried out to open the door into their shared entry.

Snowflakes melted on his eyelashes and hair, and she did her best to ignore how everything inside her seemed to shiver when his eyes lit up at the sight of her.

"Hi."

She gestured outside. "When I agreed to rent you the apartment upstairs, I had no idea you would be so handy to have around."

He gave her a wolfish sort of smile. "That's what all the girls say."

Heat soaked her cheeks, which mortified her. In reaction, she put on her most prim voice. "Don't you know you should wear a hat in this kind of weather?"

His eyes danced with amusement. "Yes, Miss Winston."

She sounded like a cranky schoolmarm, but couldn't seem to hold back the words. "It's scientific fact. You can lose up to fifty percent of your body heat if your head is uncovered, since you have little subcutaneous fat for insulation there."

"So all those times my brothers called me fathead, they were completely in the wrong."

"Yes—if you want to take the term literally."

He laughed. "I'll tell them next time—while I'm wearing my warmest hat. Thanks for the reminder."

She felt extremely foolish and wondered for a few seconds why she had come out into the hall, until her gaze caught the container in her hand. "Oh. This is for you."

She held it out. "It's white bean chili, really good on a snowy day like today. You'll want to heat it on the stove for about twenty minutes to soften the vegetables."

His expression registered his surprise. "Thank you. That's very kind of you."

"It's the least I could do, after all you did with the boys over the weekend, picking out my Christmas tree, then shoveling the walks the last two days. I owe you far more than a bowl of chili." It seemed ridiculously inadequate.

"You don't owe me anything—though now that you mention it, I could use a favor."

Jamie Caine struck her as someone who never liked asking for help. All the more reason to be pleased that he had asked *her*. "Of course," she said promptly. "What can I do?"

He made a face. "I promised Spence and Charlotte I would go to this gala for their Warriors of Hope charity on Saturday night in Hope's Crossing. I need a date."

His words took several seconds to register. She heard *gala*, *charity*, *Hope's Crossing* and *date* as if in one big blur. "A...date. In Colorado. I don't understand. Do you need me to help find you a date?"

His eyes opened wide, and then he laughed, low and irresistibly. "I would like you to *go* with me. *You* would be my date, Julia."

Before she could soak in that shock, he hurried on. "You don't have to worry about the boys. I was thinking they could fly out with us. They'll probably enjoy another airplane ride, won't they?"

"Uhhh." It was the most intelligent thing she could come up with in that particular moment.

He went on as if he hadn't heard her brainless utterance. "The gala is Saturday night. I'm supposed to fly Aidan and Eliza and Ben and McKenzie out on Friday night. Aidan has booked all the rooms at Wild Iris Ridge—that's the B and B that Lucy and Brendan operate. Lucy insists she knows a reputable babysitter who can handle all the kids, which I think would be great."

What was happening here? All she'd intended when she walked out into the hallway was to hand the man a container of soup. Now she was confronting a totally unexpected invitation.

"Why?"

He shrugged. "The boys really hit it off with Carter and Faith and Maddie over Thanksgiving. I'm sure they'd all love to spend a little more time together."

"No, I mean, why me for your date?"

He looked genuinely shocked at the question. "What do you mean? Why not you?"

She could think of a dozen reasons, starting with the fact that she had absolutely nothing to wear to a fancy charity gala that would probably involve professional athletes, business tycoons and movie stars.

"It might have escaped your notice, but I'm not one of your glamorous, skinny model types."

Far from it. She was a socially awkward, introverted librarian who was usually happiest at home with a book in her hands, surrounded by her mother's cats, even when they barely tolerated her.

A muscle flexed in his jaw, and she had the oddest feeling she might have offended him somehow.

"I don't have a glamorous, skinny model type. I like all kinds of women, remember? Including you. I like spending time with you, and I thought you and the boys might enjoy a little weekend outing. Hope's Crossing has tons of things to do this time of year."

He gave her a persuasive smile that no woman in her right mind could resist. "It will be fun, Julia. Trust me. Good food, enjoyable company, maybe a little dancing. Last year I went by myself, and I thought it would be much more fun this year to go with a…friend."

Was that how he saw their relationship? At least they had that.

"I don't…" she began, not sure what she even intended to say.

"You'll have plenty of friends there. My family already adores you and the boys. They'll love seeing you all again."

The thought of his family quieted some of the panic.

YOUR PARTICIPATION IS REQUESTED!

Dear Reader,

Since you are a lover of our books — we would like to get to know you!

Inside you will find a short Reader's Survey. Sharing your answers with us will help our editorial staff understand who you are and what activities you enjoy.

To thank you for your participation, we would like to send you 2 books and 2 gifts — **ABSOLUTELY FREE!**

Enjoy your gifts with our appreciation,

Pam Powers

SEE INSIDE FOR READER'S SURVEY

For Your Reading Pleasure...

We'll send you 2 books and 2 gifts
ABSOLUTELY FREE
just for completing our Reader's Survey!

YOURS FREE!
*We'll send you two fabulous surprise
gifts absolutely FREE, just for trying
our books!*

Visit us at:
www.ReaderService.com

YOUR READER'S SURVEY
"THANK YOU" FREE GIFTS INCLUDE:
- ▶ 2 FREE books
- ▶ 2 lovely surprise gifts

▼ DETACH AND MAIL CARD TODAY!

PLEASE FILL IN THE CIRCLES COMPLETELY TO RESPOND

1) What type of fiction books do you enjoy reading? (Check all that apply)
- ○ Suspense/Thrillers   ○ Action/Adventure   ○ Modern-day Romances
- ○ Historical Romance   ○ Humor   ○ Paranormal Romance

2) What attracted you most to the last fiction book you purchased on impulse?
- ○ The Title   ○ The Cover   ○ The Author   ○ The Story

3) What is usually the greatest influencer when you <u>plan</u> to buy a book?
- ○ Advertising   ○ Referral   ○ Book Review

4) How often do you access the internet?
- ○ Daily ○ Weekly ○ Monthly ○ Rarely or never

5) How many NEW paperback fiction novels have you purchased in the past 3 months?
- ○ 0 - 2   ○ 3 - 6   ○ 7 or more

YES! I have completed the Reader's Survey. Please send me
2 FREE books and 2 FREE gifts (gifts are worth about $10 retail).
I understand that I am under no obligation to purchase any books,
as explained on the back of this card.

194/394 MDL GMRP

FIRST NAME	LAST NAME

ADDRESS

APT.#	CITY

STATE/PROV.	ZIP/POSTAL CODE

Offer limited to one per household and not applicable to series that subscriber is currently receiving.
Your Privacy—The Reader Service is committed to protecting your privacy. Our Privacy Policy is available online at www.ReaderService.com or upon request from the Reader Service. We make a portion of our mailing list available to reputable third parties that offer products we believe may interest you. If you prefer that we not exchange your name with third parties, or if you wish to clarify or modify your communication preferences, please visit us at www.ReaderService.com/consumerchoice or write to us at Reader Service Preference Service, P.O. Box 9062, Buffalo, NY 14240-9062. Include your complete name and address.

© 2017 HARLEQUIN ENTERPRISES LIMITED
® and ™ are trademarks owned and used by the trademark owner and/or its licensee. Printed in the U.S.A.

ROM-817-SCT17

READER SERVICE—Here's how it works:

Accepting your 2 free Romance books and 2 free gifts (gifts valued at approximately $10.00 retail) places you under no obligation to buy anything. You may keep the books and gifts and return the shipping statement marked "cancel." If you do not cancel, about a month later we'll send you 4 additional books and bill you just $6.74 each in the U.S. or $7.24 each in Canada. That is a savings of at least 16% off the cover price. It's quite a bargain! Shipping and handling is just 50¢ per book in the U.S. and 75¢ per book in Canada.* You may cancel at any time, but if you choose to continue, every month we'll send you 4 more books, which you may either purchase at the discount price plus shipping and handling or return to us and cancel your subscription. *Terms and prices subject to change without notice. Prices do not include applicable taxes. Sales tax applicable in N.Y. Canadian residents will be charged applicable taxes. Offer not valid in Quebec. Books received may not be as shown. All orders subject to approval. Credit or debit balances in a customer's account(s) may be offset by any other outstanding balance owed by or to the customer. Please allow 4 to 6 weeks for delivery. Offer available while quantities last.

◀ If offer card is missing write to: Reader Service, P.O. Box 1341, Buffalo, NY 14240-8531 or visit www.ReaderService.com ▲

BUSINESS REPLY MAIL
FIRST-CLASS MAIL   PERMIT NO. 717   BUFFALO, NY

POSTAGE WILL BE PAID BY ADDRESSEE

READER SERVICE
PO BOX 1341
BUFFALO NY 14240-8571

NO POSTAGE
NECESSARY
IF MAILED
IN THE
UNITED STATES

She did enjoy the Caines, and it would be lovely to see them all again.

She had resolved before Thanksgiving to embrace life a little more instead of hiding away alone here at Winston House. A gorgeous guy wanted to fly her in his private jet to a glamorous gala in a Colorado ski resort town. How could she possibly say no?

Still, her refusal crowded her throat, ready to spill out. It was too much, too soon, like dousing a slightly thirsty person with a fire hose of excitement.

Jamie must have sensed her conflicted feelings.

"You don't have to answer me right now," he said quickly. "Think about it, and I'll check in with you later tonight."

Think about it. As if she would be able to focus on anything else all day!

"Yes. I…okay. Thank you."

"And thank you for the soup. It will be just the thing for my lunch."

She nodded, then retreated to the sanctuary of her apartment.

AS JULIA EXPECTED, she could think of little else but Jamie's shocking invitation throughout the morning as she input new items into the library computer system.

Why would he ask *her*? And how could she find the courage to accept? On a theoretical level, she wanted to try new things, taste all the adventures she had missed out on over the last decade of caring for her parents.

Theory and reality were very different.

She couldn't even drive her Lexus above fifty miles an hour. How was she going to jump on a private jet with Jamie Caine and attend a gala with a bunch of strangers?

She still hadn't made up her mind when the time came for her to leave for the Helping Hands potluck lunch at McKenzie's flower and gift shop.

"Thank you for filling in over lunch," she said to Mack Porter, her favorite clerk.

"I've been well paid by your chili," he said in his sonorous voice that always made her think he should have had a career as a public radio announcer.

Through her anxiety, she managed a smile, then carried her slow cooker of soup out to her vehicle for the short drive.

A light snowfall fluttered down like powdered sugar sifted on cake. After she found a parking spot, she enjoyed the quiet ordinariness of the small Haven Point downtown on an early December afternoon.

Inside the shop, the scene was much more chaotic, as the Helping Hands were busy preparing items to be sold at their booth during the Haven Point annual Lights on the Lake festival. All proceeds from the sale of their gifts and crafts went to a designated cause. This year it was the county battered women's shelter.

A chorus of greetings met her, and she felt some of her tension trickle away. This was her tribe, her dear friends, who always made her feel as if she belonged.

The typical routine of one of these potluck lunches was to get the work out of the way first, then eat, so she found an open outlet for her slow cooker, then an empty chair for herself next to Eppie and Hazel, and went to work tying ribbons for gift bags.

This was just what she needed, she thought, as she listened to the chatter around her. She was most comfortable listening to others talk and offering the occasional well-timed comment. She was able to put her dilemma completely out of her head while they worked together for a common goal—until the actual lunch part of the day, anyway.

When she was ladling some of Barbara Serrano's delicious zuppa tuscana into a bowl, Eliza Caine came up behind her in line.

"I understand you might be joining us this weekend in Hope's Crossing," Eliza said, beaming.

All the anxiety she had been trying to shove down seemed to bubble back to the surface. "How did you… Did Jamie tell you that?"

Eliza shrugged. "He told me earlier in the week he was thinking about asking you and the boys along. I saw him this morning and asked him about it, and he said you were still considering."

"Yes," she said, feeling cornered.

"I do hope you say yes. It's always a lovely evening. My sister-in-law Genevieve plans all the events for the Warriors of Hope, and she throws an amazing party. I'm sure this year will be no different, though she's seven months pregnant. You can count on fantastic food and interesting company—and it's for a great cause. I'm sure Jamie told you all about it."

"Not really. He only mentioned the whole thing this morning in passing."

"You know Spence and Charlotte, right?"

One didn't forget meeting Smokin' Hot Spence Gregory, who was even more good-looking than he'd been during his Major League Baseball career.

"I do."

"They run an organization in Hope's Crossing called

the Warriors of Hope, where wounded military members can spend a week in the mountains doing recreational therapy, having fun, spending time with their families. They're doing great things. Every time Aidan and I participate in a fund-raiser or event, I end up in tears somehow when I see the amazing courage of their clients and hear some of their stories about how much the organization has helped them reconnect with nature and their families. Well, you'll see this weekend."

"Ben and I went last year, and it was wonderful," McKenzie chimed in. "I've been looking forward to this gala all year long. I'm so happy Jamie had the good sense to invite you."

"Same here," Eliza said. "Usually he goes by himself. I was thrilled when he told me he wanted you to come with us. This is going to be so much fun."

Neither of them seemed at all surprised by Jamie's choice of a date, but Julia knew that was only because they loved her. If they looked at things logically, surely they would understand he'd made a terrible mistake.

"I haven't decided if I'm going yet," she mumbled.

McKenzie stared at her. "You have to! Oh, Jules. Why would there even be a question?"

Again, she could come up with a hundred reasons. Most of them she couldn't articulate, so she focused on what was probably the least of them.

"I don't have anything to wear," she finally said. "What's appropriate for the Haven Point Library would probably look out of place at a fancy charity gala."

Eliza and McKenzie both looked startled, as if that possibility hadn't even occurred to them. Of course it hadn't. They were both married to fabulously wealthy men and probably attended this sort of event all the time.

After a moment, Eliza beamed. "If that's the only objection you've got, you're in luck. I've got tons of cocktail dresses I've had to buy since I married Aidan—some I've never even worn. We're roughly the same size. I'm sure we can find you something perfect. I'll look through my closet and find you several to choose from."

"Make sure you include that gorgeous mauve silk I made you last Christmas," Samantha Fremont said. "The coloring would be *perfect* on Julia."

"Oh, you're right!" Eliza exclaimed. "And I never wore it because I was breast-feeding and was afraid Liam wouldn't be able to, er, get to the goods. I'll definitely take that one over tonight, along with two or three others I know you'll love."

Eliza was as persuasive as her brother-in-law. Julia was grateful for good friends, even when their loyalty was misguided.

"That is very kind. But even the most beautiful dress can't disguise the fact that I won't belong there."

"Don't be stupid," McKenzie exclaimed. "Why won't you?"

She sighed. "Why did he ask me? There are so many other women who would love this sort of thing."

Samantha raised her hand, with a grin that told Julia she was teasing. "I would go in a heartbeat."

"Same here. He is one hot tamale," Hazel said with a bawdy wink that made them all laugh. The woman was old enough to be Jamie's grandmother. Maybe even great-grandmother.

"What does it matter why?" Eliza said. "He wants to take you or he wouldn't have asked, and I can only applaud his excellent choice."

"You have to come," McKenzie said. "We'll have so much fun."

"Just look at it as filling your well," Samantha said. "If going to a gala with Jamie Caine wasn't on that stupid list Roxy had us make at the book club, it should have been. I might have to go home and add it to mine. You have to go with him, so you can come back and tell us all about it."

She let out a shaky breath. Was she really seriously considering saying yes? He saw her as a friend. As long as she kept that in mind, she could look at this as a big adventure, a once-in-a-lifetime chance to feel like a fairy princess going to the ball.

The biggest trick would be keeping the man from stealing her heart.

CHAPTER THIRTEEN

JAMIE WAS DIRTY, hungry and tired. He needed a shower, a sandwich and his bed, in exactly that order.

He had spent most of the day handing tools to his brilliant mechanic. Most of the time he happily left any necessary jet engine repairs to his mechanic, who was fully certified and amazing at his job, but once in a while Jamie helped out where he could. He figured every person who dared challenge the law of gravity by climbing into a cockpit ought to have at least a working knowledge of what was keeping him in the air.

He pulled into the driveway at Winston House, anticipating that bowl of soup he hadn't had time to eat at lunch and enjoying the colored lights from her tree in the front window.

Looked like the boys had finally put all the ornaments on it, at least judging from the gleam of red and gold that hadn't been there earlier.

At some point that day, Julia and the boys had hung wreaths in each of the downstairs windows that faced the street, with a single candle glowing a welcome. That festive little touch gave him an odd sense of coming home.

Winston House was truly grand, stately and graceful. It could be fussy and formal, as he'd thought earlier, yet somehow Julia was making it into a home for the boys.

He glanced at the dark windows upstairs. For the first time in his adult life, he was almost tempted to put up a Christmas tree of his own.

Where did *that* come from? Christmas was usually just another day for him. Oh, he enjoyed being with his family. He bought gifts for the whole lot of them in his travels and a few times had arranged leave to be home with them, but his heart was never in it.

His mother had loved Christmas. After she died—and then with everything that happened with Lisa, shortly afterward—the holiday had lost its magic for him.

It usually felt like a big jumble of emotions, guilt and old sadness and the sobering awareness that Christmas was meant for families, something that would never be for him.

This year, maybe he would put up a tree, he thought as he parked his SUV. He could even ask the boys if they wanted to help him decorate it, assuming they weren't tired of decorating after doing so much downstairs.

He glanced at the clock on the dashboard. After nine. The boys would probably be in bed.

Should he stop by anyway? He needed to know what she had decided. Was she going to take a risk and come with him to Hope's Crossing for the weekend? He wasn't sure how he wanted her to answer, torn between his desire to help her tick off multiple items on her wish list and his completely reasonable discomfort with his unwilling desire for *her*.

He would shower first, eat some dinner, then see if her lights were still on, he decided. If they were, he would visit downstairs.

The best laid plans. The moment he unlocked the door to the entryway, her door opened and two boys spilled through, as if they had been waiting just for him.

Jamie told himself that little flutter through his insides was just hunger pangs.

"You're finally home," Clint exclaimed.

"We've been waiting *forever*!" Davy informed him. "What took you so long?"

He didn't realize he had a curfew, imposed by a couple of steely-eyed schoolboys. Jamie had to laugh. "Hey, guys. How was your day?"

"We finished the Christmas tree tonight, and we've been waiting and waiting to show you," Davy informed him.

"Sorry about that. I was busy working on a broken airplane."

"Is that why you're so messy?" Clint asked.

"Exactly. I'm covered in oil. Maybe I'd better postpone until I clean up."

"We'll be in bed by then. Julia said we had five more minutes, and if you weren't home, we had to go to bed and would have to show you the tree another day."

"We don't want to wait. We want to show you now," Davy said.

Jamie glanced up the stairs, then toward her door, with the fancy antiques behind it. Maybe he could go in, as long as he was careful not to touch anything.

Before he could tell them as much, Julia suddenly appeared in the doorway. His insides did that weird jump thing again. She looked delectable, with no sign of the prim librarian tonight. Her chestnut hair was piled on top of her head and messy strands escaped everywhere.

Keeping his hands to himself might be easier said than done.

"Hi." She didn't smile, and his gaze sharpened on her. Something had happened. He could see it now in the strain lines around her mouth and the worry in her eyes.

"Can we show him the tree now?" Clint asked.

"Yes. That's fine with me, as long as Jamie can spare the time."

"I'm a mess. I'll have to be careful not to touch anything."

She held the door open wider, clearly unconcerned by the grease and grime on his clothes. He made his way inside and saw the tree and wreaths were only part of the Christmas decorations. A lovely crèche covered the top of the mantel, and greenery had been hung around the windows.

Instrumental Christmas music played softly, setting a peaceful holiday mood.

She was trying her best to show the boys a warm Christmas. Her efforts touched him, making him more determined than ever to give *her* a memorable Christmas, too.

The tree he had helped the boys pick out truly did look magnificent in the space. It would have been too big for most rooms but fit perfectly here.

He stopped in front of it, making a show of looking from all angles to admire their work. "That looks terrific. Great job, guys. And it smells fantastic in here, too."

That wasn't hyperbole. The pine pitch of the tree was joined by spices and vanilla, which all combined to create a scent that should have been called The Perfect Christmas.

"We made cinnamon ornaments," Davy informed him. "That's why we didn't show you the tree before, because the ornaments weren't dry. We had to wait until we could put them up. We rolled them and cut them out just like cookies—except you can't eat them or you'll be sick, because they have glue in them."

"Warning duly noted," he said seriously, which earned him a smile from Julia, though he could still see edginess seething beneath the surface.

"You boys did an excellent job of decorating," Jamie went on. "I could see your tree from halfway down the street."

"And did you see all the wreaths in the windows?" Clinton asked. "Julia said she saw a picture of the house from a long time ago, before she was born, and it had wreaths in the windows."

"I saw them. They look great. Do you want to put more wreaths in the windows upstairs?"

"Would you mind?" Julia asked him. "You don't have to, if you don't want, but I did buy enough to hang in the front-facing windows upstairs. I also picked up solar-powered, light-sensitive candles. You don't even have to turn them on. They'll automatically come on when it's dark."

"Easy enough." He glanced at the tree again. "Thanks for sharing your tree with me, guys. It's beautiful."

"Do you have yours yet?" Clint asked seriously.

He winced. "Not yet. I need to get on that, don't I?"

"You better. It's going to be Christmas before we know it," Davy said, sounding so adult it made Jamie smile.

"Maybe I'll pick one up after I'm back in town next week."

He happened to be glancing at Julia when he spoke and didn't miss the flicker of nerves in her expression. The suspense was suddenly making him crazy. Would she go with him or not? He had to know.

"Speaking of which…" he began.

She shook her head slightly, with a warning look at the boys. Clearly she didn't want to discuss the matter in front of them.

"Guys," she said quickly, "it's past time for bed."

Their groaning protests were ruined when Davy yawned.

Julia hid a smile, though she still looked distracted. "Tell Jamie thank you for stopping by, then go brush your teeth."

"Thanks," they said in unison.

"You're welcome. Good night."

As soon as they rushed off to the bathroom, he turned to her. "Okay. What's going on?"

She shifted, avoiding his gaze. "What do you mean?"

"I can see it in your eyes. Something's happened."

She sighed and looked toward the bathroom. "Can you wait for five minutes, until I have them settled? I don't want to say anything to the boys yet. I haven't told them."

"Their mother has been found." The words popped out before he thought them through. He wasn't sure how he knew, yet as soon as he spoke he had no doubt.

She looked startled. "How did you…? Never mind. Five minutes."

She hurried off to steer the boys from the bathroom to their beds, and Jamie waited in the living room, enjoying the lights and the soft Christmas music for the few moments it took her to return.

"How did you know their mother has been found?" she asked. "Did Cade Emmett call you?"

"I haven't talked to anybody. It was a lucky guess. Where was she?"

She sighed, her features distressed. "She was located in a homeless shelter in Portland, apparently, though she's now in the VA hospital there receiving treatment. It seems she went off her meds and had a mental breakdown or psychotic break or whatever you want to call it. From what little Wyn could find out, she was arrested on a minor violation, and when they ran her prints, they found out who she was and that authorities here were looking for her."

Her remarkable eyes filled with emotion. "Jamie, she doesn't remember that she has two sons. Isn't that the most tragic thing you can imagine? To forget those wonderful boys? How is that even possible?"

"She has PTSD. It can manifest itself in some pretty terrible ways."

He didn't know Mikaela Slater, but he knew too many others. He had seen it firsthand with his brother, in the long months when Dylan was recovering from the explosion that had wounded him severely and taken his hand, then the terrible systemic infection that had threatened to finish the job a kid with an IED had started.

His brother had been an Army Ranger, tough as nails, but for more than a year, until Genevieve came along, they had all been afraid Dylan would check out rather than have to live with the lasting scars.

War and the fallout from it could take tough, decent,

dedicated people and mangle them into something un-
recognizable.

"That poor woman," Julia said softly. "She's going
to be devastated when she remembers she left her boys
alone here."

The compassion in her voice touched him deeply.
Many people would be angry and judgmental, not understanding how any mother could abandon her children, no matter how messed up her mind and emotions
could be. Not Julia. She thought first about how the
woman would suffer from her actions.

Did she have any idea how remarkable she was?

He was dirty and grimy and probably smelled like
an airplane hangar. Jamie still couldn't resist pulling
her into his arms. She came willingly, clinging tightly
to him and resting her cheek on his chest for a long,
priceless moment, before she pulled away, cheeks pink.

"I don't know what or how to tell the boys. I can't
just come out and say, *Hey, guess what? Your mom took
off and left you, but it's all good. She'll be back when
she gets the help she needs*."

"Maybe not those particular words, but the gist. As
long as you focus on the fact that she's getting help and
that they've got a safe place here with you as long as
they need it, they'll be okay."

"I hope you're right," she said. "At least I don't have
to tell them the news is much worse. I was so worried
someone would find her in a field or ditch somewhere.
Or that she wouldn't be found at all. At least this way
offers hope they can one day be a family again."

"When she does remember them and her doctors
think she's up for a visit from them, say the word. I can
have you all there in an hour."

"Oh, Jamie. Thank you. I hadn't even thought about taking them to see her. I'll let you know."

She gave him a soft, fragile smile, and that dangerous tenderness seeped through his chest.

"It seems pretty unimportant, in light of this new development, but did you think about what we talked about this morning?" he asked.

Her smile slid away, and she caught her breath, then let it out slowly. "I… Yes. And I've changed my mind a dozen times. I had lunch with Eliza and McKenzie and the other Helping Hands, and they all think I would be crazy to say no."

But what did *she* think? "So is that a yes?"

"Yes—for the boys' sake, if nothing else. They're going to be upset when I tell them about their mother. They'll worry for her. Perhaps another trip to Hope's Crossing will provide a distraction from that."

Was that the only reason she wanted to go? He understood her rationale. Still, some part of him felt small and selfish for wishing she might genuinely want to spend a weekend with him.

This was all for her list, he reminded himself. It wasn't about him.

"We can certainly provide a distraction for them. They'll be so busy with Carter and Faith, they won't have time to stress about their mother."

"I hope so."

"This will be great. Can you be ready to leave about six tomorrow? We can drive together, if you want."

"I think that should work."

She was quiet for a moment. When she spoke, he had the impression this was something that had been troubling her all day. "I do have one condition."

"Oh?"

She looked down at her hands, then met his gaze. "You don't have to…flirt with me while we're there."

"What do you mean?"

"You don't need to try to charm me. We're friends, but…we both know that's all there is between us. I don't need you to pretend to be interested in more than that."

He struggled to come up with a response. Yeah, they were friends. But they'd also shared a pretty intense kiss he couldn't seem to stop thinking about.

"It's kind of you to ask me," she went on quickly. "I'm still not sure why you did, but I wanted to make sure you know the ground rules. I'm saying yes because it sounds like fun, and the boys will enjoy the chance to see their new friends, but, just so you know, I'm not interested in anything deeper. I just don't want you to worry you might…break my heart or something. You won't."

He wasn't sure whether to find that comforting or insulting.

"Good to know," he answered. "I'll see you tomorrow afternoon, then."

She nodded, and they walked together to the door. He wanted to kiss her again just to see how she responded but thought that might be petty and wrong. Too bad…

CHAPTER FOURTEEN

WHAT HAD HAPPENED to her nice, quiet life in the past few weeks?

Just a month ago, she thought she had things figured out. She had good friends, a nice job, a beautiful house, no mortgage. She knew what she would be doing from one day to the next. Her biggest challenge was trying to get along with three cats who barely acknowledged she existed.

Now she had two foster children who were filling her life with chaos and noise, and here they all were, about to get on an airplane with Jamie Caine for a whirlwind weekend in Colorado.

These sorts of adventures happened to other women. Not her.

You wanted to live a little, her internal voice reminded her. She had been longing for something beyond her staid existence, a taste of the adventure she had expected to share with Maksym after college.

This was living with a vengeance.

Her heart pounded as she followed the directions Jamie had sent her and parked near a big blue hangar with Caine Aviation on the side.

Every instinct was clamoring for her to back out. She didn't *do* things like this. She was a boring, small-town librarian who spent her days reading about other people's adventures, not living her own.

These nerves were stupid, she knew. Millions of people flew every day. It was considered one of the safest forms of transportation out there. She knew that intellectually. Now that the reality was in front of her, though, she had no idea how she would find the courage to step onto the airplane.

How humiliating, that Jamie would be there to witness her fear.

"Why are we just sitting here?" Davy asked.

Because I'm a big, fat coward. "Just trying to think if we brought everything we need," she lied.

"We have. Let's go. I can't wait for another airplane ride!"

Oh, she longed to be six again, with a tiny portion of that unwavering excitement.

She drew in a deep breath and opened her door. Before she could climb out, Jamie was there. In the afternoon sunlight, he looked utterly gorgeous, wearing a black leather jacket and a white button-down shirt and tie. It wasn't quite a uniform but close enough.

He grinned at all of them. "There you are. I was beginning to wonder if I would be flying myself to Colorado."

"Sorry about that. We had a few stops to make." She glanced around the hangar area. "Where is everybody else? I thought McKenzie and Eliza would be here."

"Change of plans. Genevieve called in a panic last night and needed emergency help with some of the decorating, so I flew Kenz and Ben out this morning. Eliza and Aidan tagged along."

No wonder she hadn't seen him all day. Some part of

her had been afraid he changed his mind and decided he didn't want to take her after all. An even bigger part wondered if the whole invitation had been a dream.

"I wish you had told me you were leaving early. I could have tried to arrange my schedule at the library so we could go with you, then you wouldn't have had to make two trips."

"Don't worry about that. In between the two trips, I came back here anyway to fly a couple of the Caine Tech execs to some budget meetings in California."

She stared. "You've flown round-trip to Colorado, then round-trip to California, and now you're heading back to Colorado? That's a crazy schedule. You've basically been working all day."

"I know. Isn't it great? Sometimes I still have to pinch myself that I get to do what I love all day."

She understood that. She loved working in the library, being surrounded by books all day. What wasn't to love about that? Some might consider it boring clerical work, but she adored organizing the library collection, working with students on research papers, helping people discover new authors.

"So we will be by ourselves on the plane?" Clinton asked.

"That's right. You okay with that?"

"Yeah!" Davy said. "We can sit wherever we want!"

Julia wasn't sure whether to be relieved or disappointed. She had been looking forward to having her friends McKenzie and Eliza along to help ease her way into her first flight. On the bright side, if she turned out to be a terrible passenger, at least there wouldn't be eyewitnesses.

"Are you ready? I can grab your luggage."

"As ever," she muttered, fighting down the panic that returned in force now that the reality of the trip was unavoidable.

She popped the back of her vehicle to open the lift gate, and Jamie pulled out the two suitcases she'd packed.

"Is this everything?" he asked.

"Yes. It's enough, isn't it?" They were only going for two nights and wouldn't have needed even two suitcases, if she hadn't had to pack bulky winter clothing.

He helped them into the plane, then spent several moments doing an inspection before climbing in himself and closing the door.

"That's it. Let's do this." She could sense his enjoyment of the process as he sat in the pilot's seat and started adjusting controls.

"You don't have a copilot?" she asked.

He turned around with a half grin. "I have three of them. You and the boys."

The low simmer of panic inside her spiked hot and fierce, and for a moment she forgot to breathe. "I don't know anything about airplanes, except from books. I've never even been on one!"

He gave her a comforting smile. "Relax. I'm teasing. I'm fine on my own. If I were going farther than Hope's Crossing, I would plan for one of my other pilots, but this is one of my smaller jets, and the flight is barely an hour. Relax, sweetheart. I'm an excellent pilot, and my girl here is in tip-top shape. Everything is going to be fine."

She forced her lungs to work again. She could do this.

"I do have a job for you."

"Yes?"

"I need you to try to enjoy yourself. Can you do that?"

"I don't know. Ask me again when we get to Hope's Crossing."

"I was nervous the first time I went on an airplane, too," Davy told her, sounding like a sophisticated world traveler instead of a boy whose first flight was only a few weeks ago. "Turns out, it was really fun. You'll see."

"I'll take your word for that."

"Be ready for your tummy to tickle," Clint said. "That's the best part."

She admired these boys so much for their courageous approach, for facing head-on all the difficult curveballs life had thrown at them.

She had told them about their mother that morning. Davy had cried a bit when she said their mother was ill and they wouldn't be able to see her for a while, but Clinton had been stoically accepting of the news, and his younger brother had eventually followed his example.

"She'll be okay, won't she?" Davy had finally asked her. Julia hadn't wanted to lie to them or give them false hope, so she'd only hugged them close.

"She's getting the best help possible right now. We can pray that she will. What you can do right now for her is work hard in school and do your best to have fun learning and growing and trying new things. That's what she would want, for you to be safe and happy."

She hadn't told them Mikaela hadn't remembered them. They didn't need to add that heartbreak to their store.

She would take the advice she had given the boys—

to embrace the world and new opportunities. That had been her once, before she slid into the expectations everyone else had of her.

She settled into her seat and kept her attention focused on Jamie competently working the controls of the plane as they started to taxi away from the hangar and toward the blinking lights of the runway. She trusted him. He would keep them safe—and the only thing left for her to do was enjoy the ride.

JAMIE LOVED EVERYTHING about flying. The power of the plane, the adrenaline rush, the view. He had logged thousands of hours up in the air, first as a helicopter pilot, then flying jets, and he never tired of it.

This time, he almost wished he didn't have to focus on the fun of it so he could sit next to Julia and hold her hand while she experienced her first flight. For several minutes after takeoff, he had to manually work the controls until they reached the altitude and point in the flight path where he could switch to autopilot.

When he was comfortable their course was set, he finally turned around to focus on his passengers.

"How are things back here?" he asked.

Julia turned from peering out the small window at the ground below them, and he had to catch his breath at her expression.

Her eyes shone, filled with wonder. "Oh, Jamie. It's amazing! Every bit as wonderful as I always dreamed. The view is incredible, and I'll never forget the thrill of takeoff, of peeling away from the earth."

"See?" Davy said. "I told you it wasn't scary."

"Make sure you take pictures. I meant to remind you before we took off," he said.

"Will it be dark when we reach Hope's Crossing? I would love to have a little light so I can photograph the town from above."

"We should be getting there just after sunset. Sorry about that, but you can get some nice night shots."

"Great."

"Hold your phone right up to the glass. That's the best way to keep out the reflection."

Most of the time Jamie's passengers considered the ride routine, mostly a nuisance. They were business executives heading from one work obligation to another, then back again. He loved sharing this thing he loved so much with someone discovering the wonders of flight for the first time.

"We've got another forty minutes to go. Settle in and enjoy. We'll fly over some beautiful mountains."

"Thank you," she said again, her features soft, lovely. That alarming tenderness bubbled up in his chest, soft and dangerous, making it hard for him to look away.

He cleared his throat. "There are water bottles in the refrigerator and an assortment of snacks beneath each seat."

The boys were all over that. While Julia was busy helping them choose between candy bars and little bags of chips, he made himself turn back to the controls. Flying was safe and predictable. He felt completely confident in his ability to deal with whatever challenge could arise behind the controls of a plane. This tangled thing with Julia was a much more complicated situation. It was much easier to focus on what he knew and understood.

Because of a little turbulence, he didn't have much chance to talk to his passengers until after he brought the plane down safely in Hope's Crossing and taxied to the hangar he used there.

When he was done with the postflight check, he finally turned to them, waiting patiently in their seats.

"So? What do you think?"

She beamed. "I think I need to plan another trip somewhere."

"Where would you go?"

"Somewhere tropical, maybe. Or Europe. I always wanted to visit Europe."

She looked down, color suddenly high on her cheekbones, and his interest sharpened. She had said she would go to the Ukraine, he remembered from a long-ago conversation. Julia had secrets. He had sensed it before. The woman had hidden depths, parts of herself she didn't share with the world.

Davy tugged on his leg before Jamie could probe. "Where are we going now? Will we have to walk there? It's cold here."

He smiled down at the boy. "Nope. I've got a car waiting for us, right over there. Do you guys think you can help me carry the luggage?"

In answer, Clint picked up a suitcase and his younger brother quickly followed suit.

"Ready?" Jamie asked with a smile for Julia. She was looking around at the mountains that surrounded Hope's Crossing, terrain similar to Haven Point but without the vast, beautiful lake.

"I am," she answered. She followed him to the parking area where he kept his vehicle.

"This looks familiar," Julia said as he loaded the luggage in the cargo area and opened the back door for the boys. "Right down to the same color as the SUV you have in Haven Point. Did you buy them in bulk?"

"I keep a personal vehicle in Hope's Crossing and at the airport we use in San Jose. It makes life easier, so I don't have to arrange a ride when I fly in and out. When they're all the same, I don't have to figure out which car is mine."

"I would have thought a man like you who enjoys… variety…in so many other aspects of his life would have a different vehicle in every airport."

"When I find what I like, I stick with it," he murmured. "At least where cars are concerned."

To his delight, color climbed her cheekbones. He loved it entirely too much when she blushed.

"What do you think about heading over to my dad's café before we head to the inn so we can grab a bite to eat?" he asked, when the luggage had been loaded and everyone piled into his vehicle.

"That would be lovely."

"Davy is starving," Clint informed them.

"We'd better take care of that, then," he said, then put the car in gear and turned toward town.

THE DOWNTOWN AREA in Hope's Crossing was packed with other vehicles, which meant it took Jamie some time to find a parking space.

"Is it always this busy on a Friday night in December?" she asked.

"The ski resort brings in plenty of tourists, sure. It's got world-class skiing. Some of the traffic might be for the gala. Still, this is much busier than normal. There must be something happening downtown—a concert or an art walk or something. I couldn't tell you for sure."

His hometown seemed vibrant and fun. As he drove around looking for a spot, Julia greatly enjoyed the charming lampposts, the holiday lights, the merchants and restaurants decorated for the holidays.

The town was set in a lovely location, too, surrounded by soaring snow-capped mountains.

She tried to imagine Jamie as a boy, wandering these streets with his friends, maybe riding his bike in the summer or hanging out at his father's café.

Why had he been in such a hurry to leave? She still wasn't sure she knew the full answer.

"Whoa. Look at that snowman!" Clint yelled out, pointing to a small, undeveloped corner on one city street where a snowman that had to be at least sixteen feet tall watched over the hustle and bustle of shoppers and tourists. The snowman's sturdy base looked taller than Julia and was as big around as an above-ground swimming pool.

"That's cool," Davy exclaimed. "Hey, Jamie, can we build a snowman that big tomorrow?"

Jamie grinned. "That's a tall order, kid. Literally. I imagine they had to bring that much snow in from a field somewhere."

"How did they get it here?" Clint asked, his expression fascinated.

Jamie was explaining about dump trucks and front-end loaders and community cooperation, when ahead of them, a big pickup truck started to exit a space. Jamie braked to give him room, then pulled into the newly vacant spot.

"This works, as long as you don't mind walking about a block."

"Walking isn't a bad idea," she said. The boys had

been in school all day, then running errands with her before climbing onto an airplane. They could probably use a little exercise before dinner.

They walked about a block, making their way past other pedestrians until they reached what looked like one of the busiest spots in town. The air inside the café was warm, and the smell of yeast and grilled meat made her stomach rumble.

Inside, Jamie stopped short. "I should have known," he muttered. "On a Friday night at the Center of Hope, you can usually find enough Caines to start a pickup basketball game."

She recognized several of his siblings and their spouses, crowded together at a pair of tables. They were all laughing and seemed to be having a great time. Charlotte was the first to spot them, and her eyes lit up with happiness.

"Jamie! I was hoping you would drop by once you got back to town."

She hugged him, then hugged Julia in turn, though Julia had only met her a few times.

That seemed to be the signal for Dermot's wife, Katherine, to jump up and hug her, followed by Genevieve and Eliza.

"You made it," Eliza exclaimed. "What do you think of Hope's Crossing?"

"It's beautiful," Julia answered. "We've only seen the ride from the airport to downtown, but I enjoyed every bit."

His brothers jumped to bring extra chairs for the four of them, wedging them in any empty space. Julia found herself seated next to Charlotte on one side and Jamie's brother Andrew on the other.

"It's so great to see you again," Charlotte said, with a sincerity that warmed her. "I have to tell you, I was so thrilled when Eliza told us Jamie was bringing you and the boys to town for the weekend and that you were going to be his date for the gala tomorrow."

Julia shifted in her chair, hoping his family didn't have the wrong idea here. Was it possible they thought she and Jamie were involved? Surely they only had to look at her to know that was completely impossible.

She wanted to set the record straight but couldn't figure out a way to do it that wouldn't sound ridiculous. "I'm looking forward to it," she said instead.

"It takes a tough woman to come back for a second helping of Caines."

She wasn't tough. Far from it. Hadn't she proven that, over and over?

"I think your family is wonderful," she said softly.

Charlotte smiled. "They can be. And they can be annoying and intrusive, too. It depends on the day. The point is, we're all thrilled Jamie brought you for the gala. It's nice to see him showing some sense, for once, and picking someone with brains as well as beauty."

Oh, dear. She had been right. Charlotte had absolutely the wrong idea.

She had to say something. Before she could, though, Clint tugged on her sleeve to ask if he and Davy could go to the bathroom, and the moment was gone.

As she had observed at Thanksgiving, a meal with the Caine family was both crazy and wonderful. The food was delicious—nothing elaborate but fresh, healthy comfort food.

She would have expected nothing less from Dermot Caine.

She would have loved to stay all evening listening to the banter. The only discordant note was the fine-edged tension between Jamie and his brother Dylan. She had noticed it at Thanksgiving and wondered if she imagined it, but seeing them together at the café reinforced the suspicion.

Jamie smiled and joked with his youngest brother as he did with everyone else, but she caught a certain tension in his jawline and murky emotion in his eyes.

"Are you sure I can't persuade you to stay with us?" Charlotte asked when the dishes had been cleared away and people started putting on their winter coats. "You know we have plenty of room."

"You're welcome in Snowflake Canyon, too," Genevieve said. "You would be our first overnight guests since Dylan finished adding on to the cabin."

"I appreciate your kind offers, but this time we're staying at Wild Iris House. Lucy insisted," Jamie said.

"Next time you're staying with us," Charlotte insisted, "even if I have to arm-wrestle Lucy for it."

"There's an idea for our next family party," Eliza said, while Julia felt a pang at the realization this was a one-time experience. She wouldn't be back. They were this close-knit, warm, intertwined family, and she was only temporarily on the periphery.

"Good night, everyone. I hope I see you again before we leave town."

"Something tells me you'll see so much of us this weekend, you'll be eating those words," Dylan said with a grin. With his scar and the eye patch, he looked like a sexy, disreputable pirate.

She smiled back at him. Out of the corner of her

gaze, she thought she saw Jamie's jaw tighten again, though she couldn't be completely sure.

When they walked outside, the night was crisp and smelled of snow. Hope's Crossing was charming, festive, and Julia resolved to enjoy every moment she was here.

"Careful there," Jamie said, pointing out a patch of ice on the sidewalk. He gripped her arm to make sure she didn't slip. To her secret delight, he didn't remove his hand as they made their way to his vehicle, with the boys walking hand in hand in front of them. Clint watched over his younger brother, as he always did.

"Sorry about that back there," he said after he helped them to his SUV and settled into the driver's seat. "I should have prepared you for the possibility of a Caine onslaught tonight before we headed to the café. My family can be overwhelming."

"I like them very much," she assured him as he pulled out of the parking space. "It's obvious they care deeply for one another—and for you."

He made a face, his attention focused on the driving for a moment.

While the boys pointed out Christmas decorations they liked, she watched Jamie out of the corner of her gaze. He still seemed distracted, on edge about something. Was it being back here in Hope's Crossing, or could there be something else going on?

"I don't know a subtle way to ask this," she said after a moment, "but can you tell me what happened to Dylan?"

His features tightened, and through the dark interior, she saw his eyes go bleak. "Afghanistan. He was in the Army Rangers. Boots on the ground. They were doing a house-to-house search when a kid with an improvised explosive device decided to check out and try to take as many Rangers as he could."

"Oh, no."

"Things were rough on him for a while. He was drinking too much and in a pretty dark place, but then Gen came along. Who would have guessed the biggest snooty society girl in town would be just the one to rattle his cage enough to help him find his way out?"

He gave a half smile, but she still sensed his disquiet when he talked about his brother. Was that the cause of it? Could he be jealous of Dylan and Genevieve?

"Were you and Gen…ever involved?" she asked, completely on a hunch.

It was the wrong one, apparently. He shifted his gaze from the road just long enough to give her a wide-eyed, shocked stare.

"Hell, no! Gen and me? I barely knew her before she and Dylan were arrested together one night—which is a long story you'll have to ask her about. Why would you go there?"

She shrugged, feeling foolish. "I just wondered if that's the reason for the tension between you and your brother. I noticed it at Thanksgiving and again tonight."

"Tension? That's crazy. Dylan and I have always been close."

He seemed genuinely shocked, and she said nothing, wishing she'd never brought up the subject. It was none of her business, anyway, and maybe she had completely imagined the whole thing.

"I'm sorry. Forget I said anything."

"What made you think something was up between us?"

"Every time I've seen you together, you have this

strange, tense expression, like you're afraid he's going to shatter in a stiff wind."

He didn't answer for several moments, making her again wish she hadn't said anything. Jamie didn't speak until he pulled up to a magnificent Victorian, roughly twice the size of Winston House.

"It's guilt," he finally said, his voice low.

"What is?"

"What you…may have seen in my expression. I didn't think anyone else picked up on the vibe. Apparently I was wrong."

"Guilt about what?"

He met her gaze, and this time she couldn't miss the bleak shadows there. "Dylan went through hell and nearly died. And none of it would have happened, if not for me."

She opened her mouth, shocked. He didn't give her time to respond, cutting her off by turning back to the boys. "Here we are, guys. Let's get you settled. We've got a long, hard day of playing in the snow ahead of us tomorrow."

Even in their tired state, the boys cheered that idea and jumped out to help Jamie carry in bags.

DAVY AND CLINT were so tired from their long day at school and the added excitement of another plane ride that they were asleep almost before she finished reading their favorite story.

"Jamie's really nice," Davy said, his eyes sleepy and his features soft. "When I grow up, I think I want to be a pilot."

"That sounds like a wonderful dream." She smoothed a hand over his hair as tenderness trickled through her.

Three weeks ago, she hadn't even known these boys. Now they were becoming so very dear to her.

Rather like—

She shied away from completing that dangerous sentence. Instead, she kissed Davy on the forehead, then his brother.

"Good night, my dears."

"Where are you sleeping?" Clint asked, suddenly concerned.

"I'll be out in the sitting room. Jamie's taking the bedroom."

He wasn't happy about it. They had argued about it earlier. She had insisted he take the bed while she could sleep on the convertible sofa, which didn't so much as fold out as fold down, like a futon.

Jamie claimed he slept on one like this at his dad's and was always comfortable, but she had pointed out he was taller than she. If he tried to sleep on this one, his legs would dangle over the edge. Eventually he had reluctantly given in, especially when she told him she preferred to be close enough to hear the boys if they awoke.

The sitting room between the two bedrooms was spacious, and she imagined those big windows would provide beautiful light during the day. Now, the room was in shadows, lit only by the crackling fire he must have lit in the beautiful fireplace and the flickering lights of a small, sweetly decorated artificial Christmas tree on a table in the corner.

"They get settled in okay?" Jamie asked, startling an instinctive gasp out of her.

"Oh. I didn't see you there! I thought perhaps you went to bed."

"Not yet. I wanted to feed the fire a bit, to make sure it would stay hot for you."

They were alone here in this beautifully appointed, romantic room. At the realization, a soft thread of intimacy unfurled between them, twisting and tangling together. All her instincts warned her she would be wise to simply say good-night and go to bed herself, though energy still hummed through her.

"Yes. I think they're likely sound asleep. You have to admit, this would be a pretty exciting day for any kid, jumping on an airplane at the drop of a hat and flying off for the weekend."

"I hope you enjoyed it, too."

"You know I did. It was amazing."

As her face heated, she sincerely hoped she didn't look like the giddy schoolgirl she felt.

Though she knew it probably wasn't wise, she didn't know where else to go, so she took the seat across from him and the fire—a plump, soft armchair she wanted to curl into with a good book.

"I love seeing your family interact," she said. "It's obvious they care about each other very much."

"We've always been close. After our mom died of cancer, those bonds seemed to tighten more."

"How old were you when that happened?"

She knew Katherine had only been married to Dermot a few years, but didn't know the rest of the story about Jamie's mother.

"I was nineteen, in college and on track to become a helicopter pilot. Only Dylan and Charlotte were left at home."

"That must have been hard on you all. How lovely that you had each other to rely on, though."

"I guess that's one of the blessings of a big family. We can support each other in good times and bad. We've had a few of the latter but plenty of the former."

"I can't imagine having so many siblings. Was it wonderful?"

"Most of the time. I always felt sorry for Charlotte. She had a pretty rough go, being the only sister of six rambunctious older brothers."

She didn't exactly feel sorry for herself for growing up the only child of two older, settled parents. The Caine household must have been sheer chaos, but six older brothers sounded perfectly lovely to her.

"You all must have spoiled her terribly."

"Tormented, more like. At least that's the way she would probably tell it. We did all adore her, but we figured it was our solemn responsibility to toughen her up. As the youngest brothers, Dylan and I were probably the worst on her."

She had been waiting for a chance to ask him about what he had said in the car after the dinner. While she didn't want to ruin this soft intimacy between them, she sensed he needed to talk about it.

"What did you mean before? When you said you felt responsible for Dylan's injury."

That muscle flexed in his jaw again, and for a long moment, she thought he wouldn't answer. The only sound in the room was the crackle of the fire. Finally he sighed heavily. "I shouldn't have said that. Forget it, okay?"

She couldn't do that. Now that he had raised the issue, she found she wanted to know more. "Jamie. What happened? Why would you even imagine you might be responsible? You weren't there, were you?"

"That was the whole point. I wasn't where I should have been."

He gazed at her, then at the Christmas tree. "We were both stationed in the same region, both in the army, though our experiences were very different. He was a boots-on-the-ground guy, special forces. In the heat of the action. I was a chopper pilot, flying guys from base to base and trying to stay out of trouble. I wasn't very good at it. Staying out of trouble, I mean."

"What happened?"

"Though we were in different countries, Dylan and I were both supposed to have leave around the same time. That rarely happened for us. Since it was the holidays and we didn't really have time to go home, we decided to do the next best thing and meet up in Qatar, hang out with friends, maybe meet some women."

She could imagine the two gorgeous Caine brothers would have no trouble finding women, wherever they were.

"It didn't happen?"

"No. Because I couldn't keep my mouth shut. I got in trouble with my commanding officer for insubordination. He was an idiot, always putting guys in stupid, dangerous situations, and one day I had enough and let him have it. As a result, he wrote me up and yanked my leave a few days before I was supposed to meet up with Dylan. I was able to get in touch with him through his unit and told him he should go ahead to Qatar without me since we already had the hotel rooms, but he decided to reschedule his leave for another time, on the chance he could match mine."

His expression was suddenly bleak, distant. "He wasn't supposed to be on that mission. If I had only kept my mouth shut for once, Dylan and I would have been sitting by a luxury hotel pool in Doha having drinks with a couple of beautiful junior officers in bikinis. Instead, he signed up to head into the field and ended up being the target of a twelve-year-old suicide bomber."

His voice was hollow, filled with regret, and it took all of her strength to keep her fingers curled together on her lap instead of reaching out to comfort him.

"Do you really think Dylan blames you for his injuries?" she asked.

"How could he not?"

She didn't know Dylan well, but remembered him at dinner talking to Davy and Clint, teasing his sister, looking adoringly at his wife. How could he possibly hold a grudge against his brother for something over which Jamie had no control?

"I won't believe it," she said firmly. "You weren't responsible for what that boy did. Nor were you responsible for Dylan's decision to go on that mission in the first place. I think you're taking entirely too much on your shoulders. Give yourself a break, Jamie."

CHAPTER FIFTEEN

SHE DID NOT know the worst of it. Jamie shifted in his chair. The ghosts that had haunted him when he returned to Hope's Crossing seemed to hover ever closer.

Someone as sweet and kind as Julia would never understand how a man's choices could sometimes ride his tail.

Yeah, he blamed himself for Dylan's injuries. Though his brother seemed to have come to terms with all he had lost serving his country and had carved out a pretty damn good life for himself here with Gen, Jamie couldn't accept it with the same equanimity. He remembered Dylan as he had been, strong and whole, fun-loving and filled with life. When he looked at his brother, he saw everything Dylan had lost.

Jamie was the older brother. Pop had told him before their last deployment together to watch over Dylan. So what if they weren't serving in the same unit—hell, not even the same *country*? That didn't matter. From the time they were toddlers, his parents used to always charge him with keeping an eye out for Dylan, and he considered it his responsibility.

He had failed spectacularly to take care of someone he loved. That was nothing new, though, simply the latest in a long string of failures.

He shouldn't have brought Julia here. What had

seemed like a good idea at the time now appeared fraught with emotional land mines.

She had asked why he didn't settle in Hope's Crossing. He hadn't lied. He did love the recreational opportunities Haven Point could provide, and it made perfect sense to be close to Aidan and his Caine Tech facility there.

He hadn't told her everything, about the regrets that followed him like those ghosts.

"You should talk to your brother, tell him how you're feeling," Julia said now. "He would probably be the first one to assure you he doesn't blame you for what happened to him."

He tried to imagine having that conversation with Dylan and couldn't see it. "Maybe."

"Do it. Trust me, life is too short to regret the things you didn't say to the people you care about."

What regrets did she carry? He wanted to ask about her own secrets, but he had a compelling need to return the conversation to the fun, lighthearted repartee with which he was most comfortable. He didn't want to think about Dylan or Lisa or any of his other regrets. It was far easier to fall back on old habits.

"I'm sure there's some truth to that," he said with a well-practiced smile. "While we're talking about regrets, let me say that I would regret forever if I didn't tell you how lovely you look. Hope's Crossing agrees with you, Julia Winston."

Those remarkable eyes looked huge in her features as she gazed at him for a long moment. He saw awareness spark to life there, as bright and glittering as the crackling fire.

He could kiss her right now, here in front of the fireplace and the cheerful Christmas tree. It would be so very easy. All he had to do was reach out a hand and tug her from her chair to his lap. He could slip his hand into her hair, feel the silk slide against his skin, draw her mouth closer to his...

As he imagined it, Jamie felt his body stir to life. It constantly astonished him, how fiercely attracted he was to this plain, quiet librarian.

She probably wouldn't push him away. That tantalizing thought seemed to writhe through his awareness. Suddenly, it became the only thing he could think about.

She let out a tiny, gasping sort of breath, then her eyes narrowed.

"I know what you're doing." Her voice was tight, suddenly, mirroring the suspicion in her eyes.

"You do?" He wished she would share, since he hadn't been sure what the hell he was doing since the afternoon he moved in to Julia Winston's house.

"I'm on to your secrets," she said. "Whenever you want to divert a woman's attention and keep her from getting too close to the heart of who you are, you whip out the old charm sledgehammer and bash her over the head with it."

"Interesting but oddly violent analogy."

"I don't know how else to describe it. With a few well-chosen words and that killer smile of yours, you take an otherwise rational woman and leave her dazed and bewildered. It's quite fascinating to watch."

"You sound like something of an expert," he drawled. Was he supposed to be flattered or insulted by her observation? He wasn't used to women who could see so clearly past his charm. It made him wonder if she had been studying him all this time, rather like he was some sort of rare, bizarre creature she stumbled over in the wild.

He wondered if she knew how much he loved to see her blush, that little tint of color in her cheeks he wanted to kiss away.

"I simply try to study the world around me," she said pertly.

"What else did you learn about me?" he asked, not entirely sure he wanted to know the answer.

"I know you love your family above everything— even flying, which is your passion. I know you're much kinder than you want people to know. And I know you long for something you don't have, but you're not entirely sure what that is."

He didn't know what to say to that, so he fell back on what she said he used as a shield. "You sound like something of an expert, Ms. Winston. You should know, then, that at this particular moment, what I'm longing for isn't a mystery at all."

He offered up that smile she was talking about and was delighted when she blushed.

"See? You're doing it again. Trying to distract me by throwing out your Jamie Caine mojo."

He laughed. "Is it working?"

"I don't know," she said, her tone exasperated. "I'll tell you when I can think again."

That was it. He had to kiss her. He tugged her toward him. "Why don't we both stop thinking, just for a few moments?" he said, then covered her mouth with his.

He had been dreaming of her mouth for days, since their one heated encounter. The reality was so much better than his memory. Her mouth was sweet and warm, and she again sighed when he kissed her, as if she had been waiting for exactly this moment. She smelled delicious, something flowery and light and sweet.

He found the unexpectedness of her, this secret, passionate side, incredibly seductive.

When he finally managed to find the strength to ease his mouth away, both of their breathing was ragged, and he was achy and hard.

Jamie didn't know what the hell to do about it. He could handle his attraction to her, but this soft, strange emotion surging through him as he held her was something else entirely.

He tried for nonchalance. "So. What did you learn there, Ms. Winston?"

She blinked at him, eyes slightly unfocused. "That you kiss really, really well—something I believe I've already discovered."

Did she know how much she made him laugh? Or how very much she intrigued him?

"So do you," he responded. "A little *too* well. You make it difficult to go to my room, when I would really love to keep kissing you all night."

That wasn't entirely true. He was a healthy, red-blooded guy. What he *really* wanted involved much more than kissing. He wanted to spend hours exploring that luscious mouth, then move on to every other delectable inch of her—exactly why he needed to say good night.

She deserved far more than a guy like him could offer her.

"But you won't," she murmured.

"Is that regret I hear in your voice, Ms. Winston?"

Her color rose a little higher, but to his surprise—and secret delight—she gave a throaty laugh. "A little, if I'm honest. But a little regret is better than great, steaming buckets of regret—which is what both of us would carry away from this, if we don't stop here."

"Where's a guy's charm sledgehammer when he needs it?" He was only half joking.

"I'm that most unique of women, someone who is apparently immune to that particular weapon."

He wasn't so sure. He had tasted the desire in her kiss, had sensed it in the trembling of her fingers in his hair and the press of her body against him.

"Are you?" he murmured.

"Yes," she said firmly. "And that wasn't a challenge. Only a statement of fact."

"Which of us are you trying to convince?" She pursed those swollen lips, becoming the prissy librarian he found so very intriguing. "I like kissing you. You're very good at it, which I would have expected."

"Should I say thank you?"

She made a face but avoided the question. "It sounds as if we have a big day tomorrow," she said. "We both should try to get some sleep."

He had a feeling he wouldn't be able to sleep any time soon, and when he did, he would be tormented by heated dreams of the impossible, but he forced himself to nod. He should never have brought her here. He should have let some other guy—some *better* guy— help her check off all those items on the list, though he hated the very idea.

"Are you sure you'll be okay out here?" he asked.

"Absolutely."

He added another log to the fire, then put the screen up to keep any stray sparks from jumping out. "The fire will probably burn for another hour or two, though the embers will stay hot for much longer. If you get cold, just throw another log on."

Or come crawl into bed with me.

He couldn't say the words, as much as he might mean them.

"Got it. Good night, Jamie."

He nodded and forced himself to turn and head into the other bedroom.

He should never have kissed her again, but at least it accomplished one objective—it distracted both of them from discussing topics he preferred to avoid.

As soon as his door closed behind him, Julia sank onto the sofa, gazing at the glittery dance of sparks. She felt like her insides were filled with embers, smoldering and crackling and spitting. She had no idea how she had resisted the man under these difficult circumstances—or how she would possibly do it the next night.

She was halfway in love with him.

The realization burned through her, in all its stark, unadorned, slap-to-the-head reality.

What a disaster. She was falling in love with a man who had basically told her not to expect anything but a few kisses from her, who shied away from any serious discussion by kissing her until she forgot what she was saying.

It was just like her to be so foolish, to throw her heart after something completely impossible.

She had to keep her emotions in check. How humiliating, if he figured out that what had started as a crush was rapidly becoming much more. She would simply have to maintain perspective, to remember that none of this was real. When the weekend was over, they would both go back to their respective lives and the roles they had created.

Jamie would continue womanizing and flying and charming half the population of Haven Point.

She would try her best to return to real life. Her house, the library, her friends. Those things were real. This weekend was only make-believe. If she could keep that in mind, she just might survive with what was left of her heart intact.

WAS SHE REALLY doing this?

The moaning of the wind through the trees sounded like a warning of impending doom while the butterflies in her stomach seemed to be auditioning for the Radio City Music Hall Rockettes.

Julia tried to relax her death grip on the ski poles she had no idea how to use. This was crazy. Sane, moderately intelligent people didn't strap sticks to their feet and head down a snowy mountainside. They stayed inside by the fire with a mug of hot cocoa and a good book.

She didn't do this sort of thing. Oh, she didn't mind winter hikes or a bit of snowshoeing, but downhill skiing was way outside her comfort zone.

"I don't think I can do this."

"Don't be nervous." In the morning sunlight, Jamie's smile was bright and encouraging. She couldn't see his eyes behind his sunglasses, but she was certain they would match his smile, an expression designed to make any woman think she was the most important thing in his world and he completely believed in her.

She was as much a sucker as the next girl.

"I'm not nervous," she answered. "I'm terrified."

"You're doing great. You aced the lesson. Just remember that. You know how to turn, and you can snow-plow and stop without any trouble at all. You didn't fall once on the bunny slope. This is just the next step. Don't worry. I'll be here the whole time. Visualize yourself with the wind in your hair and your face."

The bunny slope hadn't seemed at all threatening, but they were now atop a real mountain. All she could manage to visualize was a moving picture of herself in the middle of some spectacular cartwheel of death.

Everyone else seemed to be oblivious to any sense of fear. People were whizzing off the lift one second and heading down the mountain without even pausing to take a breath.

Even the boys had picked up the sport with astonishing speed. Brendan, along with Andrew Caine's teenage daughter, were keeping an eye on the two boys and Brendan's children.

"Maybe I could walk back down and meet you at the lodge," she suggested.

He sidestepped to her, that supportive smile pasted firmly on his face. "You've got this, Jules. We can wait right here until you're ready. Just breathe for a minute and enjoy how pretty it is up here."

Psychology 101. He was trying to calm her, distract her from her nerves. It might even work. She sucked in a deep breath and then another. The air tasted sweet and pure up here, in a way she couldn't begin to describe, and the view really was spectacular.

The vivid blue sky contrasted sharply with new powder, and she could see the reservoir they had passed on the way from Hope's Crossing up the canyon to the Silver Strike ski resort, as well as the road snaking back to the pretty town.

He pointed down the mountain. "Look how well the boys are doing. They're ripping it up."

She spotted the boys' parkas amid the sea of other skiers and snowboarders, under the watchful eye of his family members. "How do they pick it up so easily, like they've been skiing their whole lives?"

"Kids are amazing, aren't they? They can be fearless."

She, on the other hand, was suffocating under the weight of her fear.

"I don't suppose I could take the ski lift back down, could I?" She had to ask, didn't she?

He grinned. "Nice try, but that's against the rules, I'm afraid. You've got no choice here. That's one of the good things about skiing. Once you take that lift up, you're obligated to see it through to the bottom—unless you end up needing the ski patrol to carry you down on a gurney. Let's try to avoid that particular scenario, shall we?"

Oh, cripes. He had to bring up *ski patrol* and *gurney*. Now she could picture that humiliating scene entirely too clearly, her lying in the snow with some broken limb, cold and in pain and mortified while Jamie stood by looking gorgeous and concerned.

"We can take this as slow as you want."

"I think you forgot a little thing called gravity."

"You're in control of gravity up here, believe it or not. You've learned how to turn and how to stop. This is a nice, wide, gentle ski run. We're not heading straight down—we're zigzagging down from side to side. You get to decide the angle of our zigs and your zags. You want to go faster, you turn more often. You want to slow down, just ease back on the turns and make your path wider."

She let out a breath and tried to give herself the same pep talk she had delivered the day before on his jet. She wanted to experience more of life. This was something she had always wanted to do. Hadn't she put it on that stupid list she made during book club?

Two items down on her list in two days. That wasn't bad at all, if she could only find the strength to follow through.

"What if I fall?"

"Then I'll be right there to help you get back up." He gave her that teasing smile she secretly adored. "Of course, if you fall, and I have to help you, you'll have to pay me back with a kiss. It's the rule."

The matter-of-fact way he imparted that information forced a laugh out of her that only sounded a little hysterical. Or so she hoped.

"Says who?"

"It's clearly listed in the Jamie Caine ski instruction rule book."

"Given your reputation, that seems remarkably counterintuitive. If you promise a kiss every time someone falls, you would have women lined up from here to Haven Point, trying to sign up for lessons."

"It's a big job, but I'm willing to take it on. Somebody has to teach all those lovely women how to ski."

She laughed again, relieved to sense some of her fear floating away like ice crystals on the wind.

Despite his urging her to take her time, she knew he couldn't stand here forever. He was right; she had to *do* something or she wouldn't make it off this mountain.

That seemed to be an entirely too apt metaphor for the rest of her life. She wanted to live, and she wouldn't do that while she stood around dithering and giving in to her fears.

"Okay. I'm ready. Let's go."

Jamie's approving smile gave her the last bit of courage she needed. She pushed off with her poles and took off. Her stomach twirled as she headed down.

Okay. She could do this. Adrenaline sizzled through her as the wind rushed to meet her, and her heart thundered in her ears. Maybe there was something to this whole skiing business, a valid reason that might explain why the industry made billions every year.

As he suggested, she made her turns wide and slow, but momentum and gravity still carried her faster than she felt comfortable with. She did fine on her first turn, then her second and third, but somehow on the next one, her ski caught an edge. As she moved into the turn, she could feel herself losing her balance. Despite her efforts to regain it, her feet slid out from under her. At the last minute, she remembered how he had taught her to fall, and she turned her body to absorb as much of the impact as she could, keeping her arms in a braced position at her sides.

He was at her side in seconds. "You okay?" he asked, his features worried.

"I think so." She didn't bother to tell him her pride was the only thing bruised.

He reached a gloved hand to help her up, and when she was on her skis again, she stumbled into him a little. Instantly, his mouth was on hers. His lips were warm and tasted of the coconut lip balm sunscreen she had seen him put on earlier. Delicious. Why couldn't they just stand here and do this, instead of having to make it all the way down the mountainside?

"I warned you," he said with a laugh.

"You did. Maybe I fell on purpose, just to see if you meant it."

"Did you?" He sounded genuinely shocked.

"What do you think?"

"I think you continue to surprise me, Julia Winston," he said with another laugh.

Her heartbeat was still fierce in her chest, but now she wasn't sure if it was from the skiing or from the kissing.

Not that it mattered.

"If it helps, that was a textbook fall. Perfection."

"At least I've got that part down, right?" She drew in another breath and pushed off again.

She fell twice more before they reached the bottom. The first one was accidental, but the reward of his warm mouth on hers was just too enticing. What woman could possibly blame her?

When she and Jamie reached the bottom, Brendan and the children skied over. The boys seemed to glow with excitement.

"Did you see me, Julia? Did you?" Davy asked.

"You did so well," she said.

"Better than you." Jamie's nephew Carter didn't hold back any punches. "How many times did you fall down?"

"Not nearly enough," Jamie murmured, earning a surprised look from his brother, which quickly turned speculative.

Julia could feel her face heat and didn't dare look at him. "So many, I lost count."

"Should we try one more run?" Brendan said. "Maybe I should give Julia a few tips. Looks like your methods aren't working."

"Or are working too well," she couldn't resist answering.

"Are you up for another run?" Jamie asked.

"Yes!" the children all shouted in unison.

"Julia?" Brendan asked.

"Yes. You can't stop now, especially when you're beginning to get a taste for it," Jamie said.

"This time, let me take you," his brother suggested. "I'm a much better teacher than James here."

Somehow she doubted she would have the same incentive to fail, with Jamie's happily married brother. It wouldn't be nearly as fun but she would probably genuinely learn how to ski instead of merely discovering more creative ways to fall.

"That would be great. Let's go."

"I guess that leaves you with the kids," Brendan said with a grin at his brother as they all headed to the ski lift again.

CHAPTER SIXTEEN

"THANK YOU FOR letting my brother drag you here. It's so fantastic to see you again."

"He didn't drag me anywhere," Julia said to Charlotte Gregory. "I've been delighted to be here. The boys and I have had a fantastic time."

"I heard you went skiing today for the first time. How did you like it?"

Julia thought of Jamie's mouth, which tasted improbably tropical, his laughing eyes, the heat of him that had seeped through her skin despite the December chill. Her face flamed, and she prayed his sister didn't notice—or at least couldn't ascribe the cause to Jamie. "It was wonderful. I almost wish we had a ski resort closer to Haven Point."

Charlotte smiled. "Any time you want to ski, I imagine Jamie would be happy to bring you here. Maybe he'll start coming around more. We don't see him nearly often enough."

Julia didn't have the heart to tell Charlotte that after Jamie moved out of her second floor apartment in a few weeks, it was likely she herself wouldn't see him at all. What reason would they have for their paths to collide?

"You look beautiful, by the way," Charlotte said. "I love your dress."

"Thanks. It's Eliza's. She was kind enough to lend me one for tonight."

"She should give it to you. Seriously. It suits your coloring perfectly."

Julia did feel more glamorous than she ever had in her life. Tonight she wasn't a dowdy librarian. Jamie might have been feigning the stunned look when she finally came out after getting ready, but somehow she didn't think so. How could she not find that gratifying?

She and Charlotte chatted for a few more moments about some of the similarities between their respective towns until Dermot Caine wandered over to talk to them.

He kissed his daughter on the cheek, then did the same to Julia. "What are the two prettiest women in the place doing over here in the corner by themselves? Some smart guy should take one of them out to the dance floor."

"I don't know where all the smart guys have gone these days," Charlotte said with a teasing smile.

"I don't know either. I do know my sons are over talking basketball with a couple of NBA stars, which means I get to be the luckiest fellow at the gala. Too bad there's only one of me."

"I need to go talk to Evie and Claire about our Christmas party anyway," Charlotte said. "That should narrow your choice."

Her father smiled and turned to Julia. "Will you dance with me, my dear?"

He was such a darling man. How could she refuse? "Certainly. I would be delighted."

Jamie's father led her out as the jazz combo began playing a familiar ballad.

"Ah. One of my favorites," Dermot said, further cementing her adoration of him. "You should have heard the great Billie Holiday sing this one," he said.

"I like that version. It's a classic. But what about the soulful touch Nina Simone brought to the table?"

He gave her an appreciative smile. "A beautiful woman who knows her jazz. I knew you were a woman after my own heart."

She laughed, utterly charmed by Jamie's father. He was simply adorable and probably made every woman he spoke with feel as if she was the most important person in his world.

Rather like someone else she knew.

Was that why she liked Dermot so much? Because he reminded her so very much of Jamie?

His behavior wasn't feigned either, but an utterly genuine reaction. She felt like the most important person in his world because in that moment, she *was* the most important person in his world.

"Are you enjoying yourself, my dear?" Dermot asked.

"Very much. Hope's Crossing is lovely. Everyone I've met has been nothing but kind to me."

At a small dinner party earlier at the huge, luxurious home of Harry Lange, who apparently owned the ski resort, she had met dozens of people. She was likely to remember only a few of their names.

"I'm very glad to hear you're enjoying yourself. I hope this means you'll come visit us again."

"Maybe," she answered, though she couldn't imagine when she would. What would possibly bring her to Hope's Crossing again? This was a one-time visit only. The realization made her throat ache, but she quickly

swallowed the sadness. Tonight everyone had come together to celebrate and support a good cause. For her, it
was a once-in-a-lifetime experience, and she wouldn't
ruin it by being maudlin.

"I heard things are going well with those boys you
took in. I'm so glad. Makes my heart happy to hear, it
does. What a good thing you've done there, my dear."

She glowed at his approbation. "Someone needed
to. I'm glad I was in the right place to find out what
was going on."

They talked about the boys a little and about their
mother and the hurdles she faced.

"You know, Spencer and Charlotte don't just provide
services to those who are scarred or have lost limbs.
They also open their program to those whose injuries
aren't as easy to see. Make sure their mother knows
about this place. It might be just the thing for her, when
she begins to heal," Dermot said.

"I'll do that."

They lapsed into a comfortable silence as he twirled
her around the dance floor. At one point, they danced
past Jamie, who stood talking with his brothers. He was
watching her with an intense look in his eyes that made
her blush and remember those silly, spontaneous, wonderful kisses on the ski slopes earlier.

"I worry for my Jamie."

She felt her face heat more. She didn't want to talk
about Jamie with his father. She really didn't. But how
could she avoid it, when he brought it up? Perhaps Dermot would have insight into some of the mysteries sur-
rounding his son.

"Why is that?"

"He's a good boy who feels things deeply. He always

has been. Of all my children, I think he had the hardest time, after his mother's death. One might think that dubious distinction would go to Charlotte, her being so close to her mother and all, not to mention being the only girl. But Jamie. He struggled mightily. It didn't help that..."

He cut off his sentence with a rather guilty look over at his sons.

"Didn't help that what?"

Dermot pressed his lips together. "Jamie was dealing with...other problems around the same time. It was a heavy burden for a lad. Suffice it to say, I worried for him then, and I worry for him now. He's not happy being alone. He might tell himself otherwise, but a father knows these things."

She wasn't completely sure she agreed with him. If he really wasn't happy, Jamie had the power to change his life.

Just as she did.

The realization seemed sobering and enlightening at the same time. She was the only one keeping herself from living the life she dreamed. If she was tired of living her humdrum existence, she could change things.

"You should tell him that," she said.

"I have. Why would he listen to me? I'm only his father, the one who has loved him since he was no bigger than a hedgehog. We used to call him hedgehog, actually. He had the thickest hair you've ever seen, dark and bristling, just like the cutest little hedgehog. He was a stubborn one, too. You should hear the stories I could tell."

"Yes, please," she said promptly, which made him laugh and immediately launch into one.

"Pop seems to be working his usual magic," Dylan drawled.

Jamie followed his brother's gaze to where their father was spinning a laughing Julia around the dance floor. The fairy lights overhead glinted in her soft brown hair, and her eyes sparkled. Even from here, he could see their stunning color and the roses in her cheeks.

She took his breath away, all dressed up and elegant. He had known she was lovely in her quiet way. Tonight, Julia simply glowed.

She fit in perfectly with his family. The Caines could be overwhelming for anyone, but Julia took all his brothers' teasing in stride and even gave some back. And his sister and sisters-in-law had drawn her into their ranks as if she were one of them.

Now, as he watched her dance with Dermot, he couldn't shake the unsettling feeling that she belonged here.

Not necessarily here in Hope's Crossing, but here among most of the people he loved.

"I was just about to find her and ask her to dance," he said with a halfhearted pout. "Maybe Pop ought to find his own girl. Where is Katherine, anyway?"

Dylan pointed to their stepmother, who was in a corner talking with friends.

"You could always cut in," Drew suggested. "Maybe she's tired of Pop's blarney and could use a break. The man hasn't stopped talking all night."

"That is an excellent idea," Jamie said. Already imagining Julia's soft, curvy body pressed closely to his, he pivoted to head toward them, but Brendan came over before he could step away. The former NFL football player had always been fast on his feet and deadly at the unexpected block.

"That was quite a display out on the slopes today."

Was it his imagination or did his brother look disapproving?

Jamie bristled. "Don't know you're talking about," he lied.

Brendan didn't answer him directly. Instead, his gaze also found Pop dancing with Julia. "She seems like a very nice woman."

"She must be, to take in those cute kids." Dylan added his two cents. "Not to mention, to put up with you living upstairs."

Jamie knew his brothers well. Brendan clearly had come over armed with an agenda.

"She is very nice." What the hell else could he say?

"Not your usual type, though," Brendan observed.

"I wasn't aware I had a type," he said stiffly. "And are you implying the other women I've dated *aren't* nice?"

"Who can tell? There have been so many of them. We never really had a chance to find out."

Brendan's easygoing words belied the steel in his gaze. Jamie's fist curled, then relaxed. He wouldn't cause a scene at Charlotte's gala. She would never forgive any of them.

Anyway, he couldn't argue either point with Bren. He liked women…and Julia wasn't his type. She was worlds away from the casual, fun-loving kind of women who didn't take any effort on his part.

"I only wanted to make sure you know what you're doing here," Brendan said. "Julia seems very nice, and I would hate to see her hurt."

Jamie's fist curled again. They could always take it outside. Char didn't have to know…

She would find out, though, and so would Pop—not

to mention Lucy, Brendan's wife and their hostess at the inn. Jamie would probably take the blame and would never hear the end of it.

"Julia is my friend. I brought her here so the boys could go skiing and so she could be my date tonight while we hobnob with a few athletes and celebrities. That's all there is to it."

"Is it?" Brendan looked clearly skeptical, and Jamie supposed he really couldn't blame him. There was a high likelihood his entirely too observant brother had seen one or two of those lighthearted, delicious kisses on the ski slopes that afternoon.

The memory made something inside him ache, especially since he realized too well that Bren was right. He was dragging both of them too close to the edge. He couldn't have things both ways. If he wanted to be friends with Julia, to help her check off all the bucket-list items on the paper he had found, Jamie had to back off with the flirtatious stuff that came to him as naturally and mindlessly as swallowing.

He cared about her. The last thing he wanted to do was hurt her.

"That's all," he said firmly, hoping to remind himself, too. "Now, if you'll excuse me, I'm going to go grab a drink."

He hurried away from his brothers, feeling guilty and small and wishing on some level that he had never brought her to Hope's Crossing.

"THANK YOU, MY DEAR. You are a lovely dancer."

Julia smiled at Dermot Caine as the music ended, quite sure the pink in her cheeks was clashing terribly with the mauve of her dress. "It was truly my pleasure."

Jamie's father was delightful, full of wry observations, insightful comments, funny stories.

Out of the corner of her gaze she caught Jamie heading to the bar, though the view was marred by a stray lock of hair that shouldn't have been loose, and she realized that as Dermot had whirled her around, a few strands of hair somehow had escaped her updo.

Her social anxieties reared their ugly heads. She probably looked ridiculous, with messy hair and a borrowed dress.

She needed to get over herself. She could fix her hair. It wasn't the end of the world. And Jamie and his father—as well as Charlotte and all her friends—had complimented Julia on the dress. "Will you excuse me, Mr. Caine? I should find the ladies' room and do what I can to fix this hair and my lipstick."

"Of course, of course. I'll escort you there."

"I'm sure I can find it."

"Just through the main doors and down the hall to the right."

With that Irish accent, she could listen to him all night, even when he was simply giving directions to the restroom.

"Thank you," she said with one last smile, then made her way out of the ballroom.

The Silver Strike lodge was beautiful, the height of Western elegance. Even the ladies' room was lovely, with gleaming wood and copper accents.

After fixing her hair and repairing her lipstick, Julia washed her hands and was drying them under hot jets when another woman entered the room. In the mirror, Julia saw she had dyed blond hair and a dress that was pretty, if a little on the tight side. Instead of going into one of the stalls or toward the mirror, she stood directly in Julia's path.

"Did I see you come in with Jamie Caine?"

"I...yes," she answered, taken aback. What business was it of this woman's?

"Are you his girlfriend?" the stranger demanded. Her features were tight, her words a little slurred on the last consonants.

"No. We're merely friends." She did her best to inject a firm note in her voice, trying not to think about those heated kisses on the slopes. Maybe if she said it often enough, she might be able to convince herself.

"Good. If I were you, I would make sure you keep it that way."

Was that a threat or a warning? She couldn't quite tell and had no idea how to respond—or how to handle this strange interaction at all. Her instincts told her to just walk away, but the woman stood between her and the door, blocking her way.

"Jamie Caine doesn't care who he hurts. Just ask my baby sister." She wiped a hand through her hair, sudden tears spilling down her cheeks. "Oh wait, you can't, because she's dead."

Julia swallowed her shock and dismay. Who was this stranger, and why was she confronting her? She had no idea how to respond. "I'm sorry."

Now the woman's trickle of tears became a full-on deluge. "Lisa would have been thirty-five this year," she sniffled. "Five years younger than me. She was so beautiful. You should have seen her! Prettier than anybody else in there. By now she would have been married and maybe had children. She might have gone on to be a nurse, like she always wanted. She had dreams and goals. Ambition. Instead, she never made it past nineteen years old. Thanks to Jamie Caine."

She said his name like a vile curse word, spitting it out with so much disgust, Julia felt sick.

"I don't—" she began, not sure what she intended to say, only that she felt she must say *something*.

"He'll do the same to you. Just watch. If you're not careful, he'll leave you broken, just like he left my baby sister. He doesn't care about you or your feelings. He uses and he uses and he uses. Are you hearing me?"

Before Julia could come up with a reply, another woman came into the bathroom. This was someone whose name she remembered, Claire McKnight, a good friend of Jamie's sister.

She must have summed up the situation in a moment. She gave Julia a quick look of apology and empathy, then turned to the other woman. "Marla. What's the matter, honey?"

The woman looked disoriented at the interruption and at the question. "She's gone. He's here and she's gone. My baby sister."

Claire, whom Julia had already noticed seemed to be maternal and kind, put a comforting arm around Marla's shoulder. "How much have you had to drink, honey? Why don't we go find your husband?"

The woman sobbed into her shoulder and Claire made a little I-got-this gesture with her finger for Julia to go.

She wondered if she should stay and help, yet Claire seemed to have the situation in hand. Julia had a feeling her presence there as Jamie's date would only exacerbate the situation.

"Sorry," Claire mouthed to her as Julia slipped out the door.

She returned to the gala. The lights were still as glittery, the trees as beautifully decorated, but the evening had lost its magic. Suddenly, she only wanted to go home.

WHAT HAD HAPPENED? Julia was upset, but Jamie couldn't put his finger on exactly why.

He had been so looking forward to dancing with her, to holding her in his arms at last and seeing her eyes sparkle in the fairy lights.

Instead, the smiling, lively woman who'd laughed and joked with his father seemed to have disappeared, replaced by a stiff, disapproving librarian who didn't meet his gaze and who spoke to him in monosyllables.

What had he done? He racked his brain but couldn't think of anything so terribly egregious. Maybe she was annoyed at him for kissing her so often while they skied. She hadn't *acted* annoyed, but maybe he wasn't as great a judge of women as he thought.

He only knew it was clear she was no longer enjoying herself.

What happened?

"Are you ready to leave?" he finally asked. The last thing he wanted to do was torture the woman by keeping her at the gala longer, if she was miserable.

At last she met his gaze, and he winced inwardly at the relief in her eyes. "We probably should. The boys might be wondering where we are."

He doubted that. They were probably either asleep or having the time of their lives staying up late back at

Wild Iris House with Bren and Lucy's kids, under the watchful eye of his niece, Maggie.

"I'll grab your coat and have the valet bring the car around," he said.

"Thank you. I'll say my goodbyes to your family."

Did she mean that to sound so terribly final? She would see them again. He was certain of it. Eliza would no doubt invite her to her frequent parties at Snow Angel Cove, especially now that all the women in his family had come to know and adore her, too.

She was subdued when he brought her coat over, though she smiled as she gave one more hug to Lucy and Genevieve before offering a last goodbye and hurrying out of the gala.

Snowflakes swirled around their vehicle as he helped her into the passenger seat, then climbed in himself and drove away from the Silver Strike Lodge. Julia said little. She sat beside him, her hands tightly laced together on her lap and her gaze fixed out the window as if the lightly falling snow was the most interesting thing she had ever witnessed.

A jazz station on the stereo softly played a familiar Christmas carol, but Jamie didn't enjoy a moment of it. They were nearly out of the canyon before he finally broke the silence.

"Are you going to tell me what's wrong, or will you make me guess?"

He didn't want to ask but he hated this awkward tension between them more than he dreaded her answer.

She blinked at his directness, clearly not expecting it.

"I'm… I'm sorry. I had a…troubling conversation with someone earlier, and I can't seem to shake it."

He frowned. "Was someone at the gala bothering

you? Some of those celebrities Spence brings in for this event can be arrogant jerks, especially when they spy a beautiful woman who appears to be on her own."

He wasn't sure why she looked so startled. Did it shock her that he called her beautiful? She was, inside and out. It was about damn time someone convinced her of that.

"No. It…wasn't a celebrity."

She didn't seem inclined to say more, and he wondered how much he should probe. If she wanted to tell him, she would. After a long moment, she sighed. "I suppose I should come right out and ask you, instead of fretting about it."

"The straight course is usually a good way to plot a flight path." Barring headwinds, thunderstorms and weird air currents, anyway.

"All right." She drew in a breath. "Who is Lisa, and what happened to her?"

The tension inside the vehicle suddenly ratcheted to fever pitch.

Lisa.

He remembered a pretty cheerleader and the rush of first love and the overpowering guilt of his failures.

"You spoke with Marla." It was a question, not a statement. He had spied Marla Ellison at the gala, usually at the bar, glaring at him whenever she had the chance. He should have expected she would be there, since she did some administrative work at the community center where most of the Warrior's Hope activities were held. He also should have suspected she might confront anyone close to him. That was not exactly out of the ordinary behavior.

"She cornered me in the ladies' room and warned me to stay away from you."

That must have been when Julia's mood changed, when the light in her eyes seemed to go dim.

What had Marla told her? He could only imagine. The truth, most likely. That was more than enough.

"Probably advice you would do well to follow."

He couldn't keep the bleakness out of his tone. He was bad news to those he cared about. Lisa. Dylan. Everyone.

She studied him through the darkness. "Why do you say that? Can you…tell me what happened to Marla's sister?"

Wasn't it enough that he had purged his soul the night before about Dylan? By some miracle, she told him she didn't think he was to blame. He still didn't believe her, but it felt wonderful to know she didn't despise him for it.

Did she have to peer into every dark, ugly crevice of his past?

He didn't want to tell her anything about that horrible time and the things he had done. He wanted to drive her straight to the airport and fly her back home to Haven Point, where his sins couldn't touch her.

He couldn't, of course. Marla had opened the door, had brushed some of the old ugliness on Julia and he had no choice now but to show her the rest.

This was so hard. He never talked about it. How could he find the words to explain his choices and their grim consequences?

Though he hadn't really registered where he was driving, had merely turned aimlessly, he realized now that they had reached one of his favorite spots overlooking town, near the little park and bridge by Sweet Laurel Falls. Below them, the streets of Hope's Crossing gleamed with festive lights and holiday decorations. He pulled the vehicle over to an overlook parking space so he could focus on the conversation and turned off the stereo.

The dashboard control lights cast a greenish, unearthly light on her features. She still looked lovely and sweet as she waited for him to begin, hands folded on her lap.

"Lisa and I started dated our last year of high school. We were…serious, I guess you could say. As serious as you can be when you're that young. We talked about maybe getting married someday."

It seemed childish and immature now, those dreams they had spun after football games and on long, lazy summer afternoons by the lake.

"Someday?"

"In the far distant future. I wasn't in a hurry. I had dreams of flying, from the time I was young. I was completely focused on my goals."

He sighed, thinking of all his mistakes. He shouldn't have had a girlfriend in the first place. Not when he only wanted to graduate, go to college and finish his flight training.

A family was in his plans eventually, though at that time in his life, he couldn't see anything except what was right in front of him.

"I cared about Lisa—as much as a stupid punk can care about a girl, I suppose. Things weren't perfect, though. She had…problems. She was moody and highstrung. With the benefit of hindsight, I'm pretty sure she suffered from anxiety and possibly bipolar disorder, but at the time, I only knew our relationship could be rough."

That was an understatement. Things could seem fine between them. They could be hiking or skiing or at a party with friends when suddenly she would implode and start screaming at him for no discernible reason, accusing him of smiling at another girl or thinking someone else was prettier than she was.

The next moment, she would be bawling her eyes out as if she'd just lost her favorite pet, and she would be all over him with her apologies.

They could cycle through a half-dozen emotions in ten minutes and as a guy with other things on his mind, he found it completely exhausting. He was always so relieved when it was time to go back to college.

"We dated for a while after school, until I was about twenty. That was when my mother lost her fight with cancer."

She gazed at him, eyes drenched with compassion, and he wanted so much to lean into that comfort she offered so generously.

"I'm sorry," she murmured.

"It was a rough time. Mom was the center of our family. Our bedrock. With her gone, we all floundered.

"I was in my second year of college and busy with class and work and ROTC, and I couldn't deal with Lisa and her moods, on top of losing my mom then, plus trying to help my dad out at home whenever I could. Over Christmas, I broke things off with her. I tried to do it gently, going on about bad timing and needing space to clear my head. I told her maybe we could pick up again when I was in a better place, but she knew it was over."

He was quiet as the wind rattled the windows of his SUV. He had to tell her the rest, and he didn't want to.

The straight course is usually a good way to plot a flight path.

His own words echoed in his head and he screwed his eyes shut for a moment then opened them and found his bearings. "That night—the night I broke things off—Lisa went home, dressed in the prom dress she wore when I took her to our senior prom and swallowed a bottle of antidepressants."

"Oh, no," she whispered.

"I want to think it was just a cry for attention, that she wanted her parents or her sister or *me* to come in and find her so she could go get her stomach pumped or something. But she had been drinking, too, and the combination was too much. She lay down on her bed in her blue prom dress and never woke up."

It had been hell on earth for Jamie. He had still been reeling from losing his mother weeks earlier, then had received this second blow. He had been consumed with guilt, had nearly left school and ROTC. If not for his family, he very well might have.

Lisa's suicide had scarred him, had left him with a powerful fear of causing that depth of pain in someone else.

"How tragic and unnecessary," Julia murmured.

"I know. She had promise. She wanted to be a nurse and a mom and dreamed of writing children's books. She might have done all those things. If not for me."

Julia shifted in the seat to face him. In the greenish light, he saw her lovely features twist with compassion. "You're not responsible for the entire world, Jamie. This wasn't your fault, any more than you were to blame for Dylan's injuries."

"Her family doesn't think so. Marla never misses a chance to tell me it's my fault."

"When she told me that you killed her sister, I couldn't believe it. I had all these terrible visions— a car crash, maybe, or even a small plane crash. That might have been logical. This, though. Suicide is completely illogical. That's why it's so terrible. This was something she *chose* to do. You are not responsible for her actions."

"Those are easy words to say. Not so easy to believe. I broke up with her, knowing she was in a fragile place. Maybe I should have picked a better time to break up with her than the holidays. Or maybe I shouldn't have broken up with her at all, should have tried to work it out."

"Would you have continued to date her, even *married* her, simply because you couldn't bear the idea of hurting her?"

Yeah. He might have, as ridiculous as that seemed in retrospect. He might have married her, and they both would have been miserable. They would have divorced young. He had no doubts about that. He wouldn't have been able to live with her mood swings and her constant, wholly unwarranted accusations that he was unfaithful.

He gazed out the windows at the snowflakes twirling in patterns against the window.

He had lived with the guilt for so long, it felt as much a part of him as the small birthmark above his left hip and the scar on his chin from a gnarly bike crash when he was eight.

Maybe that's why he had taken on guilt over Dylan's injuries, too.

Rationally, he knew both were unwarranted, at least to the extent they haunted him.

Julia was right. Lisa had made her own choices. She had been an emotionally insecure, troubled young woman who probably needed intensive inpatient mental health counseling.

That didn't change the fact that he had been self-absorbed and thoughtless.

He had known she was upset after he broke things off. He should have called her parents, her minister, her sister. *Someone.*

He *had* left a message for her mother, telling her she might want to check in on Lisa. He hadn't known her parents were out of town and that her mother hadn't gotten his message until it was far too late.

As a result, Lisa—the pretty athletic cheerleader who had been homecoming queen—had died alone in her bedroom, in a pool of vomit.

The image haunted him along with others and left him inexpressibly sad.

"Marla's not the only one who blames me. Her whole family does," he said quietly. "Every year on the anniversary of her death, they call me. For sixteen years, they make sure I never forget what she might have become, if not for me."

"That is unnecessarily cruel, and someone should tell them so," she said.

He stared, taken by surprise at the hardness in her voice.

"They lost their child. They needed someone to blame."

"It never should have been you, Jamie, and they have to know that. You can see that, can't you? They're pushing their own guilt off on to you. They lived with her.

You didn't. If her behavior was as irrational as you describe, her parents, her sister, should have been the ones to make sure she got the help she needed. They were her parents. Her mental health was their responsibility. They should *never* have blamed a grieving young man, barely out of his teens."

For some ridiculous reason, emotion stung his throat at her compassion and concern for the heedless young man he had been. She hadn't known him then, yet she was still ready to jump instantly to his defense.

He had never talked about this with anyone. Not even his brothers. Was there something significant to be found in the fact that he had trusted this to Julia?

"*That's* why you decided to move to Haven Point with Aidan instead of coming home to Hope's Crossing with the rest of your family," she said after a moment, with dawning realization.

Nobody else understood that either.

He shrugged. "I didn't want to make it harder for her parents or for Marla, having to see me around town all the time."

Her chin trembled a little as she reached out and rested her hand on his. "You're a good man, Jamie Caine."

He let out a raw-sounding laugh. "You obviously weren't listening to what I just told you, then."

"I heard every word—and I heard nothing that would persuade me otherwise."

He again felt that tight achiness in his throat. For the first time in a long time, he wanted to be someone else. The kind of man who would have the right to pull her close and kiss her, here in the shadowed intimacy of a car parked on an overlook.

He couldn't do it.

He knew it was no coincidence that he only dated women who didn't want or need anything from him but a good time.

No entanglements. Don't break any hearts. Flirting is fine, anything more serious than that must be avoided at all costs.

That had been his modus operandi since Lisa's suicide.

Julia was soft and sweet and serious, worlds away from that casual kind of woman.

He wanted her more than he had ever wanted anyone else.

He curled his fingers around the leather of the steering wheel, the only way he could keep from reaching for her.

"Now that I've spilled all my ugly secrets, I suppose we should head back to the inn. The boys will be wondering where we are."

She gave him a long, careful look, and he wondered if she could sense the tumult inside him, the war between what he wanted and what was right.

"I hope they're in bed by now," she said. "It's been a long day, and we're flying home early."

"That's one good thing about flying your own plane. We can leave whenever we're ready—or whenever Aidan and Eliza are ready, anyway."

He checked for traffic, then pulled out. The snowy roads were quiet as he headed for Wild Iris House, all the while wishing he could have her and the boys to himself for one more day.

But something told him even that would never be enough.

CHAPTER SEVENTEEN

"DID YOU HAVE a good time in Hope's Crossing?"

Julia shifted her gaze from the cockpit—and the man at the controls of the plane—to find Eliza Caine studying her.

Oh, she hoped Eliza couldn't read the turmoil of her emotions in her expression. She quickly schooled her features into what she hoped looked casual and polite.

"Everything has been lovely. The boys and I had a wonderful time, from the moment we arrived. I've always wanted to ski, and Clint and Davy both loved it. And of course the gala was magical."

Until the last half hour, anyway, when a grieving sister had spilled her poison over the evening.

"Life back in Haven Point will seem rather staid after the excitement of this weekend."

"I don't think that's possible, especially considering next weekend is the Lights on the Lake Festival and the week after is Christmas. The boys are going to be bouncing off the walls at all the excitement. Anyone who has children in her household will be lucky to get five minutes of sleep until after New Year's."

"You're right about that," Eliza said with a sigh.

"Mama. Mama. Mama." As if to reinforce the point, the little boy in Eliza's arms chanted the word and wriggled to be let down.

Liam Dermot Caine was just over a year old, but already seemed a little perpetual motion machine.

"What else is new? At least for you," Julia said, with a smile at little Liam, who had to be the most adorable baby she knew.

"Are we going yet?" Davy asked from the row behind them.

"Not yet," she answered.

"About five more minutes," Jamie said from the cockpit without turning around. "I've got a few more preflight checks to go through before we can be on our way."

The boy turned back to the travel game he was playing with Clint and Maddie.

Nobody else seemed at all nervous about the flight, all apparently seasoned veterans of air travel. This was only her second takeoff, and she could feel the anxiety building. To distract herself, she held her arms out to the wriggling boy in Eliza's lap. "May I?" she asked.

Her friend looked grateful. "Please!"

Liam had always liked Julia, for reasons she didn't quite understand. Most babies did. He launched himself at her, and Julia scooped him up with a little laugh.

"I don't know how long he'll stay happy," Eliza said with a note of apology in her voice. "He needs a nap, which tends to make him cranky."

"I totally understand, Liam," Julia said. "I'm the exact same way."

"Everybody still buckled up?" Jamie said from the front. "This is it."

Julia made faces to Aidan and Eliza's little boy while Jamie taxied toward the runway. She enjoyed watching the baby's eyes go wide as the plane accelerated rapidly and then lifted up into the sky.

She could relate to that, too. There was something so astonishing about flying.

"That was fun, wasn't it?" she whispered to the boy, who giggled.

"Mom, did you bring any crayons? We want to color now," Maddie said as the jet seemed to level off.

"I think I've got some in my bag. Let me see what I can find."

While Eliza was busy scouring her cavernous bag, Julia rocked little Liam and hummed to him. His mother was right. He needed a nap. She could see his eyes begin to droop and feel his wriggling against her become less frequent.

She pulled a blanket over him, still rocking softly in her seat, and after about five minutes, his eyes closed completely and he seemed to sag against her.

Gazing down at his little features made her insides ache. She and Maksym had talked about children. He had wanted a round half dozen. She thought she would have been content with three or four. If things had turned out differently, she might have been a mother several times over by now.

She would have been a good mother. Though she felt over her head with Davy and Clint, something told her that with a little more practice she would find the caretaking role far more comfortable.

She had some of the most important qualities in a mother—patience and a heart that wanted desperately to love.

The baby nestled against her, his little head tucked under her chin.

"I can take him for you, if your arms are tired," Eliza said softly.

"Don't you dare," she whispered. "I would be perfectly happy holding him all day."

She may have dozed off herself—a few sleepless nights in a row could do that. When she opened her eyes some time later, she found Jamie gazing at her from the cockpit, wearing an odd expression that sent tingling heat through her.

She swallowed hard and shifted her gaze to find Eliza also watching her. Her friend's expression was more clear. She looked unmistakably worried about something. Maybe Julia was holding the baby incorrectly. She readjusted him as Jamie spoke up.

"We should be landing in about ten minutes. Make sure your seat belts are buckled and tray tables are stowed. Et cetera. Et cetera."

Liam stirred a little at his deep voice, though he didn't awaken. She cuddled the baby closer, wishing they didn't have to land, to return to real life.

The last forty-eight hours had been…earthshaking. She felt as if she were a different person than the timid woman who had climbed onto this very jet Friday.

She glanced at their pilot. He had barely exchanged two words with her after their lengthy discussion on the overlook. All through their drive back to the inn, then after they arrived to find the boys in bed, he seemed distracted, his mind a million miles away—or sixteen years, anyway.

Jamie's story about Lisa had explained so much. It must have been a seminal moment in his life, losing his mother to cancer, then his girlfriend to suicide within a short, devastating window of time. How difficult it must have been for him, especially when he felt responsible for the death of one of them.

She wished she could impress on him that he wasn't to blame for Lisa's death. How much had that guilt he experienced at such a formative age shaped the man he had become?

No wonder he was so good with casual relationships, keeping women at arm's length. His charm served as a careful barrier, preventing any women from taking him too seriously. He made sure every relationship was only surface deep and broke them off quickly because he feared what might happen if any woman grew to care for him too deeply.

He didn't want to hurt anyone.

What would he do if she told him she was afraid she was falling for him? He would panic, would do everything in his power to put a safe distance between them.

Maybe he had already started. She could feel him pulling away.

He hadn't moved out yet. She had a few weeks left with him before his house would be ready. She would simply have to savor every moment she had with him while doing her best to keep him from figuring out her feelings were already growing.

The plane landed so smoothly, she hadn't realized they were on the ground until Jamie turned back to them all.

"Here you are. Safe and sound."

Her heart gave a little squeeze, which she firmly ignored. The next few moments were filled with the flurry of unloading the plane and saying goodbye to Aidan and Eliza, then bundling into Jamie's SUV, identical to the one they had left in Hope's Crossing.

He still seemed a million miles away as he drove them back to her house, saying little to either the boys or her. Was he regretting the things he had told her? The kisses between them? Their growing closeness?

"Boys, help me carry in the bags, can you?" he asked when they reached her house. Davy and Clinton both jumped to help him. They adored Jamie, and she envied them that they could do so freely.

The cats sauntered out to meet them when she unlocked the door. While they gave affection to the boys, they merely sniffed at Julia's attempts to pet them, clearly miffed that she had left them here, to be fed by a neighbor girl.

Her house was cold, and the Christmas decorations seemed a little forlorn, until Davy rushed to the tree and turned it on.

"I think this is everything," Jamie said, still with that distracted expression.

The man who had teased her with kisses after each ski disaster had been replaced by a remote stranger.

"Thank you. Clint, Davy, what do you say to Jamie for taking us on a wonderful weekend?"

"Thanks, Jamie," they said in unison. Without prompting, they rushed to him and threw their arms around his waist. Jamie hugged them back, looking adorably awkward.

"It was my pleasure. I'm glad I had someone to come with me. I would have looked pretty silly, dancing by myself at the gala."

Predictably, this made both boys giggle.

"I wish we didn't have to go back to school tomorrow," Davy said with a sigh. "I wish Christmas was this week."

The children might be excited about it, but Julia tried to squash her panic at the thought of all she still had to do.

"It will be here before you know it," he said. "Don't wish away all the fun of this week and next. This weekend is the Lights on the Lake Festival, remember? You're excited about that, right?"

"I guess so. We've never been before," Clinton said. "We didn't live here before."

"That's right. Well, you'll have to be sure to go this year. Make sure Julia takes you."

She noticed with a pang that he made no effort to include himself in their weekend plans.

Clint must have picked up on that, too. "You won't be going?" the older brother asked.

"I'm not sure yet. I have a couple of out-of-town trips this week, and I don't know if I'll be back by then. I'll have to see."

Jamie sent a sidelong glance at Julia, a look she couldn't interpret.

"We'll get there, don't worry," she said to the boys. "We can't miss the Lights on the Lake. It's going to be another fun weekend. Meantime, both of you have homework to finish before school tomorrow. Take your suitcases into your room and put the dirty clothes in the hamper and the clean clothes back in your drawers."

The boys grumbled a little, which she took as a sign that they were beginning to feel more comfortable in her home. Despite their long-suffering sighs, they complied immediately.

"I've said it before, and I'll say it again," Jamie said. "Those are some great kids you've got there."

Julia smiled. "I would have to agree with you."

When she tried to remember her solitary life of a month ago, she could hardly recall what things were like before the boys entered her world. She was deeply grateful for whatever instinct had prompted her to follow after them that day and insist they let her drive them home. She had to believe someone else would have realized the predicament they were in with their mother gone and would have called in the authorities. Julia had been the one to come to their aid, though, and because of it, her life had been enriched far beyond her imaginings.

"Thank you again, Jamie," she said. "It was truly an adventure of a lifetime. I did two things that had been on my bucket list for a long time—flying an airplane, and learning to ski. Three, actually. I forgot! I tried escargot in those quiche things Alexandra prepared. They were delicious."

"Glad I could help," he said, his low voice thrumming along her nerve endings.

Color rose up again as she remembered those sexy ski lessons he had offered, interspersed with kisses and laughter, and twirling with him around a dance floor in a gown that made her feel like a princess at the ball.

She would remember this weekend for the rest of her life.

"I don't expect I'll be around much this week," he said. "As I told the boys, I've got a couple of back-to-back trips that will take me from coast-to-coast. I don't know how the timing will end up."

She would miss him, but she could never tell him that.

He looked at the Christmas tree and then back at her. "I didn't want to say anything to the boys because

I didn't want to end up disappointing them, but I'll do my best to be back in time for the Lights on the Lake festival on Saturday. Maybe, if you want, we could all go together."

Was he asking because he wanted to spend more time with Clint and Davy or because he wanted to be with her? She didn't know, and she was afraid to ask, even as anticipation sparkled through her.

"That would be great. The boys love spending time with you." She did as well, but that was something else she wasn't about to tell him.

"Sounds good. I'll let you know."

"Okay. Thank you again for bringing us home safely."

"My pleasure," he said. "All of it."

Was he talking about that heated embrace at the inn or those teasing kisses on the ski slopes? Or perhaps neither.

"Fly safely this week," she said. Though she knew it was dangerous, she leaned on tiptoes and kissed his cheek.

His eyes held surprise and something else. Sweetness tangled with tenderness. His mouth shifted, and he kissed her, really kissed her—a soft, gentle, almost chaste kiss that made her heart ache, for reasons she couldn't have explained.

After a short moment, he eased away. "Good night," he murmured, then hurried out the door. She listened to his footsteps on the stair treads outside her door for a long moment, then forced herself to move, aware that he hadn't even left Haven Point and she already missed him.

CHAPTER EIGHTEEN

NEARLY A WEEK LATER, Jamie headed away from the airport in Shelter Springs and turned his vehicle toward Haven Point.

He couldn't quite believe this was how he felt, but he really didn't want to see the inside of an airplane for the next few days. He had made four trips from California to New York City and back in six days, as the acquisition negotiations heated up.

They had been trying to wrap the sale up before the New Year, and it appeared that would happen. As a major stockholder in Caine Tech, he was happy about the financial benefits, but right now he only wanted to be in one place for five damn minutes.

Home.

Julia's place called to him, even as he knew it wasn't his home. He was only a temporary resident there—more temporary than he had planned, actually. A few days earlier, he'd had a phone call from his contractor, telling him his condo would be ready earlier than expected. If all went as planned, he could move in a few days after Christmas.

The prospect should have excited him. He had been so looking forward to having his own place, his first house after years of bunking in impermanent military housing.

Instead, whenever he thought about moving away from Julia and the boys, he felt an odd pang in his chest. He would miss them all. Somehow over the last few weeks, their lives had become intertwined, in a way he never would have expected.

Dozens of times over the preceding week, he had wanted to call Julia to see how things were: if she had heard more about Mikaela Slater, how Clint had done on his spelling test, if she was done Christmas shopping for them.

He had scrolled to her number on his phone more than once but had ended up not connecting the call. He wasn't sure why not. What harm would a phone call do? Each time, he had hesitated, though.

He was afraid. That was the truth of it. He was coming to care for her and the boys too much, and it scared the hell out of him.

He couldn't help the little burst of anticipation as he pulled onto her street and saw the big, gracious Victorian at the end, the Christmas tree in the window adding a cheery note of color through the snow.

He wouldn't stop downstairs tonight. No doubt they had plans, and she probably wouldn't appreciate him dropping by for no reason, simply because he had missed them all.

The moment he unlocked the outside door to the entryway, he was met by a heady, delicious smell—something decadent that involved almonds and sugar and vanilla. If he wasn't mistaken, she was baking cookies. The seductive scent made his mouth water.

Through Julia's closed door, he heard Davy singing "Jingle bells, Batman smells" at the top of his voice, loud enough to be heard through Julia's closed door.

A minute later, Clinton joined in on the "Robin laid an egg" line.

Jamie chuckled, tempted to sing along himself as he headed for the stairs. He only made it up one step before her door burst open, and both boys rushed out as if they had set some sort of trip wire to alert them to intruders.

"You're back, you're back!" Davy was practically jumping up and down with excitement. "I just saw your car in the driveway. Where were you? You were gone *so long*."

A sweet warmth seeped through him at their delighted greeting. How had these two boys managed to tangle their fingers around his heart?

He paused on the step to greet them and nearly toppled backward when they both ran at him at once for a fierce three-person hug.

"Hey, guys," he said with a smile, when he could breathe again. "How have you been? Anything fun happen while I was gone?"

"Yes. We had a snow day on Tuesday, and we went to the library with Julia, then came home and had a snowball fight and built a snow fort. It's awesome. It might be big enough for you. Want to see?"

"Maybe later, okay?"

"I got a hundred percent on my spelling test," Clint informed him. "And Missy Fitzgerald fell on the swings at school Thursday and broke her nose. There was *so much* blood. You should have seen it. It was totally gross."

"Poor girl. I hope you helped her."

"I did," the boy assured him. "I ran to get the recess teacher, and then I went to the bathroom for paper towels to help clean up. When she came back to school yesterday, I wouldn't let my friends make fun of the big bandage on her face either."

"Good job. A gentleman never laughs at people who've had a rough time, and he always tries to help out when he can."

"I know," Clint said. "I always do what I think my dad would have done."

"You can't go wrong with that," he said, squeezing the boy's shoulder.

"Guess what?" Davy said. "Tonight is the boat parade, and we're going! Do you want to go with us?"

Oh. He had completely forgotten about that. His plans for a quiet day at home, chilling in front of a basketball game with a beer, suddenly slipped out of reach.

"Don't hound the man before he even has time to put his bags inside his apartment." Julia's quiet voice cut through the foyer, and his heartbeat accelerated. He turned his head, and his heart seemed to stop altogether.

Oh. How had he forgotten in the span of a week how lovely she was?

Her stunning violet eyes sparkled in the chandelier in the foyer, and she smiled at him with that mouth he knew tasted like heaven.

"Welcome back," she said softly. He wanted to think she was happy to see him, but he couldn't quite tell.

"Thanks. It's nice to be home."

"You might want to wait until you've been home a few more moments before you say that. The boys and I are baking cookies, and they are enjoying the fruits of our labor, maybe a little too much."

By that, he inferred that they were bouncing off the walls from an overload of sugar and excitement. He might have figured that out by the top-of-the-lungs concert he had heard upon his arrival.

"We have like a zillion sugar cookies to decorate," Clint informed him. "We're selling them at the festival tonight."

"That sounds like fun."

"I'm super good at decorating cookies," Davy declared. "You should see them. We're making angels and Christmas trees and stars and ornaments. I'm best at the ornaments. Want to help us?"

"Davy," Julia admonished. "Jamie just barely got back in town. I'm sure he'd like to be home for five minutes before you try to put him to work."

"It's fine. I don't mind. It actually sounds like fun."

"Really?"

The cookie decorating didn't appeal to him as much as hanging out with the three of them. "I don't have anything else going. I was just going to relax upstairs—where, according to you, I won't get much rest anyway."

"A few more hands definitely would be welcome." Her cheeks were pink, but he couldn't tell if she was embarrassed Davy had asked or pleased that Jamie had accepted.

He wasn't sure why he had said yes. All week long, he had been telling himself he needed to stay away from her and the boys, that he was courting trouble by spending so much time with them. This playing house thing had been fun for a while. The boys were cute as hell, no getting around that, and there was something undeniably appealing about unwrapping each tight, stuffy layer around Julia Winston and unleashing the sensual woman inside.

This game was becoming far too dangerous. He was

running the risk of hurting her and the boys. He was moving out in only a few weeks, and he didn't see how he could remain a part of their lives.

Every time he told himself he needed to stay away, he couldn't bear the thought of not seeing them again.

Anyway, he hadn't helped her check all the items off her list. The previous weekend had been a good start, but he still had work to do, right?

"Just let me take my bag upstairs, then I'll be ready to get my cookie on."

"No rush. We'll be at it all afternoon. Take a rest, if you need to."

"I'm good. I'll be down in a few."

He didn't want to tell her that seeing the three of them again, being a part of their enthusiasm and infectious joy, gave him more energy than he'd had in a week.

"I THINK THIS is the last batch."

Jamie looked up from decorating a funky-looking snowman, complete with sunglasses and a beret, to where Julia stood holding a cookie sheet.

"Good thing," he said. "You don't have a spare inch of room in this kitchen for one more cookie."

"Except in my mouth," Davy said, which made his brother laugh.

Personally, Jamie couldn't see how either boy could stuff another cookie inside. They had each had entirely too many already. They were covered to their elbows in frosting, and both had some in their hair or smudged on their cheeks.

Jamie couldn't see his own reflection, which was probably a good thing. He had a feeling he would see more frosting coating his person than either of the boys.

The kitchen smelled divine, of sugar and cinnamon and deliciousness, and every available surface was covered in cookies in various stages of decorations.

"How are you holding up?" she asked.

"My wrists now have repetitive stress disorder from spreading frosting, and I'm pretty sure it will take weeks to come down from my sugar high. Other than that, I'm fine."

The lovely sound of her laughter rippled through the kitchen and down his spine. Despite his entirely legitimate complaints, he was enjoying himself more than he had in a long time.

"You are a good sport, Jamie Caine," she said, a soft smile dancing on the mouth he suddenly wanted to kiss more than he wanted to breathe.

"It's for a good cause, right?"

"Yes. The county battered women's shelter, which is in terrible shape."

"Our effort and sacrifice will have been worthwhile, then."

"Can we be done with decorating cookies now?" Davy asked, in the same tone he might have used when asking if someone could please stop slamming his hand in a car door.

She laughed and kissed the top of his head. "Yes. You guys were champs. Thank you. We're in for a long night tonight, so why don't you go read in your rooms or play quietly for a while?"

They left with alacrity, and Julia suddenly flushed. He wondered if she only now realized that ordering the boys out of the kitchen would leave the two of them alone.

"Um, you're a champ, too. I can't believe you decorated all those cookies. I have no idea how you accomplished such a Herculean task."

"Neither do I. My hands might be permanently disfigured, and I'll never be able to fly a plane again." He made his fingers into claws, and she gave a mock scowl at his teasing. It slid away quickly, into sincere gratitude.

"Seriously, Jamie. Thanks. I'm realizing now, we wouldn't have been able to finish them all without you. I would have been decorating cookies as we walked out the door to the boat parade."

"Glad to do my part for the Haven Point Helping Hands." He didn't add that his efforts had been for *her* and for the boys, not for Eliza, McKenzie or any of the other women in her group.

"I heard the boys begging you to go with us tonight. You don't have to give in to them, you know. I'm sure you're tired after traveling all week."

If he were smart, he would take the out she was offering him, but he couldn't bring himself to say the words.

"I'm looking forward to it," he said truthfully. "Christmas seems more meaningful when you can see it through the eyes of children. I don't think I ever realized that, until Davy and Clint these last few weeks."

She smiled warmly at him, looking so rosy and delicious, it was all he could do not to tug her into his lap.

"I do need to go get cleaned up before we leave. Do I have time for that?"

"Of course. Come back downstairs when you're ready. You can take some cookies up with you, if you want. We have more than enough."

"I'm not sure I will ever be able to eat another sugar cookie in my life," he said. Or at least not for a few more hours.

"THAT WAS SUPER FUN," Clint declared, as Jamie pulled out of the great parking space he found near the Haven Point city offices and into the steady traffic leaving the lakefront park that provided the best viewing for the annual boat parade.

"The best!" Davy said. "I loved all the boats and I especially loved seeing Santa Claus at the end."

"I'm glad you enjoyed it." Julia smiled at both boys, who were buckled into the backseat of Jamie's SUV. The night had been truly magical, filled with good friends, delicious food and the sense of belonging to something bigger than herself.

She had always loved the Lights on the Lake festival but this year had been exceptional.

She couldn't help remembering what Jamie had said earlier, about Christmas being more meaningful when glimpsed through the eyes of a child. He was absolutely right. The annual tradition had been sheer delight.

Everything had seemed perfect—the decorations, the musical entertainment, the food. Was it only because she was enjoying it all with Davy and Clint? Or did Jamie's presence have something to do with the magic of the evening?

"I'm really glad you came with us, Jamie," Clint said, as if echoing her thoughts.

The sincerity in his voice made her a little teary eyed. Both boys adored Jamie. How could they not? He was funny and warm and wonderful with them, like a favorite uncle should be.

He made everything more fun—and not just for her and the boys. Did he know that was his own particular gift, adding color and joy to the world?

Davy yawned, eyes already drooping. Though the drive

from downtown to her house only took a few moments, he was asleep before Jamie pulled into the driveway—and his brother wasn't far behind.

She couldn't blame them. They had worked hard to help her with the cookies, all while trying to contain their excitement at the parade and the festival—not to mention their natural anticipation of Christmas, now just days away.

"Davy. Wake up," she said softly. The boy groaned but didn't open his eyes.

"I can carry him in," Jamie said.

She decided not to argue, especially since she knew firsthand how heavy a sleepy six-year-old could be. After unbuckling Davy from his booster seat, Julia stood aside as Jamie scooped him into his arms.

"I can come back for Clint, if you'll give me a minute," he said.

"I can walk," the older boy mumbled. He climbed out, wobbling a bit in his sleepy stupor until Julia put an arm over his shoulder.

"I'll help you," she said. As long as she led the way, Clint was able to put one foot in front of the other as they made their way up the stairs and down the hall to his bedroom, where they found Jamie had settled a still-sleeping Davy onto his bed and was pulling off his parka and shoes.

"Pajamas?" he asked softly.

She found them in the drawer, and, working together, they quickly had both boys dressed in their pajamas. Julia couldn't help think about how her life might have been different, if this had been her husband, her children, coming home after a holiday outing.

After the children were in bed, perhaps she and her

husband would retire to their own bedroom to stretch the wonderful evening out as long as possible.

The thought made her blush fiercely, and she hoped Jamie didn't notice.

"I don't need to shower?" Clint asked, clearly confused, as she helped him into his pajama bottoms.

"Not tonight. You can both shower in the morning before church. Just brush your teeth. You need to wash away all that cotton candy."

The boy went into the bathroom and mechanically went through the motions. Though it wasn't the most conscientious job she'd ever seen, she decided to let it go tonight.

He slipped back into bed, and she kissed his forehead. "Good night, my dear," she murmured.

"Night," Clint said. To her shock, he suddenly threw his arms around her neck.

"Thanks for taking us, Julia," he said sleepily. "You're the best."

She was already feeling strangely emotional. His words sent her over the edge and forced her to fight back a sniffle.

Embarrassed, she tried not to show how his words touched her as she and Jamie slipped out of the room and closed the door behind them. She knew she hadn't succeeded when Jamie squeezed her arm.

"Are you okay?" he asked.

The concern in his voice sent the emotions bubbling over, and she blinked back a tear—or two, or maybe ten.

"That boy. How sweet was that?"

"Sweet as your sugar cookies," he said.

"Davy has seemed happy here, almost from the beginning. Maybe because he's younger, I don't know, but

I do know the transition to living with me hasn't been as easy for Clint. I think he misses his mother more."

"Because he's the older of the two, he probably has a little more understanding of the situation. He understands she's ill and maybe won't ever be well enough to care for them."

The situation made her ache, for the boys, for their mother and for herself, too, if she were honest. They would leave her at some point. It was as inevitable as the dawning of a new year.

She wasn't sure how she would go on without them.

"You're doing a good thing for them, Julia."

"Am I? This is just a temporary placement. Social services could decide to yank them away at any minute. I want to think Wynona Emmett would fight to keep them here with me, but she doesn't have power to make the ultimate decision. I'm constantly worried that just when they have begun to feel comfortable here, they'll be shuttled somewhere else."

He gazed at her for a long moment, uttered what sounded like a curse word under his breath, then pulled her into his arms.

He'd taken off his outerwear while helping the boys and wore only jeans and a soft cable-knit sweater. She leaned her cheek against it, wishing she could stay there forever wrapped in the circle of his arms, blocking out the rest of the world and the reality that awaited.

"Whatever time you have with them, you're making a difference. Remember that. Your impact in their lives won't be in vain, whatever happens. They will never forget how you rescued them."

A tear or two spilled over, but she hid her face against

his chest and wrapped her arms around his waist, grateful for his strength and his wisdom.

They stood that way for a long time while the cats snored on the sofa and the lights of the Christmas tree gleamed against the cold night.

She was in love with him.

As he held her, as she listened to his steady, dependable heartbeat beneath her cheek, the truth of it seemed to seep into her bones, her skin.

She loved him. She loved his strength, she loved his kindness, she loved the man he had become in spite of the tough times he had endured.

Oh. She had to be the world's biggest fool.

The man had *keep away* written in huge letters around his heart. He had spent his entire adult life trying to avoid commitment and the very sort of love she wanted to offer. She had no idea how to break through those barriers he had built, or if she should even try.

How had she let it happen? She knew how dangerous he was. Long before she ever agreed to rent her upstairs to him, she had been aware of his reputation and the danger he might pose to her heart. Somehow she had let him in anyway.

He seemed content now to continue holding her, and she couldn't bring herself to pull away. Along with the shock of realizing her feelings for him, she was also aware of something else.

She wanted him. Rather desperately. The strength of his arms reminded her of everything she had lost and everything she had given up. Everywhere their bodies touched, little starbursts of heat seemed to form, then expand.

If he kissed her again, she would be lost.

That would be a disaster. She'd already made enough of a fool of herself.

With supreme effort, she forced herself to back away and pasted on a polite smile. "Sorry. I didn't mean to blubber all over you. You're a very kind man, Jamie Caine."

The look he gave her smoldered with heat. "You think so?"

"Yes. But I'm sure the boys and I have taken enough of your day, between the cookies and the boat festival. Now you've helped with bedtime and let me sniffle all over your chest. Yes, you're a kind man and you've done more than enough. You're probably sorry you ever asked about renting my upstairs apartment."

He opened his mouth, then closed it again. She had the oddest thought that perhaps he might need her and the boys as much as they needed him. She dismissed the idea almost as soon as it came to her. Jamie needed *something* in his life, but it certainly wasn't a harried librarian and her two troubled foster children.

"I'm not sorry," he said. "I've enjoyed every moment of it. After everything Clint and Davy have been through, they deserve to have a wonderful Christmas."

"I hope I can give them that," she said. She was certain as the holidays approached, the boys would be missing their mother terribly. She had no idea how to compensate for what they had lost.

"You already have," he said firmly. "They know they have a safe, warm place with someone who cares about them. Right now you, Julia Winston, are exactly what they need."

She wanted to cry all over again as warmth bloomed in her chest. Oh, she loved him. Her heart was already breaking, anticipating the inevitable pain around the corner.

"Thank you. That was the perfect thing to say."

"I meant every word."

"I know." She forced herself to smile. "As I said, you're a very kind man. A little too kind. You're not very good at saying no, but I promise, we will try not to bug you about anything for the next few days. I promise, I'll make sure the boys leave you in peace for at least a few days."

Oddly, as he let himself out and headed up the stairs, she thought he didn't seem as relieved about that promise as she might have expected.

CHAPTER NINETEEN

A FEW WEEKS EARLIER he never would have believed it possible, but Jamie was beginning to dislike the overpowering stillness of his apartment.

Either his downstairs neighbors were avoiding him or their schedules were suddenly in direct opposition. The day after the festival, Julia and the boys seemed unusually busy, coming and going all day. He had his own errands to run that day, and it seemed like every time he pulled up, she was driving away with the boys in the backseat. And every time he seemed to be leaving again, he passed her on her way back home.

Monday morning, he had to leave again for the East Coast so the Caine Tech brass could have one last acquisition meeting before the holidays.

By the time he returned late Thursday afternoon, he found himself eager to see Julia and the boys again. When he spotted her sporty little SUV pulling into the driveway just ahead of him, he figured the fates had finally conspired to do him a favor and give him his wish.

She didn't pull into the detached garage, as she usually did, but parked just off the side door that led to her kitchen. When she hurried to the backseat, he thought she might be helping the boys out, but instead she struggled to remove several large, bulky shopping bags. He hurried forward.

"You've been busy," he said.

"Hi," she said, rather breathlessly. "This is the result of several weeks of shopping. I didn't do all this in an afternoon, I can assure you."

"Good to know."

"Andie Bailey is having a Christmas party for a bunch of the children, complete with pizza and games. I think she's doing it to give other parents a chance to squeeze in some last-minute shopping."

That was the sort of thing people in Haven Point did for each other, throw impromptu parties to help other harried parents. "Good idea."

"I know, isn't it? I thought this would be the perfect chance for me to bring Clint's and Davy's Christmas presents home from my secret hiding place at the library, so I could wrap them at a time they're guaranteed not to walk in."

"Good thinking."

"I'm running out of time, since tomorrow is the last day of school for them and I have to run to Boise for a library association meeting."

"No reason you can't get this out of the way tonight, then."

He took two of the large bags from her and picked up two more from her backseat before carrying them inside the house and into her living room.

Her cats immediately scampered to him as if they hadn't seen him in weeks.

"Hey, girls," he said to them, and was greeted by a chorus of meows.

His arms were too full to pet them, but they didn't seem to care. They followed him inside anyway.

"Where do you want these things?"

With one of her bags, she gestured to a room he hadn't been in.

"Just put everything on my bed. I already set a folding table up in there, thinking I could lock the door if the boys come home early. Andie promised she would call and warn me when she was on their way with them, but I don't want to take any chances. You never know what might happen."

"Look at you, figuring out this whole sneaky Christmas thing."

She shrugged. "Andie is really saving the day for me, and I don't think I'm the only one in this boat. I wasn't sure when I would have the chance to wrap everything. I've been afraid to do it at night, since Clinton is a restless sleeper. He has bad dreams."

Poor kid. Jamie's heart ached for both boys. "How's their mother?"

"Okay. From what I understand, she finally remembers the boys, but doesn't seem to understand they're her sons. Her doctor suggests we take the boys up to Portland. He's hoping that will jog her memories. I don't know if they're up for that. I told him we would have to see."

He would go with her, he decided. Though he had been trying to tell himself he needed distance, he couldn't let her undertake such a stressful thing on her own. "Say the word. I can make it happen."

"Thank you." Her features softened for a moment, then turned brisk again. "What am I doing, standing here wasting time talking, when I have presents to wrap?"

She hurried through the doorway, and he followed her into a room that completely took him by surprise.

He had seen her bedroom before, when he helped her in during her illness, but it struck him now how sensual it was, decorated in rich, vibrant colors, with Persian rugs, tasseled pillows, a big bed covered in a brocade canopy and shelves and shelves of books everywhere he looked.

For the first time, he realized her bedroom was directly below his own. The thought of her sleeping in that big bed, all tousled and warm only a few feet beneath him, sent heat curling through him.

He eyed the presents piled on the bed. "How long is the party supposed to last?"

"Andie assured me they would be going until about seven. That gives me an hour and a half."

"You'll never make it. There's no way you can wrap all these presents by yourself in that amount of time. I'd better give you a hand."

She opened her mouth as if to argue, then quickly closed it again. "Do you think I went overboard on the gifts? I've never been Santa Claus before. I think I went a bit crazy in the toy store."

"They will love everything," he assured her. "How could they not? They're kids who will have new toys at Christmas."

"I hope you're right." She shrugged out of her coat, and he saw she was wearing a blue sweater with tiny silver bells embroidered on it. She looked festive and cheerful and completely adorable.

They were in a bedroom, alone in her lovely house. Something told Jamie this was a potentially dangerous situation, that he would have a tough time keeping his hands off her.

He could handle it, he told himself. He shifted.

"Where do you want me to start? I should warn you I'm not the best at wrapping gifts."

"Now you tell me, when I'm counting on you!" She smiled. "Why don't you do all the books? They should be easy enough to wrap. I'll grab another folding chair."

He picked up a roll of wrapping paper and went to work. After she set down the chair she brought in, she turned on a wireless speaker by her bed and found a Christmas station.

It was an odd, comfortable experience, sitting in her cozy bedroom and wrapping presents while they talked about Christmases they remembered.

She told him about the stockings her mother sewed every year and filled with small, meaningful gifts that came from the heart and showed him the stockings she had hand-sewn for the boys with their names on them. He told her about the craziness of Christmas morning with seven kids, all vying to be the first to open gifts.

"Where did you travel this week?" she asked, when the conversation began to lull.

"New York," he said. "We flew out Monday and came back this afternoon. I had an extra day in the middle there to twiddle my thumbs."

He had gone shopping and had picked out a few more things he needed to wrap himself, but he didn't mention that to her.

"Do you like New York?"

"It's a great city all the time but particularly at Christmas," he said. "I know that sounds like a cliché and everybody says that, but it's a cliché because it's true. There's music on every street corner, special shows in some of the theaters, wildly decorated windows. It's vibrant and exciting."

And the entire time he had been there, he had longed to be home, here in Haven Point with Julia and the boys.

"I would love to see that someday," she said, a soft, wistful note in her voice.

He came within a breath of telling her he would take her the very next time he had to fly out for Caine Tech, but the words caught in his throat. He couldn't tell her that. Nor could he take her to New York City. He was moving out in a little more than a week, and he still needed to find a way to tell her.

Before he knew it, they had gone through three rolls of gift paper and finished wrapping everything in the bags.

"Is that the last of it?" he asked.

"I think so." She peered around the room and even under the bed to make sure they didn't miss anything. "Yes. That's it," she said.

"Where do you plan to hide the stuff? You can put it upstairs at my place, if you want."

"I have a secret in my closet," she said with a mischievous smile.

"Now that sounds intriguing," he answered, trying to ignore how desperately he wanted to kiss her.

She led him to a small walk-in closet that he thought might once have served as a place for a baby crib off the master bedroom. He had a feeling Winston House had many secrets still to reveal.

Her closet smelled like her, clean and crisp and delicious, of vanilla and fresh apples and other scents he couldn't identify. He wanted to close his eyes and just inhale.

It seemed a very intimate thing to be standing in her closet, surrounded by her clothes. He could hardly believe that he had once thought she was a boring librarian. Julia was far more than she appeared on the surface.

Her expression was almost impish as she slid aside several dresses on hangers to reveal a panel painted the same color as the drywall around it. The panel was about eighteen inches across and perhaps four feet tall.

"What's this? A secret tunnel?"

"My father said his grandfather built it during Prohibition, when this was a dry county. He had a still in here and made his own corn whiskey. I love imagining that. He looks so stern and forbidding in every picture I've ever seen. Somehow it makes me so happy to know he had this hidden dangerous side, too."

Like his great-granddaughter. Jamie doubted she would see any similarity but he could. She was serious and somewhat formal on the outside, but that layer concealed someone who loved to ski, thrived on adventure and kissed like a dream.

"You're sure the presents will be safe from prying eyes in there?"

"The boys have no idea this hidey-hole even exists. They'll never find my stash."

"Who knew you could be so sneaky?"

She beamed as if he had just handed her a bouquet of glorious roses. "Now we just have to find room for everything in there."

"You'll also have to make sure you don't misplace any presents in the deep, dark corners of your hiding spot."

"Right, especially after we've gone to the trouble to wrap them all."

The two of them took several trips to carry presents into the small closet. It required a little effort and geometric calculations, but they finally were able to stack the boxes in a manner that ensured everything fit.

"That's the last of it," she declared, stuffing in a small box he knew contained a baseball.

"Great."

Did she have any idea he was dying here? Every time she brushed against him, trying to wedge one more present in the space, he could feel his heartbeat ratchet up a notch.

Working together in this contained space had been torture the last ten minutes. The scent of her overwhelmed him, taunting and tantalizing. With every breath, he inhaled her.

"Thank you," she said. "You're right. Without you, I couldn't have finished in time."

Jamie forced a smile, desperate to leave the confines of the closet.

"Glad I could, uh, help."

She studied him. "Is something wrong? Your voice sounds odd. Can I get you a glass of water or something?"

He sighed. "Water isn't what I need right now."

"What is?"

"You."

The word slipped out before his internal censors could shut it down. It seemed to hover between them, a living, breathing thing.

"Oh." She gazed at him, eyes huge in her features and her soft mouth slightly parted.

"Yeah. Oh," he muttered. "Sorry. I'll get out of your way."

"Jamie."

She said only his name, her voice pitched low, but it

was enough to tell him he wasn't the only one feeling this tug and pull.

He wasn't sure if he made the first move or if she did. He only knew that an instant later, she was in his arms, and he was kissing her with all the pent-up heat he had been trying to shove down all week.

She tasted better than she smelled, like Christmas and birthdays and every wonderful thing that had ever happened to him. He felt the soft weight of her arms around his neck, the delicious curl of her fingers in his hair. She pressed her curves against him, and his body hardened instantly.

All he could think about was holding her, touching her, tasting her. Skin on skin, mouth against mouth. Her softness, his hardness.

They kissed for several heady moments, there in the cloistered silence.

"Why are we standing in the closet?" she finally murmured against his mouth. "I have a perfectly good bed only steps away."

Heat raced through him at her words. "Excellent point."

She tangled her fingers with his and tugged him out into her bedroom. After the intimate confines of her closet, the bedroom felt airy and cool.

It provided a bracing reminder that he shouldn't be doing this, but it disappeared the moment she pulled him to her bed and kissed him with that sweet, willing passion.

He would only kiss her a moment, he told himself. They would stop before things went too far. The boys would be home soon, anyway. He couldn't walk away yet. How could he? They could play this dangerous game a few moments more, before the rest of the world intruded.

He lowered himself to the bed and pulled her with him, loving the way her body rose to meet him. When she whispered his name and framed his face with her smooth, soft hands with a tenderness that made him ache, he totally forgot about the boys, about the presents, about his vow to leave shortly. All he could focus on in this moment was Julia and this tangle of emotion between them and how fiercely he wanted her.

The skin of her back beneath her sweater was the softest thing he had ever felt, warm and smooth and amazing. He couldn't get enough and wanted to explore each inch. Heat swirled between them, especially when she shifted until she was astride him, her softness cradling his hardness in the most perfect way. She gasped and arched against him, restless and hungry, making small gasping breaths against his mouth as she slid back and forth, searching, searching. With all the layers of clothing between them, this simulation of making love—close but so very far away—was agony and incredible pleasure at once.

A moment more and then he would stop, he told himself. He kissed her, sucking her tongue deep into his mouth.

And then it happened.

She gasped and arched against him, and he felt the delicious shudders ripple through her before she seemed to turn boneless against him.

Watching this woman who could sometimes be so prickly and serious come undone in his arms was the single most erotic moment of his life.

Her eyes closed, her lips parted slightly, her entire

body seemed to pulse with energy and life. She was beautiful, and he was achingly hard, more aroused than he ever remembered being. He wanted desperately to take off the rest of their clothing and find release inside her this instant, but he couldn't.

She wasn't ready.

She might be physically ready—her spontaneous orgasm was evidence of that—but he couldn't take that final step.

After a moment, she rolled over, and he saw her features were fiery pink.

"You don't have to look so smug," she said, a cross note in her voice that made him smile, despite his aching need.

"Not smug at all. Overwhelmed at how beautiful that was."

She gave an embarrassed-sounding laugh. "It's ridiculous. We barely touched. It's just…it's been a long time for me."

"How long?" He couldn't help asking.

"It doesn't matter. I'm not a virgin spinster, if that's what you were wondering. I'm not a virgin *or* a spinster."

When he said nothing, only continued watching her with great interest, she sighed. "It is a long and twisted story for another day."

"*Twisted.* You are full of surprises, Miss Winston."

"Not twisted as in kinky. Twisted as in…complicated."

He was more intrigued by her than ever. Though he was still fiercely aroused, he loved lying here holding her.

"Tell me," he said.

She gazed at him for a long moment, then sighed.

"I don't think this is the right moment. You're still…" She vaguely gestured toward him, and a blush heated her cheeks.

"I'll live. I promise." If a guy had to have an orgasm every time he was aroused, no teenage boy would ever make it out of the bathroom.

He didn't want to move from this spot, but he sensed this would be easier for her if he gave her a little space. He eased away slightly, though their hands were still entwined. "What is your long and twisted story? You don't have to tell me if you don't want, but I would like to know."

He wanted to know everything about her, all the winding roads she had followed that had made her into the incredible woman she had become.

"It will shock you," she warned.

"Then, by all means, go on."

She smiled a little, then sat up and adjusted her sweater slightly, as if vying for time.

"I was briefly married when I was twenty-one," she finally said.

Of all the things he had imagined, that wouldn't have even hit the list. Not that it was some kind of deep, dark scandal, only unexpected. "Married? Seriously?"

She sighed. "Yes. My parents didn't approve, so we married at the courthouse without telling anyone. It was our secret, just like we were a couple from one of the gothic novels I loved when I was a girl."

"Why didn't they approve?" Other than the guy must have been an asshole if he didn't want to yell to the entire world that he was lucky enough to be married to Julia Winston.

"He was from another country. The Ukraine. We met

when Maksym was finishing his postgraduate work in engineering at Boise State. My parents wouldn't even meet him. He was ten years older, and they said he was only interested in me so he could stay in the country. They also worried because we came from different cultures, religions, backgrounds. I think they also were afraid that if he didn't want to stay in the US, he would take me to the Ukraine and I would leave them alone. I was all they had, and they were older and not well, even then."

Parents weren't supposed to commandeer their children's lives for their own needs. They also weren't supposed to tell their young daughters that the only reason a man might want her was to stay in the country.

"You married him anyway."

"It was the one and only time I ever defied them. He made me happy. We were in love and that's all I could see, so we married the week I graduated. We only spent a week together before Maksym had to go back to his country to wrap up loose ends, then he planned to return permanently."

She was silent, her fingers playing along the edge of her comforter.

"What happened?" he finally asked.

"He disappeared. He stopped answering my emails and letters, and I couldn't reach him by phone. His parents were dead but he had a younger sister, and I tried to track her down but couldn't find her. I only knew her first name, not her husband's name or surname."

He could imagine it would have been challenging to track down a woman in another country.

"That must have been tough."

"He was supposed to be back at the end of the summer to start school again, and he never showed up. No one seemed to know where he was. Not the engineering department, not the foreign student office. I even called the consulate in Seattle but couldn't find anything out."

"That sounds suspicious."

"According to official records, he returned to his country, but no one could find record of what happened to him after that. That's what they claimed, anyway. The man I spoke with there told me that maybe Maksym didn't want to be found."

That must have hurt, especially if her parents had convinced her the man didn't really want her.

"He said most likely Maksym had a girlfriend at home that he had reunited with. It was a reasonable theory. He *did* have a girlfriend at home before me and had told me about her. I thought maybe he was right."

He heard the echo of old pain in her voice, of self-doubt and rejection. She must have felt so betrayed. He wanted to fly to the Ukraine, find this Maksym dude and drag him back here to make things right.

No. Jamie didn't want him anywhere near Haven Point. Maybe he could fly to the Ukraine, find the dude and at least beat him to a bloody pulp for what he had taken from her.

"Did you have the marriage annulled?"

She shook her head. "I didn't do anything. I didn't even tell my parents about it. I was too ashamed to tell them they were right about him. They sensed something was wrong but thought I was just sad about breaking up with my first real boyfriend."

She gave a rough-sounding laugh, and he reached for her hand and squeezed it tightly. After a moment, she turned her hand over, tangling her fingers with his.

"I was in a strange sort of limbo. In my heart—and on paper—I was still married, so I didn't feel like I could date anyone, at least the first few years. Then my father was diagnosed with Alzheimer's, and I moved back to help my mother with him. I didn't have time to date. That's the reason it's been…a while for me."

"Did you ever find out what happened to your… husband?" He tried not to let his tone convey his disgust at the man.

"Eventually. About three years ago, I was finally able to make contact through social media with a childhood friend of his, someone he had once mentioned to me."

She gave a smile that didn't conceal the sadness beneath it. "I found out Maksym was killed in a car accident, just a week after returning to the Ukraine. He hadn't told his sister he was married, so she had no reason to notify me as next of kin. I don't know why the consulate couldn't get me that information. It would have saved me years of wondering what I had done wrong."

Jamie wanted to gather her close, to kiss away the pain in her voice, the heartache of a young woman who had felt betrayed and unlovable and then had learned she was a widow, and had been for many years.

"Oh, sweetheart. I'm so sorry."

She pushed her hair away from her face. "It happened. I can't change it. I grieved at first when I thought he had just used me and then left me for some reason I couldn't understand. I grieved again after I learned he had been gone all this time and I hadn't known. Mostly I grieved for all those lost years.

"I've been living in limbo for ten years," she went on, "first because of Maksym, then while I cared for my parents. I decided a few weeks ago I was tired of it. It was time to break out and embrace life, as I did when I was young."

"I'd say you're doing a pretty good job."

"I'm trying."

They had both suffered early heartache. While he had responded to his pain and guilt over Lisa's death by becoming even more gregarious on the surface but keeping everyone at arm's length, Julia had protected herself by cloistering herself away here at home with her elderly, ailing parents, where she was safe.

He kissed her forehead, wishing he could kiss away all the hurt she had suffered but knowing that would never be enough.

He started to slide his mouth down to hers but froze when her telephone rang.

Her eyes looked soft, unfocused. "That will be Andie with the boys."

"You'd better get it."

After a pause to collect herself, she sat up, smoothed down her skirt, then reached for her phone.

"Hi, Andie. No. You didn't interrupt. I was, um, finished."

She blushed and gave him a sideways look that, despite everything, made him want to laugh.

"Yes. Ten minutes will be fine. Thank you again for doing this. I'm so happy they all had fun. Yes, I took care of what I needed. And then some."

This time she didn't look at him, but he could detect a certain tart look in her eyes and had to chuckle. She turned slightly and pressed a chiding finger to her lips. She might have looked like every caricature of a stern librarian, if her hair wasn't coming out of her loose updo and her sweater wasn't askew and if he didn't have the image burned in his memory of how beautiful she had looked a few moments earlier.

"Yes. Thank you. Goodbye."

She ended the call and turned to him. "They'll be here in ten minutes."

"We'd better hide all the evidence, then."

She looked confused for a moment, until he gestured to the table, scattered with ribbon and wrapping paper and tape.

"Oh. Right." She glanced at the bed, then back at him. "Jamie, I'm sorry that turned out to be so…one-sided."

He stopped her with a kiss on her forehead. "Don't. I had a great evening. Every moment of it. If you don't mind, though, I'll help you clean up the wrapping paper mess, then I think I should head upstairs. I'm predicting the boys will be wild enough after a Christmas party. I tend to rile them up more than I intend, and I don't want to make it completely impossible for you to get them to sleep on a school night."

"Thank you for that. And for…everything else."

He laughed. "It was my pleasure. Believe me."

After they finished cleaning up, he kissed her one last time, then slipped out of the apartment. The gravity of what had happened between them seemed to build with each step away from her.

Something had changed during that heated encounter. He wanted her more than any other woman in his life and ached to be free to touch her fully, to explore the passion seething beneath her skin.

He didn't know what to do with this yearning. More troubling than that, he could feel the emotional ties tightening inexorably between them, especially after all she had told him.

He cared for her, deeply. Somehow in the last few weeks, she had slid right past his defenses, with her kindness, compassion, her sly sense of humor.

How had he let this happen? Since Lisa and her tragic death, he hadn't let any woman this close to him. How had his uptight, quiet librarian managed to wriggle her way into his heart?

It didn't matter. He couldn't pursue a relationship with her. Julia deserved to be happy—to be cherished and adored by someone who would see her for the amazing woman he had come to know this last month.

That someone couldn't be him.

She had already been hurt enough by the implosion of all her hopes and dreams. He couldn't drag this out further.

Jamie had figured out a long time ago that he wasn't the sort of man who could stick around for happily-ever-after. Sure, he was casual and fun and could make a woman smile and sigh and maybe have an unexpected orgasm out of the blue.

He couldn't make her happy for the rest of her life, as she deserved.

He would move out as planned and then do his best to extricate himself from their lives. She would be hurt, yes, but not irreparably.

He would rather walk away now than drag this out more and hurt her even worse.

"My presentation went well," Julia said over the phone to Mack Porter. "They seem to like our summer reading program ideas, and I've already had three libraries ask me to send them information about how we set up our incentives."

"That's because you're so brilliant. Before you know it, they're going to want you to run for the board of the library association."

Julia shuddered at the idea. She was happy to volunteer and participated in a couple of different committees for the association, but she had no interest in leadership. "The reason I called is to let you know I'm leaving Boise and should be back in town by two, but I'm taking the rest of the afternoon off."

"Got it. It's pretty quiet here. I guess people have better things to do a few days before Christmas Eve than return their library books."

"Like what?" Julia said in a disbelieving tone that made Mack laugh. "Nothing is more important than that."

"Truth."

"Anyway, I told the boys this morning not to go to the library after school, as they've been doing, but to meet me at home. If they forget in their excitement about it being the last day of school before the break, they might show up there. If they do, call me and I'll pick them up."

"Okay. You're leaving now?"

Out her Lexus's window, she could see a few stray snowflakes twirling down from the sky. Nerves tightened in her stomach. If it was snowing at all, she would have to take the other road back to Haven Point, which added at least forty-five minutes. The longer, more circuitous route always felt safer for her, where cars weren't whizzing past her at sometimes eighty miles

an hour, pressuring her to go faster than she was comfortable.

"Yes. Right now."

"Drive safely," her friend said in his deep voice.
"And merry Christmas."

"Same to you. I'll see you next week."

She pulled out of the parking lot of the Boise library
where her committee meeting had been held and drove
toward the road that would take her home.

Only a few more snowflakes fell as she continued
toward the route. When she reached the last intersec-
tion before she had to decide whether to take the freeway or the slower road, Julia dithered.

She really wanted to save forty-five minutes of driving, but was it worth risking the stress of driving on the
freeway in the snow?

The car behind her honked, and Julia realized she
had to make a decision.

In an odd sort of way, she felt as if she were at a
crossroads in her life, literally and figuratively. She
could continue to be afraid to reach out, to live in her
safe little world where she took no risk and thus enjoyed no benefits from that risk. Or she could give in
to the part of her that longed to go fast, to live hard, to
embrace everything life had to throw at her.

She knew which one she wanted to do. Jamie had
shown her that over the last few weeks. She had experienced the wonder of flight. She had gone to the fancy
gala dressed like a fairy princess. She had kissed him
on the ski slopes and under a starry sky and in her bedroom, where he had brought her indescribable pleasure.

He had helped her achieve so many things she had

dreamed about, and in the process she had come to know herself a little better.

How hard was driving on the freeway, anyway, even in the snow? One used the same driving skills. The same turn signals, the same steering wheel, the same cruise control. She only had to employ the skills she already had a little faster.

She could do this.

She could do anything she wanted.

The back roads had their advantages sometimes. It was beautiful there, and she could slow down and enjoy life a little. But when she was in a hurry, like today—when she had boys who would be looking for her after school, eager to tell her about their last day of school before Christmas break—she didn't want the slower pace.

Empowered in a way she never would have imagined, she used that turn signal now and moved into the lane that would merge her onto the freeway. Heart pounding, she accelerated up the on-ramp. A car changed to the inside lane to give her room, and a moment later, Julia was doing it. She was driving at freeway speeds in the middle of December in her little Lexus that was designed to go even faster.

Exhilaration burst through her, and she laughed out loud. The driving was a small thing. A symbol, really. The accomplishment was the important thing—the fact that she had taken a risk, confronted something that frightened her and conquered it.

Her happiness seemed too big to be contained inside the small space, so she rolled her window down and gave a shout of glee. A woman driving past in a blue minivan gave her an odd look, but Julia didn't care.

Of course, she could only keep her window down

for so long. It was December, after all. After a moment, she rolled it back up, turned on the stereo and drove the rest of the way home to Haven Point singing along to her favorite Christmas carols.

When she reached her house, she was delighted to see Jamie's vehicle in the driveway. She had to tell someone. To others, it might seem like such a stupid thing, but for her it was huge.

She opened the door, unlocked her apartment to dump her bags inside, then hurried up the stairs to his. He answered on the second knock.

"What's wrong?" he asked instantly.

"Nothing. Absolutely nothing. It's been a terrific day. May I come in?"

He held the door open with a confused look. The apartment appeared just as it had when he moved in, with the addition of a little more clutter and a couple of open moving boxes. For a moment, the sight of those boxes dulled the excitement sparkling through her veins. They served as a stark reminder that his time here was temporary, that he would be moving on before she knew it. She felt sadness clutch at her stomach but quickly pushed it away. Today was for celebrating.

"Guess what just happened?"

He gazed at her. "Judging by how excited you look, I'm thinking you either won the lottery or were just named Librarian of the Year for the state of Idaho."

"Neither of those things, though a girl can always dream. Maybe next year. No. This is something better." She paused for dramatic effect. "I just drove home on the freeway! And it's December. And it's snowing!"

"Seriously?"

"I know it sounds stupid, but driving on the freeway

always made me nervous, especially in the wintertime. When I was a new driver, I was bringing my dad back from a doctor's appointment in Boise when it started to snow, and black ice formed. We were involved in a twelve-car pileup. Neither of us was hurt seriously, but somebody else in the pileup was killed. Ever since, I've been afraid to take the freeway."

"You never do?"

"I rarely go to Boise, in the first place. When I do, I'll take the freeway there and back if it's a sunny day, but the rest of the time I take the long way home." She shrugged. "Today, I decided it was stupid to be afraid. I could handle whatever comes along, and I had more important things to do than give in to my fear."

"That is amazing! Good for you!"

"I know it's a little thing, but it was important to me." She paused. "Thanks for not thinking I'm a stupid scaredy-cat."

"I don't think that at all. I think you're brave and adventurous and incredible. Come here."

She had been waiting for him to say just that, and she wrapped her arms around him and lifted her mouth for his fierce, approving kiss.

What would it be like to have this all the time, someone to share her joys and triumphs and sorrows with? Another person who wanted her to succeed, who saw the good in her she often overlooked?

She sighed, remembering those moving boxes. He was a temporary part of her life, and she had to accept that. He was here now, though, and she wouldn't waste time worrying about the future.

He drew back, smiling. "You know what this means,

right? The only thing left on your list is kissing somebody special under the mistletoe and getting a puppy!"

It took a few seconds for his words to pierce her
happy glow. List. Mistletoe. A puppy. They made no
sense...until they suddenly did.

Icy shock crackled through her as dawning realization poured over.

Somehow, Jamie knew about her list. That stupid,
juvenile bucket list that Roxy Nash made them write
at the book club, when she had been well on her way
to being wasted on sangria.

Julia felt all the blood rush from her face, her hands,
her toes.

"How... You saw that list?"

"Yes," he said warily.

"You saw the list," she repeated.

He eased away and scratched his chin. "Not on purpose. When you were sick and I was taking care of the
boys, it fell out of a book. I wasn't snooping, but I...
happened to read a few lines, then of course had to
read the rest."

That pathetic, ridiculous list that she hadn't even
wanted to make in the first place! Humiliation burned
through her, replacing the icy shock. She felt exposed,
laid bare, as if he had read her private journal on a live
internet broadcast and revealed all her secret dreams
to the world.

She remembered the events of the last few weeks and
suddenly saw them through a new filter. All the things
he had done with her, the adventures he had provided
for her and the boys—taking her up in his airplane,
teaching her to ski, the gala. It was all because of her
stupid book club list.

She tried to remember everything on it, each humiliating detail. Suddenly her lungs contracted, and she couldn't breathe.

The day before, her bedroom.

She had written that on the list. *Have an orgasm with someone else.*

She wanted to die, to curl up into a ball and disappear.

That was the reason for everything he had done. None of it was real. Jamie Caine didn't care about her. It was all some stupid effort to help the poor, wretched, boring librarian check off the pitiful items on the list.

"I have to go." She pointed vaguely at the door, then forced her frozen feet to move toward it.

"Julia, wait."

She shook her head and kept moving. She couldn't face him. Not now, maybe not ever. She had to get out of here.

Gripping the polished railing that had been made by some ancestor or other, she rushed down the stairs and to her door. She was so consumed with her mortification that she didn't realize he followed her until his hand on the jamb stopped her from slamming the door closed behind her.

"Julia. Wait. Listen to me."

"I can't. Everything you did, everything we shared the last few weeks, was for that list. Because I'm a thirty-something introvert who has let life pass her by. You felt pity for me and wanted to help me accomplish things that most normal people would have done by the time they were out of their teens."

"Pity had nothing to do with this," he insisted. "I liked you and I liked the boys. I thought it was a great thing you were doing for them, taking them in when they had nowhere else to go. I admired that. When I saw the list, I wanted to do something nice for you in return. That's all."

That's all.

She had completely lost her heart to him while he was being *nice* to her.

"And you succeeded admirably. Thank you. Now will you excuse me? I have to go find a certain book about filling your stupid well and burn it."

"Why are you angry?"

She stared at him. Did he really not get it? Did he not see how absolutely humiliating this was for her, to know that the only reason he wanted to spend any time with her the last few weeks was to help her check off a stupid list with items she never should have written down in the first place?

"It doesn't matter. You did a nice thing. I'll never forget all the adventures you gave me. Skiing, flying. All of it." She couldn't add the rest. She just couldn't. "Now you can enjoy your Christmas with the warm glow of knowing you've done your good deed for the year."

"It might have started out that way," he said. "But somewhere along the way, I forgot all about that list. I was only doing it for you, because I wanted to make your dreams come true."

His words sent treacherous warmth seeping through her. She wanted to lean into that warmth, but then she remembered. This was Jamie Caine, notorious charmer, who could persuade a woman to do anything he wanted.

None of it was real. How could she have been so stupid to lose her heart to him, to actually think he might be interested in her?

Her jaw tightened. "That sounds lovely. Did you read it on a Christmas card somewhere?"

She heard her own acid words as if from far away and wanted to take them back, but she was too miserable, too hurt.

"I mean it. I care about you."

She might have scoffed. Or coughed. Or maybe it was a sob that she couldn't quite manage to restrain.

Jamie stepped forward and reached for her hand. His expression was solemn, but there was something there she couldn't read.

"I shouldn't have just blurted it out like that. I was going to tell you I saw the list at some point. I thought maybe we could have a laugh about it."

"A laugh." That's all she was to him. She tugged her hand free and twisted it around the other one. Her fingers were shaking, but she couldn't have explained why.

He ran a hand through his hair, a muscle flexing in his jaw. When he spoke, his voice was low, intense. "Would you be this angry if I told you that somewhere along the way I started to fall in love with you?"

For a brief, magical moment, joy exploded inside her like Roman candles on New Year's Eve.

Jamie Caine. In love with her.

She thought of the tenderness she was almost certain she had seen in his eyes, the sweetness he showed to the boys, how safe she felt in his arms.

She wanted so desperately to believe him. Sometimes Cinderella really did get Prince Charming, right?

That was a fairy tale, though. The kind of story that could be found in her library books. Not real life. In real life, gorgeous pilots who could have any woman they wanted didn't choose the dowdy librarian who had spent most of her life living for others, afraid to take any chances for fear of the hurt that might be waiting on the other side.

She didn't believe him. He was baring his heart to her, and she didn't believe him.

Jamie could see the doubt in those spectacular eyes after his stunning declaration.

He hadn't meant to tell her. The words had slipped out somehow. Still, they resonated with truth—at least to him. He loved Julia Winston. Yes, she was serious and studious and a bit reserved. Those were some of the things he loved about her. Everything was different with her. *He* was different.

He might not deserve a woman as wonderful as Julia Winston, but he wanted to deserve her. He ached to be the man who could make her laugh and take her to new places, literally and figuratively. He wanted to embrace his feelings for her instead of running from them.

How could he convince her?

The irony didn't escape him. He was finally willing to let a woman into his heart, and she couldn't accept that this was different and beautiful and right.

Usually he knew just what to say to a woman, but he felt completely out of his depths here. He had to say something, though. The silence was dragging on way too long.

"It…took me a while to figure it out," he began, the words sounding rusty and awkward. "I've never felt like this…depth of emotion for a woman before. I've never *let* myself feel it. Since Lisa's death, I've been afraid. That's a tough thing for a guy to admit to himself, let alone to someone else, but it's true."

She gazed up at him and he thought maybe he was making progress, but she quickly looked down again.

"I care about you, Julia. Somehow over the last few weeks when I thought I was doing something nice for you, I fell in love with your smile and your sweetness and the way you put your whole soul into everything you do. I don't know how it happened, and I certainly never intended it, but it did. You make me happy."

She swallowed and lifted her eyes to his. He couldn't read the expression there before she shielded her emotions.

"Stop. I... That's a lovely speech, and I appreciate the kind words, but...they're not necessary. I know you are worried about hurting me. Put that out of your head. My heart was never involved."

Her words sliced through him like a machete, but she didn't appear to notice.

"I'm embarrassed you saw that stupid list," she went on in an unnaturally chirpy voice, "but I'll survive. I'm naive but I'm not stupid. You're Jamie Caine. You flirt with everyone. Like every other woman in town, I had a crush on you, and it was fun to...to have you pay attention to me. To dance with you at the gala and kiss you and maybe flirt back a little, though I'm obviously not very good at it. You don't have to lie and tell me your feelings were involved. I knew all along you weren't serious."

Except he was. For once in his damn life, he was.

He opened his mouth to tell her as much when the outside doorbell rang unexpectedly, making Julia jump as well as all three of the cats, who appeared to have been watching their interaction with interest from the back of the sofa.

"I should get that," Julia said.

Now? He wanted to tell her to let the damn thing ring. They were in the middle of something here, possibly the most important conversation of his life. Whoever was at the door could freaking come back later, couldn't they?

Before he could say the words, Julia hurried from her room to answer the outside door.

He heard her open the door, heard an exchange of conversation, then he heard a long, tense silence.

Audrey Hepburn flattened her ears and hissed, and Empress arched her back, her tail curved menacingly. Wary at their unusual reaction, he moved out into the foyer, where he discovered Julia staring at the well-dressed couple who stood on the other side of the door.

She had been upset by their conversation, he knew, but something told him her sudden paleness and the utter stillness of her muscles had nothing to do with him.

He started to move up beside her, wanting to lend his support if she needed it, when he spied someone else on the porch. Wynona Emmett, Julia's friend who worked for the county social services agency.

Surprise flickered in her gaze. "Jamie. Hi."

She looked visibly upset as well, and he was filled with sudden foreboding. "Hey, Wyn. What's going on?"

She didn't smile as she gestured to the couple. "This is Paul and Suzanne Bernard. Davy and Clint's aunt and uncle. They've come for them."

TEN MINUTES LATER, he wasn't any more clear on what the hell was going on.

"So you're telling me these strangers can just walk in here, throw some papers around and take the boys away? How do we know they're even who they say they are?"

Julia hadn't glanced at Jamie once since she let the couple into her house and they all sat down in the living room, but now she gave him her quelling librarian look.

"Sorry," Paul Bernard said stiffly. "Tell me again, what relationship are you to Julia Winston? I was under the impression she lived here alone."

"Jamie rents my upstairs apartment. He's been a... good friend to me and to the boys."

He had been a hell of a lot more than that to her. He wanted to burst out with the words but knew this wasn't the moment.

"I care about all of them," he said. "And I want to know why you think you can suddenly drop in and yank them out of a place where they've been happy. Where were you when those boys were living alone in a house without heat and eating peanut butter sandwiches for every meal?"

The woman, Suzanne, twisted her fingers together in her lap, her eyes filled with sorrow. "We had no idea. Mikaela said everything was going well, and we believed her. Whenever we would talk to her, she gave no indication that she had lost her job, that she'd been kicked out of her condo, that they were living in those deplorable conditions. We didn't know."

"You've been out of the country," Julia said, as if defending them for their negligence.

"Yes. Paul's company transferred him to Jakarta for the last six months, but all along we've been communicating with Kaela and the boys via Skype."

"How could you not know when the background on the video call changed?" Jamie demanded.

"She said she moved the computer to another room. She said she was going through some things and needed space. I…we gave her a few weeks, and then she stopped answering any of our calls or emails. Finally I told Paul it didn't matter what it took, I was coming here to find out what was going on. I was sick when I went to the address she had given us and saw that empty house."

"A neighbor told us the boys had been taken by social services," Paul Bernard said. "We followed the trail to Mrs. Emmett, who verified our information and led us here."

"That's great. I commend your concern. But they're happy here with Julia. What gives you the right to just waltz in and take them?"

"They still have the custody papers Mikaela gave them when she was deployed three years ago," Wynona explained. "They've never been revoked. Besides that, they're family. The boys know them and love them. They spent several months living with them when both parents were deployed, before their father was killed."

"You're going to take them to Jakarta?" he asked.

Suzanne Bernard shook her head. "No. That was always a temporary assignment. Paul has been transferred back to Southern California. We still have our place there, and we would like to take the boys home."

Julia made a small, involuntary movement, and he wanted desperately to gather her up and hold her close, to comfort and protect her. *This* was their home. She had given them love and care when they had nothing.

She drew in a ragged breath and opened her mouth, closed it, then opened it again. "I… The boys should be home any moment. They'll be so happy to see you. I'll start packing their things."

All the life and color seemed to have seeped out of her, like a piece of cloth left out in the elements. She sounded like the stilted, stiff landlady who had shown him around his apartment when he first moved in, so very different from the vibrant, compassionate woman he had fallen in love with.

"You can't do this," he said again to Wyn.

She had always struck him as a smart woman, not afraid to go to the wall for the things she cared about. Hadn't she even taken a bullet for Andie Montgomery Bailey a few summers before?

"I don't have a choice," she said softly. "I'm sorry."

"We could wait until after the holidays," Suzanne Bernard offered, her features distressed, as if she was only now beginning to comprehend the wrenching pain their sudden appearance would cause in Julia's world. "It's only a few more days."

Julia swallowed and shook her head. "No. I'm sure you're anxious to be on your way."

Those words had just left her mouth when Jamie heard the thud of small boots scrambling up the steps and a moment later, the outside door burst open.

"Last day of school! Last day of school!" Davy yelled.

"Hey, Julia," Clint called, "somebody's here. There's a couple strange cars in the driveway."

The boys came into the living room and stopped dead for about two seconds, then Davy let out another yell and launched himself straight at the woman.

"Aunt Suzi!"

She squeezed him tightly, tears spilling out. Paul Bernard rose and hugged Clint, and for a moment, it looked like one of the many reunions he would see on base from families who had been separated too long by circumstances beyond their control. Hugs, kisses, pats on the cheek and the arm, as if to make sure the other person was really there.

The boys were thrilled to see their aunt and uncle. Happiness simply beamed out of all of them.

Julia sat by herself, watching the celebration with a remote expression, but Jamie felt emotion choke his throat. It would rip out her heart to see the boys go. She had completely opened her life to them this past month, something that was so very difficult for her.

"I should...pack their things," she said again.

"I can help," he offered.

"Jamie flies airplanes. We went on his plane two times, and it was so fun," Davy was saying to his aunt. He hadn't let go of her for a moment. She had been his maternal figure during a formative age, Jamie realized, and it was obvious the boy loved her like a mother.

Julia moved stiffly into their room, and he followed her.

"Jules," he said softly, when they were away from the others.

"Don't talk to me," she demanded fiercely, not looking at him. "Just go away. I don't want your help."

"I'm not going to leave you to deal with this on your own."

"I don't want your help," she repeated.

Apparently there was pain enough to go around tonight. He couldn't force her to accept his love, but he would damn well make her take his help right now, when she was forced to go through this terrible loss.

"Too bad," he snapped. "I'm staying."

She gazed at him with a blank, shocked sort of look, then turned back and started pulling clothes out of the drawers. After a moment, he pulled the suitcases he had brought from Hope's Crossing from under the bed and they both went to work.

CHAPTER TWENTY

SHE COULDN'T BEAR THIS.

How would she possibly find the strength to say goodbye to these sweet little boys who had completely changed her life?

She had been so looking forward to Christmas morning with them, just a few days away. The anticipation, the joy, the excitement on their faces when they unwrapped the gifts she had so carefully bought and wrapped for them.

They had brought color and light to her life. Bedtime stories and sloppy kisses and Christmas cookies. She didn't know how she would possibly endure being once more alone.

She picked through the clothes and toys in the room, choosing first the ones they had brought with them, then their favorites among the items Jamie had collected so very long ago. It seemed another lifetime ago, that Thanksgiving when they had first come to live with her.

It was. She had been another person.

Jamie worked beside her without saying anything beyond the occasional question about which toys to pack. She knew at some future date she might be grateful for his presence, for his solid strength and support. Right now she was too raw and broken.

"Is that it?" he asked, when she paused to look around the room.

"I don't think we can fit anything more."

His features stony, he zipped the suitcases, then carried them out to the living room, where Wyn waited with the Bernards and the boys.

She knew she was being a coward—putting off that inevitable, horrible moment when she had to paste a smile on her face and wave them off as they drove away—but she lingered in the room as dozens of memories paraded across her mind.

On some level, the depth of her pain struck her as excessive. This was always going to be a temporary arrangement; she had known that from the beginning. Either their mother would be deemed well enough to care for them again or a more permanent placement would be found.

Being with their family, an aunt and uncle who clearly loved them, was far preferable to going to yet another foster home. She accepted that, and, for their sakes, she tried to be unselfish and happy for them.

But, oh, it hurt.

She let out a sigh. Staying here was only prolonging the inevitable misery. Better to rip off the bandage and endure the stinging agony for a few moments, so that she could begin the process of healing.

She forced herself to go out into the living room.

"I think that's everything. If there's anything else you guys want, you can let me know, and I can send it on to you."

Though Julia tried to smile, Suzanne Bernard still gave her a worried look. "Are you sure you don't want us to stay until after the holidays? We can change our flight."

She had the room for them here, but it would be so very awkward to have them all here and would, again, only prolong what she knew was coming. No. Better to be done.

"It's fine," she lied. "The boys will love being in familiar surroundings for Christmas. Davy has told me all about your pool and how close the ocean is to your home. It sounds lovely."

"You're not coming with us?" Davy looked thunderstruck, as if the reality of the situation had just occurred to him.

She shook her head, fiercely trying not to cry in front of the boys.

"Why not? I thought you liked us." His plaintive cry drove another icy shard into her heart.

She went to him and hugged him close, trying to memorize the warm, small weight of him. "I do, honey. I do. So much. But I can't go with you. You're going back to California with your aunt and uncle. I have to stay here and take care of the cats, plus I have my job at the library and my friends and this house."

His forehead furrowed as he tried to process this. Clint, she noted, looked as if he didn't know how to feel. She could tell he was excited about going with his aunt and uncle, even as he didn't want to leave her. She could only pray this was the last tumultuous change these poor children would have to endure for a long, long time.

"Will you come visit us sometime?" the older boy asked. "Maybe Jamie can take you to California on his airplane. He goes there all the time."

She didn't dare risk a glance at Jamie. He seemed

increasingly remote, though she knew that was entirely her fault.

"Maybe," she answered.

Somehow over the last few weeks when I thought I was doing something nice for you, I fell in love with your smile and your sweetness and the way you put your whole soul into everything you do. I don't know how it happened, and I certainly never intended it, but it did. You make me happy.

His words from earlier echoed around and around in her head. She wanted so desperately to believe him, especially now when she needed something beautiful and hopeful to cling to.

"We can also talk on Skype whenever you want."

Clint came over and wrapped his arms around her, too.

"You won't forget us, will you?" he asked in a small voice.

The words from this sweet boy whose own mother had done exactly that completely shattered her.

She choked back a sob. "No, darling. Never ever."

She grabbed him close and held on to both boys. She felt scoured raw. Still, she managed to maintain the tight hold on her emotions as the boys hugged her one last time, then returned to their aunt and uncle.

"We should go," Paul said to his wife. "We have to drive back to Boise and try to get the boys on our flight."

"Yes. Yes. Of course."

The next few moments were a flurry of activity as he carried the suitcases out to their rental car and the boys kept remembering certain toys and school papers they couldn't leave behind.

While she was gathering a few things, she saw them have a hurried conversation with Jamie, who nodded solemnly throughout before lifting them both up at once for a tight hug that made them giggle.

Finally after a few more hugs, they were settled into the rental car. Paul and Suzanne offered their thanks one more time to Julia. She tried to be gracious, but inside she wanted everyone to leave—please, God—so she could fall apart.

At the last moment, she remembered one more thing.

"I'm sorry. Can you wait a moment?" she said to Suzanne Bernard in a low voice so the boys wouldn't hear. "I had Christmas presents for them. They're already wrapped and everything. I know you probably don't have room for much, but would you…do you mind taking a few things you could give them from me?"

"Of course not." Suzanne hugged her again.

This would all be so much easier if she could hate the other woman, but she actually seemed very loving and kind. It was obvious the boys adored her.

"I'll be right back."

She hurried to her room and into her closet, trying hard not to remember those cherished moments with Jamie as he helped her wrap the presents.

After looking at everything hidden away, she pulled out only the stockings that were on top, the ones she had hand-sewn at night after the boys were in bed.

The stitches were crooked on the letters that spelled out their names, but she had to hope the boys wouldn't notice that. She picked a few other small, meaningful presents that would fit in them for each, then wrapped them twice in leftover shopping bags to conceal them fully.

She still had a closet full of toys. She would donate them, she decided. It was probably too late for the Toys for Tots donation, since the day after next was Christmas Eve, but McKenzie or Wynona might know of a needy family that would otherwise slip through the cracks.

Giving the boys the stockings she had made them was a small gesture, but somehow it made her feel a little better, not quite as powerless amid the events swirling around her.

She carried them out and handed them to Suzanne.

"Thank you," the woman said. "I'll make sure they get them Christmas morning."

"Please. Take care of those boys. I have loved having them here."

Suzanne's chin wobbled, and she grabbed Julia one last time into a fierce embrace. "Thank you for rescuing them. You did a wonderful thing, and we can never repay you."

She didn't tell the other woman she had been repaid a thousand times over by their hugs, their laughter and the joy they had brought into her world.

Finally they were all settled into the rental car, and the terrible moment she had been dreading could no longer be avoided.

A few stray snowflakes stung her face, and wind blew through her sweater, but she didn't go inside until their taillights faded.

She was aware as she stood in her driveway that she wanted to climb into her own Lexus and drive away into the night. Not necessarily after them, just anywhere but here.

She didn't want to go back inside and face the echoing emptiness.

Wyn was still inside, though, and Jamie, and she knew she couldn't stay here all night, or she would freeze to death.

On bones that seemed to creak and groan as much as her old house, she slowly mounted the steps. Jamie was waiting on the porch. She was aware of him watching her, worrying for her, but she couldn't deal with it. Not yet.

Wynona was waiting in the entryway.

She immediately wrapped her arms around Julia. "I'm so sorry," her friend said. "I had no idea this would happen so fast. I wish I could have given you some warning."

Julia stayed in her embrace for a moment, then tried to subtly edge away. "This is the best possible outcome, right? They've been reunited with their family, people they love and who love them in return."

"But right before Christmas. It sucks."

That was one word for it. As someone whose entire vocation involved collections of words, she had a few choice others she could use.

"You did your job," Julia answered. "I know none of this was your fault."

Wyn hugged her one more time. She adored her friend and was grateful for her sympathy, but right now Julia needed her to leave so she could break down in peace.

"Call me if you need anything," Wyn said. "Seriously. Even on Christmas Eve. In fact, why don't you come to Mom and Uncle Mike's new place for dinner

Sunday? There's plenty of room, and we would all love to have you."

"I'll be okay. I promise. You'd better go. I'm sure Cade is wondering where you are."

Wynona finally drove away reluctantly a few moments later, which left only Jamie.

"Thank you for your help today."

Tension seemed to thrum between them as his earlier words continued to echo through her mind. It was all too much. The last few hours had been the worst sort of emotional roller coaster, and now she felt like she did the few times she'd gone to an amusement park—hot and sticky and nauseous.

"Is that all you have to say? Don't you want to talk about this?"

She shook her head. That was the *last* thing she wanted.

"I can't."

"Julia. Sweetheart. Don't shut me out."

She longed so much to fall into his arms, to cry and cry and cry until this sadness began to ease.

He couldn't make this better, and if she allowed herself to lean on him, her heartbreak would be so much worse when he left, too.

She forced a smile. "I'm really okay," she lied. "As I said to Wyn, this was the best possible outcome for the boys, to be with their family. I get that. I'm sad for me, yes, but I can't be anything but happy for them. Thanks for your concern. If you don't mind, I really need to be by myself right now."

Before he could argue, she slipped into her living room. She closed the door firmly behind her, then locked it, leaving him standing alone in the foyer.

Jamie stood on the other side of her door, listening to the lock snick home and wondering what the hell he should do.

His instincts were telling him to knock the blasted thing down. She was obviously *not* okay. He had seen the devastation in her eyes, the raw pain she had gone to such lengths to conceal.

What was a guy supposed to do when the woman he loved was hurting and wouldn't let him help? He stood for a long time, frozen with indecision. She wouldn't appreciate him banging on her door relentlessly. Should he call someone? He couldn't help remembering Lisa and how his indecision in that case had resulted in such tragic consequences.

Julia wasn't Lisa. She was one of the most courageous women he knew, with incredible strength and grit. She would get through this, he knew.

He wanted to help her, but she had asked to be alone. Maybe the best thing he could do for her right now would be to respect her wishes. Instead of thinking about what would make him feel like a hero, maybe he needed to respect that she knew what she needed.

If that wasn't him right now, he would have to accept that.

What if she never let him in again?

Panic pooled in his stomach. Julia couldn't believe he truly loved her, and he had no idea how to prove he did—or even if he should try. Maybe he should take this literal and figurative door she had closed between them as a sign.

She didn't want him.

I'm naive but I'm not stupid. My heart was never involved.

He inhaled sharply as the stinging pain of her words hit him all over again.

He didn't want to believe it, but maybe that was his damn arrogance again. It was entirely possible that he had fallen head over heels for the one woman who seemed immune to his celebrated Caine charm.

Tomorrow he was supposed to fly to Hope's Crossing to pick up his family again for Christmas at Snow Angel Cove.

He would give her time to come to terms with her loss. If by the day after Christmas Eve, she still wasn't talking to him, he would accept that she meant her words.

It might prove the toughest thing he ever tackled, but he would move out of her house and try to go on with his life without her.

JULIA FELT EXHAUSTED, wrung out and achy and heart-sick. She had cried more in one evening than the last five years combined.

For once, the cats had come through. Audrey Hepburn hadn't left her side since the Bernards drove away, and even Empress had bounced onto the sofa and curled up next to her.

It had been an unexpected blessing, a small tender mercy.

Jamie had come down early. She had been sitting by the Christmas tree wrapped in a blanket when she heard his boots on the stairs. He'd paused outside her door, and she almost thought she could hear each steady breath, but a moment later the door opened and he was gone.

She probably shouldn't have shut him out like that,

she thought now as she gazed at all the presents she had pulled out of her closet.

In retrospect, it wasn't fair. He had cared about the boys, too, had spent many hours with them. She hadn't once considered his pain and sadness, only her own. If he were still here, she would apologize to him for her selfishness.

The long weekend stretched out ahead of her, hour upon hour she needed to fill with something. She couldn't spend the entire holiday weekend, a time that should be centered on joy and hope, having a pity party.

The boys would be happy with their aunt and uncle, she had no doubt. She would continue to pray their mother would be able to heal mentally and emotionally and eventually find herself healthy enough to care for them. Meanwhile, the Bernards would provide continuity, would shower the boys with all the love and attention they needed.

How could she be selfish enough to deprive them of that, simply because she loved them, too?

Meantime, she had all these presents to take somewhere. She could always join the throng of unhappy gift recipients and return them after the holidays, but she would feel better if the gifts could go toward helping someone else.

While she fixed a quick breakfast, she called Wyn to ask if the social worker knew anywhere she could take them.

"Are you sure you want to do that?" Wyn asked, concern in her voice.

"Positive," she said firmly.

"I can think of a half-dozen people who might benefit. One in particular stands out, a woman in Shelter

Springs who just took custody of her grandchildren, two boys the same age as Davy and Clint and a little girl who is about three. The children's mother was arrested in Boise on drug charges last week. This all happened pretty suddenly, and the grandma, Janet Wells, is on Social Security and doesn't have much money to throw together a last-minute Christmas for the kids."

"I don't have anything for a girl," Julia said. "But if you'll give me a few hours, I can fix that."

"Are you sure? The stores will be crazy on the last Saturday before Christmas."

"Positive."

"Let me call Janet to make sure it's okay with her. If she is willing to accept your generosity, I'll call you back with her address. I can come with you, if you want."

"No. I would like to do this."

Ten minutes later, Wyn called back to tell Julia that Janet had wept tears of gratitude and said she had, that very moment, been praying for some miracle so she could give her grandchildren a few little presents from Santa.

"How does it feel to be a miracle?" Wyn asked with a laugh that sounded rather teary.

While she was sad about her own loss, at least she would be able to brighten someone else's holiday. She could take some solace in that.

"It feels great. I guess I'd better go shopping."

In the end, she braved the crowds at the box stores in Shelter Springs for not only a cart full of little girl toys, but enough food to feed the family for a week.

She paid a fund-raising Girl Scout troop at the front of the store to wrap the gifts, packaged the food in a large basket, then proceeded to the address Wyn had given her.

The house was neat but showed signs of neglect. It could have used new shutters and a new paint job. Maybe when the snow melted, she could organize the Helping Hands to take on another project…

The moment Julia pulled up, Janet Wells came out of her house wearing a threadbare coat and house slippers. She hurried to Wyn when she climbed out of her Lexus and gripped her hands.

"You are an angel from heaven," the woman declared.

Julia smiled and hugged her. "I'm glad I could help."

"I asked my friend Florence if she could watch the kids for me for an hour, so they don't suspect anything. I'd like to surprise them on Christmas, if you don't mind."

"Absolutely. Christmas surprises are the absolute best. I can carry them in for you."

The woman cried twice more before Julia was done unloading the two boxes of gifts and the basket full of food.

"A precious angel from heaven," she repeated several times. "How will I thank you?"

"Just hold your grandchildren close and make sure they know they're loved," she answered. "Merry Christmas."

At least she could feel good that the things she bought for Davy and Clint would go to a good cause.

SOMEHOW SHE MADE it through the rest of Christmas Eve Eve, as the boys had called this day before Christmas Eve.

Though the library was closed, she went into work for several hours, taking advantage of the quiet to catch up on paperwork. When she returned to her house late, she saw no sign Jamie had come back. His vehicle wasn't here, anyway, and she could see no fresh tracks in the driveway.

She was relieved, she told herself. She spent the rest of the evening watching a favorite Christmas movie, frosting the extra cookies she and the boys had made to give to the neighbors, and ignoring multiple calls from her friends, who all left messages inviting her over the next day to spend Christmas Eve and Christmas with them.

She was *not* waiting for Jamie, she told herself.

That was probably good, as she listened all night and he didn't come home.

CHRISTMAS EVE MORNING she woke up with a long-ingrained bubbly anticipation, the expectation that this was a day for wonder and miracles.

Only a few seconds later, she remembered, and the excitement died.

The boys were gone.

She indulged in another good cry, telling herself firmly that this was the last one. She fed the cats, straightened up a bit, then dressed for church services.

The program was lovely, with beautiful, soaring music and a touching, inspirational sermon, then a children's Nativity program that made her ignore her own stricture of earlier and become weepy all over again when she saw the missing spot where two freckled angels should have been.

Several of her friends cornered her afterward to repeat their voice mail invitations to join them for their holiday celebrations. She thanked them but told them she had plans.

Jamie still hadn't returned when she drove back to the house through several inches of new snow.

The house seemed too big, too empty. Even after filling an hour tromping though the snow to deliver the plates of cookies to her neighbors, the remainder of that day and the next stretched out ahead of her.

This would not do!

Christmas was a time for joy. While she didn't want to intrude on someone else's family celebrations, she refused to spend the day moping around her house alone except for her mother's cats, even if they were being freakishly nice to her these days.

The previous year, she had spent the holidays with her mother at the care center in Shelter Springs. Why not go there again? She knew plenty of residents who would have no visitors over the holidays, and the staff could probably use her help serving up their Christmas Eve dinner.

With more enthusiasm than she'd had for anything in nearly two days, she put on her favorite Christmas sweater, loaded her car with the last few plates of cookies for the staff, then backed out of the driveway. As she turned away from the house on the road that would take her to Shelter Springs, she spotted a familiar vehicle coming in the opposite direction, toward the house.

Jamie.

She saw him behind the wheel and had the odd impression that he looked tired. She couldn't be sure. How could she possibly tell when they drove vehicles moving in opposite directions?

For one brief instant, his gaze met hers, and he slowed down and lifted a hand in greeting.

As she looked at his dear, familiar, gorgeous features, all the misery she had been trying so hard to outrun seemed to swell, expanding to fill every available inch inside her Lexus.

While she was sad about the boys leaving, everything seemed so much worse without Jamie beside her to help her through it.

It's your fault.

She gazed out the windshield as the words seemed to ring over and over in her head. He had tried to support her, and she had pushed every effort away. No doubt, he despised her, with good reason. She wasn't very fond of herself right now.

All the progress she had made the last month to stretch herself seemed for nothing. She was still too afraid to reach for what she wanted. Though she yearned to follow after him, to lean on his strength, she didn't have the courage.

With one hand curled in a fist against the pain in her stomach, she accelerated and drove away.

WELL. THAT WAS CLEAR ENOUGH.

Jamie drove the rest of the way to her house and parked in his usual spot in the driveway.

A weird, aching pain had lodged under his breastbone. After flying into Hope's Crossing to pick up family members, he had been trying to get back to Haven Point to talk to Julia for two days. First he had engine trouble, then bad weather had closed the Hope's Crossing airport, then his car wouldn't start and he needed Aidan to jump his battery.

He only wanted to see her, to talk to her, to try to make things right. He never expected he would run into her on the street—or that she would quite deliberately drive away from him.

He was half-tempted to turn around, to drive after her and have this out once and for all. After he pulled into the driveway, he put his SUV in Reverse with the intention of doing just that.

At the end of the driveway, he hesitated, then pulled forward to his usual spot again and turned off the ignition.

No. She clearly didn't want to talk to him, and he couldn't force her to.

His main reason for returning to the house was for a shower and change of clothes, but as he slowly walked up the stairs to his apartment, he realized he couldn't stay here anymore. Not with things so tense between him and Julia.

His condo would be ready in a few days. Meanwhile, he could just stay at Snow Angel Cove with the rest of his family. Eliza had plenty of room. If Julia wanted space, he would give her space.

It only took him three trips to load up his things, then he placed the house keys in an envelope. He grabbed a piece of scratch paper and penned a quick note, slipped it in with the keys, then wedged the envelope between the door and the jamb, where she would be sure to see it.

He had something else for her, too, but he wasn't sure if he should leave it. For several long moments, Jamie sat on her beautiful polished wooden steps, the gift bag in his hands as he tried to make up his mind. He almost carried it back to his vehicle, but at the last moment, he hung it on her doorknob, then slipped outside, closing the door behind him.

He had told her he loved her. If she didn't believe him, if she *wouldn't* believe him, he would have to accept that and figure out how to go on without a sweet, kind, funny librarian.

He had no idea how the hell he would manage that, but he didn't see that she had given him any other choice.

THE STREETS OF Haven Point were quiet on Christmas Eve as Julia drove through the lightly falling snow toward home. Christmas decorations lit up nearly every house, and through some of the open windows, she could see people celebrating, families gathering.

She yawned, then shot a quick glance at the clock in her car. It was barely 8:00 p.m. She shouldn't be this tired, but the day had been long, and she had spent most of it on her feet—serving meals, singing carols, reading favorite holiday stories, pushing various nursing home residents from room to room so they could deliver their gifts to each other.

It had been an oddly fulfilling day, a chance for her to forget her own pain briefly while serving the elderly residents who had been friends with her mother.

As she drove home, she couldn't shake the memory of one particular resident. Agatha Chestnut had been the librarian in Haven Point for many years. Cranky and forbidding from the time Julia was small, Miss Chestnut rarely smiled and would lecture children for any infraction of the rules, from talking too loudly in the stacks to smudging a book page to, heaven forbid, incurring late fees.

She was in her eighties now and seemed painfully unhappy, withered and tired and lonely. Miss Chestnut had received no visitors today and hadn't joined in any of the celebrations. She had given no gifts and had spurned any cheery gesture the staff or other residents tried to offer.

She had sat in a wheelchair under a crocheted afghan the Helping Hands had made for the residents a few years earlier and had watched the singing, the stories, the celebration as if from her own private bubble.

Julia had tried hard to talk to the woman, thinking her job as a librarian might offer some common ground, but after being rebuffed several times, she had been forced to give up.

She knew perfectly well why she had tried so hard.

She was Agatha.

If she didn't change something about her life, in fifty years she would be that joyless old woman, alone in a nursing home somewhere on Christmas Eve, snapping at anyone who tried to brighten her world.

She was already there. Hadn't she done the same to Jamie? He had only wanted to help her, give her support when she had needed it most, and she had shut him down. She remembered the hurt she thought she'd seen in his eyes as she was closing her door against him that last time.

He said he loved her.

Why would he possibly say that if he didn't mean it? He wasn't a cruel man. She had seen evidence of exactly the opposite, over and over.

She needed to talk to him. Tonight. No matter how late he came in, she would wait for him. She would give him the gift she and the boys had picked out for him and finally would accept the incredible gift he had tried to offer her.

His love.

Though nerves shivered through her, the Christmas

lights seemed to glow brighter, the night seem more peaceful and beautiful as she turned on to Snow Blossom Lane toward her house and him.

Some of her excitement seeped away when she pulled into her empty driveway. Not unexpected, she reminded herself. He had told her several days earlier he would be spending Christmas Eve at Snow Angel Cove with his family.

She could wait, all night if she had to.

When she let herself into the house, she noticed two things immediately—an envelope wedged into her door with her name written in his handwriting and a large gift bag hanging on the doorknob.

Her heart started to pound as she picked up the bag and the envelope. Both were weightier than she might have expected. She opened her door and carried the two things to the sofa, where she sank down without taking off her coat.

The cats wandered in to investigate, sniffing at both things, while Julia tried to work up the courage to open them.

She picked the envelope first and her heart sank when she saw the keys inside. There was a note as well, and she pulled it out with fingers that trembled.

Dear Julia,
Thank you for letting me stay in your upstairs apartment. My condo is nearly finished, so I would ask to be released from my short-term lease at this time, as we discussed at the beginning of our arrangement.
Yours,
Jamie.

It was cool, impersonal, the kind any tenant might write a landlady, except for that final *yours*. Did he mean it? Was he still hers? The tone of the letter would indicate otherwise.

Tabitha by now had knocked the gift bag over and was trying to peek inside, but Julia pushed her away.

"That's mine," she said sternly.

The cat meowed at her, then flounced to the other side of the room to stare haughtily at her, as if to ask what was taking so long.

Her stomach in knots, Julia picked up the bag, removed the crumpled tissue paper and reached in, then had to press a hand to her mouth as a sob escaped.

A stocking. The man had given her a stocking, just as her mother had done every year until her death.

It looked store-bought, except for the block letters that spelled her name. They were cut out of red and green fabric and clumsily sewn on. She could see the ragged edges, the crooked stitches, and another sob joined the first.

Jamie had sewn on those letters himself. Somehow she knew he had. Her big, tough, gorgeous former military pilot had spent probably hours hand-stitching this, simply because she might have mentioned how much she missed the stockings her mother had made her.

She looked at it from every angle, so touched by the stocking itself, she almost forgot to peek inside. When she did, she started to cry in earnest.

It was as if he had remembered every conversation they had ever had. She pulled out item after item, things they had talked about together, things she had mentioned in passing, things she hadn't even thought twice about. A book of poems she had mentioned. A ski pass to the nearest resort to Haven Point. A slim leather journal with an engraved compass rose on the front, indicating it was meant to record travels.

Finally, near the bottom of the stocking, she pulled out a little cellophane-wrapped package with the plant inside, tied with a little red bow. It took her a moment to realize what it was.

Mistletoe.

One of the last items on her list, kissing someone special under the mistletoe.

She found a sticky note on it in his bold handwriting. "Keep this handy. You never know when you'll find the perfect person."

She did. She did know. She had known all along. Jamie wasn't perfect, but he was absolutely perfect for her.

No other man would ever do. She had given her heart to him completely and could never imagine kissing anyone else—under the mistletoe, on the ski slopes, anywhere.

She had to find him. Now, tonight. He wasn't coming back to her house; the keys he had left were evidence of that, so she would have to go to him.

Did she have the nerve?

For a moment, her old anxieties bubbled up. What if he didn't really want her? What if this was only one more nice thing he was doing for the poor, pitiful Haven Point librarian?

She looked at the items spread out under her tree as calm assurance washed away all her doubts, once and for all.

Jamie saw her. Truly saw her. He knew the heart of her and loved her anyway.

He believed she was the kind of woman who would

embrace adventures, and she wanted to be that woman. She *was*, she only had to find the strength inside her to reach for what she wanted.

This time, she couldn't rely on anyone else. She thought about Roxy's book that had started everything, with its message about pursuing things you wanted. First, you had to figure out what exactly you wanted, and Julia knew, 100 percent.

She wanted Jamie's love. She wanted a future with him.

"I'm sorry," she said to the cats. "But I have to go. Merry Christmas."

She grabbed the mistletoe and her car keys, then hurried out the door.

CHAPTER TWENTY-ONE

"Everything okay? You've been mighty quiet all night."

Jamie looked over at his father, seated in his favorite armchair in the vast great room at Snow Angel Cove.

Around them was sheer chaos. Children were running, dogs barking, Christmas carols playing. Just another crazy holiday with the Caine family.

"Sure. I'm fine."

His words sounded wooden, stiff, but he couldn't help it. He felt broken.

"I sure wish Julia could be here," Pop said, with the uncanny insight he always showed. "Breaks my heart that she lost those boys. She sure loved them."

He hadn't told his family, but Eliza apparently had heard it from Wynona Emmett and now all the Caines seemed to know.

"She did love them," he said.

Pop looked over his reading glasses with a compassion and understanding Jamie wasn't ready to see. "All the more reason she needs to be here with us. After suffering a heartbreak like that, a woman should be surrounded by people who care about her. I can't believe you didn't make her come."

His jaw flexed. That might have been possible, except she wasn't speaking with him. She had pushed him away at every turn.

"I'm not sure if you know this, Pop, but kidnapping is technically against the law."

"I thought you could persuade any woman to do anything you wanted," Dylan piped up from the sofa, where he had ostensibly been looking through a picture book with little Liam. "Usually all you have to do is throw out a little of that Jamie Caine mojo."

He had never wanted to punch his brother more than he did in that moment.

"I do hope she's all right," Eliza said softly. "I tried to talk to her at church this morning, but she hurried out so fast I didn't get a chance. She won't take my phone call or anyone else's in the Helping Hands. Wyn did talk to her yesterday, but other than that she's keeping to herself."

"What did she say, do you know? Did Wyn mention how she sounded?" He hated to ask, but he was becoming desperate.

Eliza frowned. "Wyn said she seemed oddly calm. Apparently she took all the toys she bought Davy and Clint to a needy family Wynona found in Shelter Springs."

"Oh, what a lovely gesture," Pop said.

"That couldn't have been easy," Charlotte said. "I bet her poor heart was breaking."

His own heart couldn't take much more. It felt swollen with tenderness, so big he could hardly breathe around it. She was amazing, reaching out to someone else even when she was hurting.

Was it any wonder he loved her?

"What do you think, Jamie?"

He turned to his sister-in-law Lucy. "Sorry. I didn't hear you. What?"

"I was wondering if you thought Julia might let me take a look at her house while I'm in town. You know how much I love old places, and from what Eliza has described, Winston House sounds stunning."

"I don't know," he said, his voice tight. "You'll have to ask her."

He really didn't want to talk about Julia anymore. His emotions were too tender and raw. To his relief, after another insightful look, Pop changed the subject to distract everyone, bringing up a memory of a long-ago holiday trip they had all taken to the ocean.

For the next hour, Jamie did his best to participate in the family holiday. He played a game or two with his nieces and nephews, he tried to eat a few things, he pretended to laugh at stories he barely heard.

Mostly, he just wanted to escape to the small guest room Eliza had found for him.

When Pop picked up the old family Bible to read the Christmas story in Luke, as he did every year, Jamie decided he would leave right after.

Not to his room, he decided abruptly. He would go to Julia's house. He couldn't kidnap her, but he could try one more time to make her talk to him, at least.

"And it came to pass…" Pop began, when suddenly the doorbell rang.

"I'll get it!" Maddie shouted. "Maybe it's Santa!" She hurried to the door with Aidan close behind.

A moment later, Aidan came back into the great room with an odd look on his face.

"Um, it's for you," he said to Jamie.

Behind him, tugged along by Maddie, was Julia. She looked beautiful, with her hair up in some kind of soft updo and a green sweater that set off her lovely complexion and those stunning eyes.

"I...didn't realize everyone would be here. I should have called. I'm sorry."

Why had she come? His heart began to pound, and he realized she carried something in her hand. Like a schoolboy caught in a prank, his face suddenly felt hot, and he wanted to grab it from her, to hide it away.

That ridiculous stocking.

It had been a complete impulse the night the Bernards left. He was trying to think how he might make her feel better and remembered the stockings she told him her mother sewed for her every year. He had run into Shelter Springs for the stocking and the material to cut out the letters of her name, feeling foolish the whole time.

"You made me a stocking," she said softly.

He was aware of Aidan and Dylan watching with interest and wanted to grab the thing out of her hands and stuff it up his shirt.

"It's terrible. You don't have to keep it."

"I didn't know you could sew."

"I, uh, don't. Not really. Mom used to make sure we all knew how to sew on a button or mend a ripped shirt, but that's it. I watched a couple videos online. That's all."

Out of the corner of his gaze, he saw Charlotte and Eliza exchange shocked looks that made his face burn. He did *not* want to have this conversation in front of all these prying Caine eyes.

"Seriously. You can throw it away."

"Are you kidding?" She clutched the stocking closer. "Never. I love it. It's beautiful. You didn't have to do that."

"I know. I wanted to." He paused. "That wasn't anything from your list. That was only me, Jules. Straight up."

She gave a sigh, looking helpless and confused, and he didn't know what to do. He was *never* out of his depth when it came to women, but with Julia, he felt like he was drowning in all the things he didn't know how to say.

"Are you sure you won't stay?" Pop asked. "We're about to read the Christmas story."

She shifted her gaze to his father with a look of deep affection. Wow. He really had it bad if he could be jealous of his own seventy-year-old father.

"That sounds lovely, but I don't want to intrude. I only came to thank Jamie for my Christmas stocking. And to do this."

She was blushing fiery red now as she moved closer to him. His entire family had fallen silent, even the little ones, and Jamie didn't know what the hell was going on.

She pulled something from the pocket of her wool coat with hands that seemed to be shaking. She held it out, and he recognized the mistletoe he'd picked up on a whim when he saw it in the checkout line, with all the other novelty items.

She moved closer, to stand right in front of him, gripping the mistletoe tightly. "There's only one person I want to kiss under the mistletoe," she whispered, loud enough only for him to hear. "Or anywhere else. The man I love with all my heart."

That was all he heard. All he needed to hear. He yanked her toward him and kissed her hard, joy rushing through him so fast and so hard he felt dizzy with it.

After only a few seconds, he snatched the mistletoe

from her, tossed it over his shoulder at his family and tugged her outside.

He *really* didn't need an audience now, especially not his beaming father, his dewy-eyed sisters-in-law or his hooting idiots for brothers.

He took her out the front door and onto the porch of Snow Angel Cove, which was surrounded by greenery and ribbons and twinkling fairy lights. There, he kissed her again, holding her so tightly she couldn't slip away again.

"Julia. I've been so miserable since the boys left, afraid you were shutting me out forever."

"I'm sorry. I'm so sorry. I wanted to talk to you yesterday, but…you didn't come back."

He explained to her about the engine trouble, about the storm and the delays.

"We're here now. I can't believe you came here and faced my family like that."

She looked embarrassed. "I really didn't think it through, or I would have realized there might be thirty witnesses."

"Why did you come?"

In answer, she kissed him, and Jamie felt all the bruised sections of his heart begin to heal. "I needed to see you. To apologize."

"You don't have anything to apologize for," he said gruffly.

"Yes, I do. I'm so sorry I didn't believe you when you said you…loved me. I was afraid. And then I saw that stocking today and all the wonderful gifts inside, and I realized something. You would never hurt me. You see the real me more clearly than anyone else in my life ever has. Better than I see myself."

"I see an amazing, courageous, beautiful woman who gives away her own carefully purchased and wrapped Christmas gifts to strangers in need."

She blushed. "And I see a man who cares enough about a woman he barely knows that he'll do whatever it takes to make her dreams come true. I love you, Jamie. I've loved you forever. You were my secret crush from the time you moved to Haven Point, but it was only after I saw how sweet you were to the boys, how kind you were to your family, that I came to love the real you. The one beneath the teasing and the flirting. That's the man I love."

He had to kiss her again after that, of course, a kiss he never wanted to end.

He only wore a sweater against the December wind and snow, but with her tucked up against him, he didn't feel the cold.

Christmas was magical. Why hadn't he ever fully realized that? It was a time of miracle and hope and second chances.

She was everything he had been looking for all his life, all the things he never realized he needed.

"It's cold," he said after several more long moments. "I can't keep you out here all night."

"I wouldn't mind, as long as you were with me. I'm fine going inside, too. If you want to. We've probably missed the Christmas story, but I'd love to see your other family traditions."

He wanted to take her back to her house, to tuck them both under that beautiful, sensuous canopy and spend hours keeping away the cold.

There would be plenty of time for that. The future

stretched out ahead of them, full of kisses and laughter and adventure.

"You know my family is crazy, right? Full disclosure. If we go back in there together, they won't give us a moment's peace. My brothers can be relentless."

She smiled, not looking at all cowed by the prospect. She loved his family, and it was clear they all adored her.

"You know they only want you to be happy," she said.

He kissed her again as the snowflakes swirled just beyond the porch and the Christmas lights glittered around them. "They will get their wish, then. I am happier than I ever believed possible."

They turned to go inside, to join his family in celebrating this season of miracles.

EPILOGUE

"AND THEN WE went to the beach and we walked out on the pier and we saw surfers and people riding bikes without coats on and we even saw two whales!"

"No way!" she exclaimed to Davy. He beamed out of her computer screen at her, so vibrant and alive that she had to smile, deeply grateful for the miracle of technology that allowed her to see them through a video call, if not in person.

"How was your Christmas, Clint?" she asked the older brother, who stood just to the left of Davy.

Clint smiled, though a little less exuberantly than Davy had. "Pretty good. We loved our stockings you made us. Thanks."

"Yeah, thanks," Davy said. "We're drawing you pictures to say thanks, and Aunt Suzi said we can mail them tomorrow."

"I will look forward to getting them," she said. "Mail is one of my favorite things. And you're very welcome. I'm glad you enjoyed the stockings."

"I already started reading that book you got me, the one about the dragon," Clint said.

"Oh, I'm so glad. It's a great one. I think you'll love it."

"Did you get our presents?" Davy asked.

She thought of the gifts Jamie had pulled out from under the tree, the hand-painted scarf and beaded earrings he and the boys had secretly purchased during the Lights on the Lake festival.

When she'd opened the gifts, she had wept for the boys she had only been able to love a short time, but this time she had Jamie to hold her. The pain of losing them hadn't been as intense with him there to share it.

She would be forever grateful she'd had the chance to get to know these two sweet boys. They had changed her, had helped her open her heart.

Maybe she could enter the foster parent program through traditional channels. There were many children out there who needed love, and she had a heart overflowing with it. They talked a few more moments about their bedrooms and swimming in their pool and seeing their friends again.

"Do you think we could Skype with Jamie?" Clint asked. "Is he home upstairs?"

"He's not. He had some errands to run."

She didn't tell them Jamie was no longer living upstairs. He was still at Snow Angel Cove but would move into his condo later that week.

She would have loved to have him closer, but they both felt it would have been too strange for her to rent to him now, at this new stage of their relationship. Neither of them was quite ready to move in together, though she knew in her heart this was real and right.

Every moment she was with him only strengthened her love for him.

"Will you have him call us?" Clint said.

"Yeah. I want to tell him about the airplane we flew to California. We had to wait forever to get on it. It was *huge* and we were way in the back of the plane and all they had to eat were pretzels," Davy said with a note of disgust.

She swallowed a laugh. These two little boys would be forever spoiled for regular air travel, considering their first trips had been on a private jet.

"I'll tell him."

"We gotta go. We're gonna go ride bikes. I'll call you again, okay?" Davy said.

"I'm counting on it. Goodbye, my dears."

After the call disconnected, she gazed at her screen for a long moment, aware of the tiny ribbon of sadness curling through her.

She couldn't be too sad, though. The boys were both obviously very happy in their new lives, in a home where people loved them. She was just closing her laptop when her door opened, and Jamie walked in carrying a large white box wrapped in a red ribbon.

"What's this?" she asked. She didn't need more gifts. Not when she had already enjoyed the most joyous Christmas she could ever imagine.

He gave her a wide-eyed, guileless expression that didn't fool her for a second. "I don't know. I found it on the porch. Look, it has your name on it."

"Christmas was three days ago, Jamie."

"I know. Weird. I guess maybe somebody couldn't quite get this one to you on time. Maybe you better open it."

He set it on her coffee table, then stepped back with that same air of innocence that left her more than a little wary—and completely charmed.

She was so in love with him. She never would have believed she could be this deliriously happy. It didn't matter that it was December, that they were in for a blizzard, that the clouds were heavy and full of snow. Her world had never seemed so sunny and bright.

Cautiously she opened the lid of the box, then gasped at the sight of a little tan fur ball of a puppy inside. He was adorable, with the squished-up face and sad-looking eyes of a pug.

"Where did you...where did he come from?"

"I've got a friend who works at the county animal shelter. I asked her if she knew of any well-mannered little dogs in the shelter. She told me about this one. He's a pug, obviously, with a little mutt thrown in, and he's four months old and almost house-trained."

"Almost?"

He grinned. "Think about how much you love a challenge. Plus, you work at a library and can check out all the books on puppy training in your entire collection."

She laughed and shook her head. The little guy was truly the sweetest thing she'd ever seen. But a puppy! She couldn't take on a puppy right now. Could she?

She scooped him up, and he immediately licked her hand and wriggled with delight when she petted him. Oh, he was adorable.

"His name is Humphrey Bogart. How perfect is that? And I haven't told you the best thing yet."

"What's that?"

"He adores cats."

As if on cue, Empress, Tabitha and Audrey Hepburn sauntered in the room to investigate. Their backs arched, their tails curled and they looked positively appalled to find a puppy in their midst.

Julia set him down, and Humphrey happily waddled from cat to cat to introduce himself. He seemed completely unfazed, even when they hissed at him balefully.

Eventually, he plopped into the middle of the floor and started chewing a little toy Jamie pulled from the box. Only then did the cats wander closer, and within minutes the contrary things seemed to be vying over who got to sit next to him.

"What do you think?" Jamie asked. "You don't have to keep him. I told my friend at the shelter that I would find someone else to take him if you thought it was too much."

"You're not taking him anywhere," she said, her heart bursting with love for this man. "He's perfect. I love him."

She had no idea how she would juggle caring for a puppy in her already busy life, but she had figured out how to take care of two little boys. How hard could one cute pug be?

"*Get a puppy.* That was the last thing on your list," Jamie said with a grin. He sat on the sofa and pulled her down onto his lap. "Look at you, Miss Overachiever. It's not even New Year's Eve, and you've accomplished all your goals. I bet nobody else in your book club can say the same."

She laughed, rolling her eyes as she kissed him. That stupid list had completely changed her life. She owed Roxy Nash far more than a pitcher of sangria.

"*Now* what will you wish for?" Jamie asked, after several long, glorious moments.

"I have no idea," she said honestly. "What does a girl wish for when she has everything she ever wanted?"

"Fair enough." Jamie gave that wicked smile she was coming to adore. "I guess that means it's time we start working on my list."

He whispered something in her ear, something that

made her laugh so hard she couldn't breathe. And while the three cats vied for the pudgy puppy's attention and the tree lights twinkled and snowflakes danced outside, they made each other's dreams come true.

* * * * *

SPECIAL EXCERPT FROM

H HARLEQUIN®

SPECIAL EDITION

*Ella Baker is trading music lessons for riding
lessons from the wild twin McKinley boys—but it's
their father who would need a Christmas miracle to
let Ella into his heart.*

*Read on for a sneak preview of
the* RANCHER'S CHRISTMAS SONG,
the next book in New York Times *bestselling author*
RaeAnne Thayne's *beloved miniseries*
THE COWBOYS OF COLD CREEK.

Beckett finally spoke. "Uh, what seems to be the trouble?"

His voice had an odd, strangled note to it. Was he laughing at her? When she couldn't see him, Ella couldn't be quite sure. "It's stuck in my hair comb. I don't want to rip the sweater—or yank out my hair, for that matter."

He paused again, then she felt the air stir as he moved closer. The scent of him was stronger now, masculine and outdoorsy, and everything inside her sighed a welcome.

He stood close enough that she could feel the heat radiating from him. She caught her breath, torn between a completely prurient desire for the moment to last at least a little longer and a wild hope that the humiliation of being caught in this position would be over quickly.

"Hold still," he said. Was his voice deeper than usual? She couldn't quite tell. She did know it sent tiny delicious shivers down her spine.

"You've really done a job here," he said after a moment.

"I know. I'm not quite sure how it tangled so badly."

She would have to breathe soon or she was likely to pass out. She forced herself to inhale one breath and then another until she felt a little less light-headed.

"Almost there," he said, his big hands in her hair, then a moment later she felt a tug and the sweater slipped all the way over her head.

"There you go."

"Thank you." She wanted to disappear, to dive under that great big log bed and hide away. Instead, she forced her mouth into a casual smile. "These Christmas sweaters can be dangerous. Who knew?"

She was blushing. She could feel her face heat and wondered if he noticed. This certainly counted among the most embarrassing moments of her life.

"Want to explain again what you're doing in my bedroom, tangled up in your clothes?" he asked.

She frowned at his deliberately risqué interpretation of something that had been innocent. Mostly.

There had been that secret moment when she had closed her eyes and imagined being here with him under that soft quilt, but he had no way of knowing that.

She folded up her sweater, wondering if she would ever be able to look the man in the eye again.

Don't miss
THE RANCHER'S CHRISTMAS SONG
by RaeAnne Thayne,
available November 2017 wherever
Harlequin® Special Edition books and ebooks are sold.

www.Harlequin.com

Copyright © 2017 by RaeAnne Thayne

New York Times bestselling author

RaeAnne Thayne

**welcomes you to Haven Point, a small town full
of big surprises, hope and second chances...**

Order your copies today!

www.HQNBooks.com

PHRATHPS16

SPECIAL EDITION

Life, Love and Family

Save **$1.00**

on the purchase of ANY
Harlequin® Special Edition book.

Available wherever books are sold, including
most bookstores, supermarkets, drugstores
and discount stores.

Save **$1.00**

on the purchase of any Harlequin® Special Edition book.

Coupon valid until December 31, 2017.
Redeemable at participating outlets in the U.S. and Canada only.
Not redeemable at Barnes & Noble stores. Limit one coupon per customer.

Canadian Retailers: Harlequin Enterprises Limited will pay the face value of this coupon plus 10.25¢ if submitted by customer for this product only. Any other use constitutes fraud. Coupon is nonassignable. Void if taxed, prohibited or restricted by law. Consumer must pay any government taxes. Void if copied. Inmar Promotional Services ("IPS") customers submit coupons and proof of sales to Harlequin Enterprises Limited, PO Box 31000, Scarborough, ON M1R 0E7, Canada. Non-IPS retailer—for reimbursement submit coupons and proof of sales directly to Harlequin Enterprises Limited, Retail Marketing Department, 225 Duncan Mill Rd., Don Mills, ON M3B 3K9, Canada.

U.S. Retailers: Harlequin Enterprises Limited will pay the face value of this coupon plus 8¢ if submitted by customer for this product only. Any other use constitutes fraud. Coupon is nonassignable. Void if taxed, prohibited or restricted by law. Consumer must pay any government taxes. Void if copied. For reimbursement submit coupons and proof of sales directly to Harlequin Enterprises, Ltd 482, NCH Marketing Services, P.O. Box 880001, El Paso, TX 88588-0001, U.S.A. Cash value 1/100 cents.

52615131

5 65373 00076 2   (8100)0 12308

® and ™ are trademarks owned and used by the trademark owner and/or its licensee.

© 2017 Harlequin Enterprises Limited

HSECOUPRT0917

New York Times bestselling author

RaeAnne Thayne

returns to Haven Point, where there's no sweeter place to fall in love...

"Entertaining, heart-wrenching, and totally involving, this multithreaded story overflows with characters readers will adore."
—*Library Journal* on *Evergreen Springs* (starred review)

Complete your collection!

www.HQNBooks.com

PHRATHPS17

Turn your love of reading into
rewards you'll love with

Harlequin My Rewards

**Join for FREE today at
www.HarlequinMyRewards.com**

Earn **FREE BOOKS** of your choice.

Experience **EXCLUSIVE OFFERS** and contests.

Enjoy **BOOK RECOMMENDATIONS**
selected just for you.

PLUS! Sign up now
and get **500** points
right away!

Earn
FREE
REWARDS
HarlequinMyRewards.com
Join
Today!

MYR16R

Get 2 Free Books,
<u>Plus</u> 2 Free Gifts –

just for trying the *Reader Service!*

YES! Please send me 2 FREE novels from the Essential Romance or Essential Suspense Collection and my 2 FREE gifts (gifts are worth about $10 retail). After receiving them, if I don't wish to receive any more books, I can return the shipping statement marked "cancel." If I don't cancel, I will receive 4 brand-new novels every month and be billed just $6.74 each in the U.S. or $7.24 each in Canada. That's a savings of at least 16% off the cover price. It's quite a bargain! Shipping and handling is just 50¢ per book in the U.S. and 75¢ per book in Canada.* I understand that accepting the 2 free books and gifts places me under no obligation to buy anything. I can always return a shipment and cancel at any time. The free books and gifts are mine to keep no matter what I decide.

Please check one: ☐ Essential Romance ☐ Essential Suspense
194/394 MDN GLW5   191/391 MDN GLW5

Name _____ (PLEASE PRINT)

Address _____ Apt. #

City _____ State/Prov. _____ Zip/Postal Code

Signature (if under 18, a parent or guardian must sign)

Mail to the **Reader Service:**
IN U.S.A.: P.O. Box 1341, Buffalo, NY 14240-8531
IN CANADA: P.O. Box 603, Fort Erie, Ontario L2A 5X3

Want to try two free books from another line?
Call 1-800-873-8635 or visit www.ReaderService.com.

*Terms and prices subject to change without notice. Prices do not include applicable taxes. Sales tax applicable in NY. Canadian residents will be charged applicable taxes. Offer not valid in Quebec. This offer is limited to one order per household. Books received may not be as shown. Not valid for current subscribers to the Essential Romance or Essential Suspense Collection. All orders subject to approval. Credit or debit balances in a customer's account(s) may be offset by any other outstanding balance owed by or to the customer. Please allow 4 to 6 weeks for delivery. Offer available while quantities last.

Your Privacy—The Reader Service is committed to protecting your privacy. Our Privacy Policy is available online at www.ReaderService.com or upon request from the Reader Service.

We make a portion of our mailing list available to reputable third parties that offer products we believe may interest you. If you prefer that we not exchange your name with third parties, or if you wish to clarify or modify your communication preferences, please visit us at www.ReaderService.com/consumerchoice or write to us at Reader Service Preference Service, P.O. Box 9062, Buffalo, NY 14240-9062. Include your complete name and address.

STRS17R